Two, One … Now Three

How Can That Be?
by
Anna J. Small Roseboro

D1737585

TWO, ONE, NOW THREE: How Can That Be?

© Anna J. Small Roseboro 2022

For permissions contact: ajroseboro@comcast.net

Cover Art by Manvi Semalty
Dehradun, Uttarakhand, India
manvisemart@gmail.com

Interior art from Microsoft Office 365 Online Art in Public Domain

Lyrics for quoted songs other than "He Rescued Me" used by permission of lyricist, Ms. Rochelle Jones, are songs in the public domain. Sources consulted include https://www.pdhymns.com/ and https://hymnary.org

Please note the in-text citations for other quoted or paraphrased contents. Discussion questions adapted by those posted by Michelle Boudin.

Copyright 2022
ISBN: **9798834308010**

Table of Contents

Dedication   5

Introduction   6

THE REVEAL   **8**

     Lillian Reflects Alone   19

     Glendella is Propositioned   29

     Lillian Wonders   40

     Louis Reflects Alone   48

     Claude Reflects Alone   58

     Learn about GEMS   60

     Meet the Teens   65

     Beth-El Community Church   74

FIRST WEEK   **80**

     Church Choir Director Imagines   85

     The Twins Arrive and Wonder   90

     The Couple is Back to Work   106

     Lillian's Department Chair Makes Offer   112

     Claude Suspects   122

     Lillian and Louis Walk and Talk   126

     Louis Hears Radio Sermonette   129

     Delphi's Back Story and Lillian's Front Story   132

     Glendella Learns and Leaves   138

     Lou Junior Questions Mom   145

     Louis Calls Radio Minister   147

SECOND WEEK   **156**

Pastor Reflects on Meeting 167

Teacher Saw Something 173

Louis Meets with CEO 181

Old Neighbor Becomes New Neighbor 187

Consulting with Marriage Counselor 192

Time is Taking Its Toll 201

Teen Neighbors Talk in Text 204

Reveal at Letchworth 208

THIRD WEEK **220**

Lou Junior Reflects on the Reveal 224

Twins Call Camp Counselor 227

Sisters Journal about the Reveal 234

Claude and Glendella Plan 243

Delphi's Admission 252

Basketball Coach Wonders 254

FOURTH WEEK **260**

Reveal at Beth-El 260

Decision Time 265

EPILOGUE **268**

No Dinking with the Dinka 268

Acknowledgments **273**

Discussion Questions **275**

About the Author **277**

Dedication

To God who prompted the seed story
and guided the manuscript preparation.

To my husband, William,
who advised me to consider the secret eyes of life.

To the contributors who shared
verbal and written narratives reflecting different attitudes
and aspects of sexuality.

To courageous readers who understand that,
as Rudine Sims Bishop told us,
stories may be mirrors, windows or sliding glass doors
that allow us to see ourselves, view others
, and even step into a situation for a short time.

To curious readers who, recognize the telescope image of
Stephanie Tolliver
. who says reading can take us "up close and personal?"

Introduction

This work of Christian fiction is a woven tapestry comprised of a seed story that I wrote and the contributions of fifteen other persons. They were invited to assume the voice of a character introduced in or alluded to in that seed story, which is now Chapter One of this novel. Each writer responded with a first-person narrative describing at least one scene in which their character encounters a member of the Robertson family mentioned in Chapter One.

Then, I switched the metaphor from growing a seed that blossoms into a novel and became a weaver. I threaded the loom with the warp of the main story and extended it. Next I interlaced the weft of the contributed narratives to create a portrait of a family responding to a revelation.

The texture of this weaving reflects the distinctive voices that come through each author's style, their description of settings, creative dialogue, and use of dialect. As you read from section to section, chapter to chapter, and scene to scene you will become privy to back stories, side stories as well as the private thoughts of the variety of characters whose experiences make up the plot of the novel, TWO, ONE … NOW THREE and eventually answer the question of the subtopic, "How Can That Be?"

THE REVEAL

They'd worked in the same building for years and often ate lunch together in the little café on the first floor. Lillian and Louis were getting on in years during a time when most women were married and mothers of one or two children by their twenty-fifth birthday. Lillian had wanted to marry, but she was somewhat overweight, and men in her circle seemed more attracted to her svelte co-workers.

Lillian worked in the accounting office of one of the chain stores whose regional offices were on the fifth floor. She'd been there since graduating from her local community college, where her professor recommended Lillian do an internship in the office. The company hired Lillian, so she never went on to acquire a higher degree. She thoroughly enjoyed working with numbers and being an inside voice for people of color who sometimes were marginalized in terms of jobs in the company and grace for paying bills.

Louis had spent years getting focused training, honing his skills, and now led the building crew who kept the place in good repair. He, too, had gone on to college, did well, and like Lillian, was hired by a company he'd worked for while a student in a tech school across the state. When their office moved here, he came with them.

As African Americans in their late twenties, both had solid careers but little chance of moving up in the business for which they each worked. So, they decided they may as well get married and start a family. Maybe their children could progress further up the ladder if their parents invested time and money in providing them with a good home and a little more education. Seventeen years later, on a weekend when Louis and Lillian were home alone, planning to watch a movie together, Louis settled in his comfy recliner, turned to Lillian, and cleared his throat. "Lillian?"

"What is it, dear?" she responded, setting the newspaper aside and looking at her husband of nearly two decades. His smooth blue-black skin and short kinky hair had become precious to her. Some friends asked how she could stand being married to someone so dark, and she'd respond, "Simple! I've come to care for him. He respects me and takes good care of me and the kids."

"Lillian?"

"Yes?"

"We have to talk!"

"Sure. About what? The kids are fine. The twins won't be back till morning. They're on that sleepover with the girls in the GEMS youth group at the church down the street. I'm really glad that the non-denominational Christian group is so close. I was in Pioneer Girls when I was their age, but they don't have one around here. The group is planning a big summer event for the Fourth of July weekend. Can't wait to hear about it. What's up? You look a little odd."

"Yeah, that's right. Alysa and Alvyra will really be stoked for that. Think they'll be twirling batons or playing their clarinets in the marching band? They may offer to set up some kind of stand to sell some of their weird artwork!"

"And, you know, Lou Junior's gonna be at the baseball camp till Sunday afternoon. You know I hate for him to miss his senior Sunday school class, but there will be scouts from the State College there. Louie may get a college scholarship. Won't that be great!" "Yeah, I know, Honey. So, that's why I thought this would be a good time to talk."

BEEP, BEEP, BEEP.

Louis' cell phone alerts him to a text message. He's on-call this weekend and has to answer.

"Yes, this is Mr. Robertson. What's up? … Oh! … That's no problem. Call Frank. He'll take care of that for you. Yeah? Really? Well, congratulations to the family. Gotta go, now. Bye." He turns down the volume before putting the phone back on the table next to his chair. "Lillian!" he says a little louder than normal. "We have to talk!"

"This sounds serious, Lou. Something the matter?" "

No, not really. I just decided to come clean with you."

"Clean about what? You keep this place nearly spotless as it is! There's seldom a day you're not sweeping off the porch or mopping the kitchen or bathroom floors."

"I'm not kidding, Lillian. There's something you ought to know." "Okay, Louis, my man. Tell me" Lillian settled back in her chair and oted out of the side window that her neighbor was out cutting the grass. Lillian and Louis set pretty high standards for the neighbors, and few allowed their front yards to go too long without cutting, trimming, or watering.

"I wanna move upstairs with Claude."

"With Claude! Whyever, would you want to move up there?" "I'm in love with him. And we thought it was time to tell you." "Wait a minute! You're in love with Claude?How can that be?You're married to me! We have a family! When did this happen?"

Ding-a-ling. Ding-a-ling. Ding-a-ling. Now it's Lillian's phone disrupting their supposedly quiet evening at home. She picks up her phone and sees it's her sister, Glendella. Could be important. So, she answers.

"Yeah, Sis. Can this wait? I'm busy now. What? Really. That's no big deal. Huh? Okay. Let me step into the kitchen. Louis is setting up a movie for us to watch. Say, Louie. I'll be right back."

Lillian is glad for a reason to leave the room to process what she's just heard. Still, she's not ready to talk about any of it to her only sibling, her older sister, Glendella. They've been close since they were children growing up in the trailer park near the Finger Lakes in Upstate New York. Glendella had married early and had left town with her husband. She's just recently moved back.

"No, Glendella. I don't really have time to talk. Let's meet Monday. I gotta stop by the Nourish Your Curls shop after work to pick up some hair products. We can meet there and pick up dinner. Monday is Louis' day to work late, and the kids will be studying for their AP exams … Sure…Okay. See you at church tomorrow." Lillian turns off the phone and leaves it in the kitchen to avoid being disturbed again. She knows how important scores on those advanced placement exams are for some college admission packets.

She takes a deep breath, returns to the living room, and takes a seat. This time she turns to face her husband. "Tell me again. When did you and Claude start up? I haven't seen anything different." "It didn't just happen. Claude and I have been together for some time now. Claude and I met in college. He didn't know I was here. I saw our college logo on this car in the office building parking lot and looked up the owner. Later that week, we met for lunch to catch up as alums. I learned he'd done better in college and got that job in the business office.

"No! Well, not 'No' about his job. But, 'No" about you, two!"

"Yes, Honey! That's why he moved upstairs when you and I bought this two-family house last year. In fact, he helped me with the down payment. I'd been saving for a house since we married, and when this two-flatter came up for sale not far from our apartment, Claude and I decided to buy it. We knew the kids wouldn't want to move very far from their friends.

"You and Claude!" Lillian sat trembling in disbelief. Louis kept talking, nearly gushing as though a dam had burst, and he was finally able to talk.

"We figured it would be big enough for a growing family with the basement so clean and dry. We knew that Lou Junior would be fine in the basement 'cause there was a half bath down there with a shower. The twins would be delighted to have their own bedrooms even though they still have to share a bathroom. And with a master bedroom suite for us, you thought it was perfect. Claude knew he'd be fine with the two bedrooms on the second floor.

"Wait a minute! You and Claude?! After all this time?" Lillian looked around. Ah, the sound of the lawnmower will block whatever is going on over here.

"Well, now, I want to move up there with him. BEEP. BEEP. BEEP. "Oh no! Not again! Hold on." He picks up the phone and turns it over. "It's Lou Jr."

Louis, Sr., takes a deep breath, puts on his Daddy hat, and answers, "Hello, Son. How's it going at camp? He did! That's great. I'll tell your mom. Yeah, she's right here. We planned to watch a movie tonight. With all you kids gone, we can do some grown-up stuff. No…. not that! Cut it out!" The father grins a little and shoots a smirk over to his wife with the "If he only knew" look in his eyes. "Well, Junior. Gotta go. You take care, now. Okay. See you tomorrow evening."

Louis clicks off the phone and, this time, holds it up to show Lillian that he's turning the sound off completely. They have stuff to talk about and don't need to be disturbed.

Lillian had leaned forward when she heard the call was from their son but relieved; she leaned back when she realized he was calling to share the good news. The scout from State college had pulled Lou, Jr. aside for a quickie interview. Apparently, the scout has promised to contact the family during the summer. Their son is finishing his junior year in high school, and all are hoping he gets a sports scholarship to go to their state college.

But now, Lillian jerks nearly out of her chair when her husband declares, "Lillian, I'm bisexual! I've known I am gay since I was a teenager. But, with my job, I couldn't be open about it. My guys wouldn't work for me as they do."

"Yeah, but… you married me!" She leans forward, shaking her head. "Yes, I married you because I like you as a person, and I wanted to have children. I can't have children with Claude. He understood."

Louis leans forward, trying to make eye contact, hoping she'd understand. "'He understood!' You mean you talked to Claude about marrying me? And now this? Is that why you've been spending so much more time with him this past year or so?"

"Yes, we've decided to come out of the closet and live openly. Lil, Honey. You know he loves our children as much as I do. That's why he encouraged them to call him Uncle Claude. He doesn't want to lose them, and he knows I plan to take care of you all financially forever. In fact, Claude has already been saving to help send the girls to college."

"Wait a minute, Louis! This is coming at me too fast. You and Claude have been together for nearly two decades, and you're just now telling me about it!"

"Yes. He and I are tired of living a double life. You seem to be doing fine and don't seem to miss the decreased physical relations this past year. It looked like you could take'em or leave'em."

"I can't say all that is true. But I've never really had a strong sexual drive. And you were so gentle with me that it was not difficult to go along to have the children. Once they were born, I didn't miss not being intimate with you in that way."

14

"I know, Babe. But I have continued with Claude. The passionate side of our relationship seems to be less of a drive, but we want to live as a couple."

"A couple? But Louie. You and I are a couple. Claude was the best man at our wedding, for crying out loud! We got married in the church! 'The two shall become as one.' We've been one happy family for over fifteen years!"

"I've been married, content as a breadwinner, and delighted as a father, but I've not really been happy- happy unless I've been with Claude." Lillian, still in shock, sits shaking her head and swaying left to right in her leather lounge chair. He answers her questioning eyes.

"Claude understands that my first priority will always be my family. Now, he would like family to be him, too. He knows I want to stay near you all and continue to care for you to the best of my ability. That's not going to change if I just move upstairs."

"Louis! This is too much!" Lillian slams her hand on the side table, nearly sweeping off the colorful crystal bowl he'd bought for their fifteenth anniversary. Her husband was like that. He was a celebrater.

He'd been living pretty much on his own since he graduated from college and no longer had any relatives living in town. Lillian and the kids are his family. Or that's what Lillian thought. Yes, Claude had always been around as Louis' best friend, and what Lillian viewed as his "play brother."

Now, she learns her husband, Louis, Sr., and Claude have been lovers all this time? What? Now, they want to come out publicly, move in together, live as a couple and reside upstairs from her and the three children. Too, too much!

"What about our kids? They're teenagers! What will they think? What about their friends? What about the church? We're all active members of the same congregation where we got married just two blocks away. You and Claude are ushers for crying out loud! I sing in the choir! In fact, I have a solo tomorrow! Oh, Louie! Will they throw us out? Oh, God! What're we gonna do?"

What would Jesus do ?

*****

Louis watches Lillian's batting eyes and bobbling legs, swinging nervously up and down. He's sitting now, leaning back in his chair, listening to Lillian's flood of questions. He's freed himself and now is being swamped in her shower of emotions. He has told her, now what? Lillian obviously is shocked, but he is relieved. He now can live more openly with the loves of his life. Yes, he loves Lillian, just not in the same way he loves Claude. His three children, the fruit of this marriage, are pure joy to him, even on days they disappoint him in one way or another. They're teenagers, growing into individuals he's proud to say he has fathered.

"Lillian?"

"What do you want, now, Louis?" turning her head away as though she cannot bear looking at him anymore.

"Let's watch the movie. It'll give us a break, and then we can decide when to tell the children."

"You gotta be kidding! I don't want to be watching no movies!" To moisten her throat, Lillian reaches for her cup of tea, but she can tell it has grown cold, much like her current feelings for Louis. After knowing this man, her very own husband (bound by spiritual law? - suggestion) for nearly twenty years, she finds she doesn't know him at all. He's bisexual. Has been in a relationship with Claude all this time. What are they going to do?

"Lillian, do you want to be alone for a while? I can put on the music channel. Anyway, I better go talk to Claude. He'll be wondering how this went. You know we've been praying about this for weeks. How shall we tell the family?" "The family? Louis, you, and I are family. I don't understand. We are the two who have become one, and we now have three children together. What's gonna happen now?

"I don't know, Lillian. It's just that the pressure has been building up with Claude and me. We didn't want you or the kids to learn about us from somebody else."

"From somebody else?" Lillian jerks straight up in the chair. "Who else knows?" Her back stiffens as she envisions the looks she will get when people learn about her husband and his long-time lover. How had she not seen this earlier? Why had she not suspected something was different this past year?

"That's hard to say, Lil. Folks see Claude and me all the time. We've worked in the same building for years. Who knows what signals we've emitted that suggest we are more than alums of the same college?"

"I never noticed anything particular. I just knew you were good friends and enjoyed golfing together. When you two were out of the course, the kids and I were glad 'cause we could do sloppy things at home." Lillian smiles, recalling the hands-on projects she and the kids often chose to do when Louis was out for hours on Saturdays playing golf with Claude. Or were they just playing golf? Lillian shakes her head again, then looks up and flicks her hand at Louis, signaling she'd had enough.

"Get out. Go on outback with Claude." She repeats the hand-flicking gesture. "I know he's out in the shop working on something. I imagine he's anxious as all get out to know whether you're still alive! Go on!" she flicks again. "I need space and time to think." Louis picks up his cooling cup of tea, selects a quiet music station on the TV, and sets the remote control on the table next to his wife. They'd bought a triangular table to go between their lounge chairs. It's narrow in the front, so their chairs sit angled toward the big screen TV. The rear of the table is broad, and that's where they set the light snacks he and his wife allow themselves to eat in the TV room.

Walking back to the kitchen, he glances at the photos on the ledge under the window. He sees their wedding photo along with some snapshots of the children on their birthdays. "Yes, my wife. She'll always be my wife, the woman I chose to marry, and the mother of our children. We have a good life together and can continue doing so if I just move upstairs with Claude, the other member of the family." Family. Two, One, Three. Three what? Three children. Now three adults?

In the kitchen now, Louis looks out the window at the garage, where he's set up a narrow workbench with a sturdy top and just enough room to do minor repairs that don't need much space. Before heading outside to update Claude, Louis steps over to the counter to set down his cup. He sips the cooling tea, then spews it in the sink. "Yuck!" What was he thinking? That all he had to do was tell Lillian the truth? The truth would set him free. Of what? He's still a father. He, Claude, and Lillian still work in the same office building. He still is an usher at church. How will things change once he and Claude start living openly?

*****

"Well?" Claude queries with a puzzled face. Louis steps across the raised wooden plank and into the garage where they keep their lawn care tools, and Claude works on his small wood projects. Claude is the artist and has taught the kids all sorts of ways to convert chunks of wood into weird works of art. Often, when the kids were younger, and Louis and Lillian needed time away, Claude had been their on-call babysitter. The family, yes, the family had gotten into the habit of Saturday mornings or afternoons with Uncle Claude.

Lillian Reflects Alone

When the three children were in elementary school, Claude planned outings for them every other Saturday. As the children entered their teens, they started spending time with church or school groups, and the outings with Uncle Claude were less often.

Now that they are teenagers, they still look forward to late lunches at one of the independent restaurants around town that serve different national and international cuisines. The girls researched online to see how many other restaurants they could try that they hadn't sampled yet. The organized Lou, Jr. alphabetized the list by names. Over the past two years, they managed to get through half the list. Uncle Claude still takes them out to late Saturday lunches when the cuisine served is the same, but portions may be smaller and a little less expensive than the dinner time options. "Get the most for your money" is what his Daddy had taught him. "Shop carefully. Spend wisely."

Louis and Lillian found these outings to be a nice break from parenting and great bribers when they lived in the apartment. The kids couldn't go until they'd changed the linen on their beds and de-junkified their rooms. In addition, they each had an assigned cleaning task in the family part of their home. The girls had to run the vacuum and dust the furniture, and Lou Jr. had to empty the trash cans and clean their one and only bathroom. Knowing these chores had to be done before an outing with Uncle Claude was a great incentive.

*****

"What time is it?" Lillian calls out from the kitchen, where she is finishing the grocery list by checking the pantry shelves.

"Mom," Alvyra reminds her, "it's nearly eleven o'clock, and Uncle Claude will be here at eleven on the dot."

"Okay. You know what's next. Call your Dad. He's down there decluttering the car. No matter how many times he tells you guys to clean up after yourselves, there's always something he notices that you've left in that back seat."

By now, all three are in the kitchen, dressed in their Saturday best, ready for their afternoon culinary adventure. When they hear the front door open, they turn like members of a military front line. Dad's back, and he will have to check their rooms before they can leave.

"Well, you three. You ready for inspection?" Dad asks as he washes his hands at the kitchen sink and rips a section of paper towel from the vertical stand on the shallow countertop.

"Yes, Dad, we're ready," Lou says, speaking for the three of them. "Can you hurry?"

"Sure! Let's start in the front room." Dad leads the way, and the kids follow in reverse order of their ages. Lou Jr. walks in back to see that the girls get where they're going. He sometimes acts like he's their guardian, just 'cause he's the oldest and a male. Oh well. That comes in handy when the family is out shopping, and the girls start wandering off. Their parents know that their son takes care of the girls, though he's only a year older than they.

Dad swipes his finger across the wood surfaces and nods. Yes, they've been dusted. He does the same in the bathroom when he pulls aside the shower curtain to see if his son has cleaned the edges and rolled the rim of their old-fashioned clawfoot bathtub. Dad nods and heads to Lou's bedroom. He just sticks his head inside the doorway, sweeps the room with his eyes, nods, and turns to the girls' cluttered space. The three children stand outside the door and watch their dad go to the corner where the girls have a skinny table where they store their book bags and stuff. The legs of the table are narrow and straight and easy to vacuum around.

"Hmm," both girls mumble softly. A few months ago, Dad had noticed the twins slacking off with their cleaning, so he hid quarters in the corners of their bedroom. When neither one came to him with quarters, Dad asked them if they had found any money in their room. They looked at each other and back at him, but neither looked guilty as though they'd found the quarters and sworn secrecy? Anything. So, he walked the girls to their room and pointed to the corners at each end of their twin beds. Ah! That was the last time he had to do that!

"You won't find anything wrong in here, Dad. We vacuumed twice and didn't hear any money clanking in the metal pipes!" Alvyra smirked, then stood up straight.

"Okay, cleaning crew. You're cleared for departure!" Dad grins and gives them each a pat on the back as they tramped down the short narrow hallway back to the kitchen. Mom tightens the multiple-colored beads on the end of the braids the girls have begun wearing. They chose bead colors to match whatever they planned to wear that week. Off the three go for an outing with their uncle, leaving their two parents at home to do what mommies and daddies do.

*****

Now, out there in the garage, Louis and Claude are wondering how the teens will act around their dear Uncle once they learn about the relationship between the two adult men who have played such crucial roles in the lives of their family. But then, first, the lovers must deal with Lillian's response.

"Lillian is incredulous! But she seems to be processing the information. She did shoo me out!" Louis pauses pensively and cocks his ear toward the door, then looks at Claude, raising his shoulders and shaking his head. Have I missed something? Well, one step at a time.

"Now for the next step." He scoots the stool over to the corner to sit out of the way while Claude sands a rather intricate-looking piece of wood. "You know we gotta find the time and place to tell the kids. I don't think I wanna do it here, though."

"Why not?" Claude asks, stopping his sanding and looking up. "It should be somewhere private where they can talk if they want to."

"Well. That's true, but if Lou Jr. gets upset and starts having a hissy-fit, I don't want any of our stuff to get broken."

"You really think the kids will be all that surprised? I don't see how much will have to change. We've been living together in this house for almost two years now. The kids won't see much difference. Things won't look much different from the outside, either."

"Yeah, you're right. The neighbors are used to seeing us working out here together. We still will be using the same common front entry to the vestibule or this side door leading to the door to my flat or upstairs to yours."

"Most of the houses on the street are built like ours. So, no problem there."

"True. While you have a locked door to go up to your place and we have a locked door to enter our space, things won't look that much different."

"But, Lou, things are going to change. If we're going to live openly. Things will have to change. I've shared you with Lillian all these years. I want more of your time and attention if we're to be a true couple. I'm tired of living a double life! It feels like I'm living a lie."

"What's the truth, Claude? I'm a married man with a family!"

*****

Inside, the music wafting around her, Lillian sits, again frozen in her chair. Her eyes dart around, looking at family photos on the ledge under the side windows. Her daughters have arranged the pictures chronologically, starting on the left with the formal wedding picture of Louis and Lillian with Claude as best man and Lillian's sister, Glendella, as Matron of Honor. Next, in modest frames from left to right are collages of birthday party snapshots the girls have pulled together into single 8" x 10" frames when the narrow wooden shelf became crowded with the yearly photos. More recently, the girls have done similar collages of the siblings' school pictures. There are a few photographs of other family members here. What a range of melanin in the skin tones of her family.

*****

In her sophomore year of college, taking Women's Lit, Lillian experienced the award-winning movie Daughters of the Dust by Julia Dash. Her professor was into reading the book, then watching the film version, and, of course, discussing the ways seeing and reading evoked different mental images. Lillian was distracted from the class assignment when she watched the interactions of the women of Ibo Landing on Dataw Island. It was their physiques that caught her attention. With the skin tone of Yellow Mary and the girth of the plump supporting actresses, Lillian looked like she could have been one of that women's relatives. o

From looking through her mother's Polaroid photos, Lillian recognized early on that she inherited her generous hips from her Gullah Geechee grandmother. Viewing the Julia Dash movie, set on what now is known as St. Simons Island, off the Georgia coast, seemed to validate the stories her mother had told her. Buxom women run in our family. You see, Lillian's grandparents had been among the people of color who joined the Northern Migration in the 1930s and 40s. During that historical period, six million sons and daughters of former enslaved Black folks left the rural South. Many sought jobs in the manufacturing, assembly lines, and processing plants that sprang up in the North after the first World War.

Lillian's warm coffee with cream skin color also reflects the genes of her Iroquois grandfather. About that time, in the 1930s, when former sharecroppers were moving North, the Iroquois Nation on the Canadian border near the Great Lakes were being dispossessed of their native lands due to unenforceable treaties with the US government. In his early twenties, Lillian's grandfather, who had been sent to an American Indian Residential school, had gotten a job in one of those chemical processing plants on the Finger Lakes, not far from Lake Ontario. At lunchtime, in the segregated break? spaces, he learned how mis-educated he really was.

He then scrimped and saved enough to enroll in the community college not far from the plant. That's where he met Lillian's grandmother. She, too, was attempting to improve her chances of moving out of poverty by getting more education. The two college students clicked, married, and settled on a small plot of land not far from the Iroquois tribal lands. The companies tended to "rent" nearby land to employees, so they'd have no excuse for being late to work. Some of the folks from the south said it was almost like sharecropping. They worked the land, but the owners got the profits.

Lillian's mom and dad bought a used mobile home and settled on what probably was ancestral native land. From this location, Lillian's grandfather could easily travel by motor scooter back and forth to work. The mobile home area resembled automobile manufacturing plants in Lordstown, Ohio. Lillian didn't know for sure, but that's what she envisioned. Folks new to the area settled in economical housing within easy access to the plants where they worked.

Nobody planned to stay long anyway. Working inside the plants was a way to earn money to get out of the town. Work, college, and out of there! Perhaps, out of guilt, administrators renamed the community colleges sprang up with Iroquois nation names, like the Onondaga Community College near Syracuse. Their website claimed (and still claims), and the family found it true: "We pride ourselves on offering a quality education at an affordable price … which provides students with flat-rate, predictable pricing for textbooks and technology." Unfortunately, the flat rate was still too much for Lillian's grandparents to pay once they became parents.

During the winters in those early years, one of the workmates would pick up her grandfather. The friend just rolled up at a spot on the highway that ran by an ancient oak tree. Granddad would have snowshoed to the highway and tossed the lace-framed snowshoes in the back of the truck before riding to the plant with his friend.

Snowshoeing was the traditional way indigenous peoples in the north navigated in the winter. The webbed footwear made walking easier and faster. It kept their feet from sinking into the sometimes waist-high snow during the long winters around the Finger Lakes. Mom said that Lillian's granddad shared the cost of weekly gas for his buddy's old truck. That was less expensive than buying a vehicle of his own that he really couldn't afford.

Lillian had been born in that mobile home. Unfortunately, neither of her parents could afford to continue as students at the community college once they got married because they needed both incomes to pay the rent on the land. But birth control options known today were not available then. Lillian's Mom had soon birthed two daughters, and the couple decided she should remain an at-home mom. By this time, due to union pay scales, her dad, though never earning much, had a little more reliable income. With mom's careful money management, they'd done all right for themselves.

Once a week, Lillian's Mom would take the girls, Glendella and Lillian, to the library in town. Their neighbor's husband worked the night shift, and she had access to the car during the day. Ms. Geneva was glad to get her preschoolers out of the house so she wouldn't have to shush them all day so their dad could sleep. It was reading that kept both families from going crazy in their tight mobile homes. By reading, the moms could get out without going out other than to get the free to borrow books, thanks to the Andrew Carnegie tradition of establishing neighborhood libraries.

Over the years, as Glendella and Lillian grew into their pre-teens, reading remained a central family activity. The family chose not to spend money on cable TV and got tired of the silly shows on the networks. Besides watching The Cosby Show and reruns of Father Knows Best, few programs kept their attention for long. So, they read. In fact, it was a quotation on the wall in the library that encouraged them all to read widely.

Years later, as a grandmother, Lillian's mom encouraged her and Louis to read regularly to their children. You see, her mom had been impressed by a quotation on the bulletin board in the library's teen section that they passed on the way to the back room where the preschoolers and their parents or caretakers met for Storytime. As an adult, Lillian sometimes sees the same quotation on a poster in their local library here in town. Though no author appears on the poster, it sounds like something by Dorothy S. Strickland. "…the single biggest predictor of high academic achievement and high ACT scores is reading to children." Although her mom wasn't sure, at that time, what ACT scores meant, she knew about academic achievement.

The quotation was long, and mom said she had checked the wording out for the month the quotation was on the wall. It went on," Not flashcards, not workbooks, not fancy pre-schools…." No problem there; they could not afford a non-fancy pre-school. "…not blinking toys or computers…."

Heck, they didn't even have cable TV! Ah, here is the line that encouraged their family to continue the habit of reading. "…but Mom and Dad taking the time every day or night (or both) to sit and read them wonderful books." When raising her own children, Lillian followed the same reading advice.

Mom taught the girls the word "wonderful" could mean "amazing, eye-opening, even "awful.." During their teen years, Mom or Dad would ask Glendella and Lillian, "What did you read or learn that was "wonderful" today?" Their Mom had taught them to quote from the text and then explain their answers in their own words.

Lillian has continued the practice with her three and hopes they will use that skill on the AP exams they are scheduled to take these next couple of weeks. She is confident that the practice of reading and writing regularly is one of the reasons she and her older sister, Glendella have done well on the entry exams for college and continued to be successful students. Both completed a couple of years of community college and got satisfactory jobs with reputable companies.

Glendella and her husband encouraged their nieces and nephews to read wonderful books. For birthdays and holidays, Aunt Glendella and Uncle Quinten regularly sent books when Lillian and Louis' children were younger. In their pre-teens, gift certificates to independent bookstores. As high school students, they started receiving coupons on Amazon to select e-books or print books of their choice. No guessing for the kids. If it's from their only aunt and other uncle, it's gonna be a book.

*****

Lillian, still looks at the photos, moving from those of her parents to one of Glendella and her husband. Ah, Glendella.

Glendella is Propositioned

"Pens up!"

"Whhhaaatt?' Glendella, startled, looks up and asks. "Exam is over. Put that test sheet on top of your blue books and pass them forward right now!"

Glendella and the other hundred or so students in the exam room do as the professor says. They know from talk around campus that if you do not get that blue book upfront right away, he will not accept it even a few seconds late. And, since final exams are 30% of the course grade, few students challenge his unspoken rule.

"That's it, folks. The last gathering of English 230, Rhetoric: Oral and Written. Your oral presentations last week were pretty good. I expect comparable quality in your writing." The professor stands upfront, nodding to each of the exam proctors as each affirms that the count is right for the exams they have collected. Then, he announces with a flick of the hand to the doorway, "You're dismissed!"

Typical rumbling and bumbling arise as students reach under the desks and pull out their backpacks. Glendella slips her hand inside hers to check for her wallet with the bus pass. The next bus home leaves at 3:15. "Good," she says aloud, touching her wallet and twisting her wrist to check the time. It's just 2:35. "I got a little time."

"Great. Can I talk to you a moment?" Glendella swings around and bumps into a student just a little taller than her five feet eight inches. His bright brown eyes, about the same color as his milk-chocolate brown skin, sparkle as though he is excited about something. He reaches up and sweeps back his longer-than-usual wavy, straight hair.

"Who are you, and what do you want?" her eyes roam over his chunky shoulders bulging in a V-neck sweatshirt with a crinkly white undershirt showing. He is rather chunky. So is she. He is muscular; she is waistless. But who cares? He is still looking at her like he knows who she is. "I'm Quintin Sanchez, Afro-Panamanian, at your service, Ma'am!" he chuckles.

"Do you always include your racial lineage when you introduce yourself?" By this time, they are in the queue of students heading out the door to the arboreal quadrangle near their building. Though this is a two-year college, the expansive campus has land space enviable of many four-year institutions of higher learning.

"Yeah, I do. Folks usually wonder why a Black man has a Spanish name. My folks came over after the Panama Canal was built and have lived here since the early twentieth century. And what do I want?

"Yeah. Why are you crowding me?"

"I have a proposition for you. Wanna go out and sit under the old oak tree? I doubt many will be stopping to sit around since this is the last exam of the Spring term. Most are heading out to celebrate or commiserate with one another. I saw some folks shaking their heads as they read the opening questions on the exam."

"A proposition? You got a job offer for me? I was hoping to have something lined up by now. This is my last semester. I'll be getting my associate's degree in a couple of weeks. What about you?"

"Yeah, I'll be getting one, too. Much good it will do me. There aren't many jobs for high techs around here, and I can't afford to move right now. That's what I want to talk to you about. You thirsty?"

"As a matter of fact, I am. What you got in there to drink?" Glenda asks, pointing to his dusky canvas navy-blue backpack.

"I got some sweet tea!"

"Sweet tea? I love me some sweet tea!."

"How you know I like sweet tea?"

"Your Mom told me."

'My Mom? How you know my mother?"

"I know her from the library."

"How do you know she's my mom?"

"I saw you talking to her and asked her when you left."

"Okay, this is sounding weird. But I'm thirsty. Let's head on over to the big oak and get some of that sweet tea."

It's nearly 2:45 by the time the two students have crossed the grassy quad and are pulling their backpacks from their shoulders. There's a high-back metal bench under the tree, and they plop their packs in the middle and drop down to sit, each leaning against the high armrests at their end. The two lean back, almost in unison, and stretch out their legs.

They both put their arms behind their heads and take a deep breath. The late Spring fragrant lilac blossoms still remain on some of the trees. A light pre-summer breeze whistles through the leaves of this ancient oak tree that probably has been here since the Iroquois nation held powwows on this land.

"Um, you mentioned sweet tea," Glendella reminds Quinten.

Smiling, he quickly reaches into his backpack and pulls out a plastic bag with a squat purple cup in it. He hands it to her, then swishes out a tall silvery thermos bottle. He removes the cap and hands that to her before he twists off the inner cap. Like a bartender, he holds the tipped thermos high over the cups and pours in the tea until the cup is two-thirds full. He twists, then tilts his wrist back to stop the flow of tea, then begins the same flashy pouring into her cup. She takes a sip.

"Hmmm. This is tasty. Why'd you bring sweet tea today? Do you drink it all the time?

"Not really. I brought it today, hoping you'd share it with me while I tell you my proposition. You ready?"

"I'm not sure. But I am ready for a little more tea. This is really good. What kind of tea do you use?"

"Oh, some of that herbal tea we sell at the restaurant on Milton Street."

"On Milton Street?   That where you work? I go there all the time. Why haven't I seen you?

"Few folks notice the wait staff. That's the way we are trained. Be present, but invisible."

"You kidding me, right?"

"No, I've been working there since high school 'cause we earn pretty good tips. So many regulars from the business office across the street come for lunch and dinner. It's turned out to be a good place to work as a tech student. I get to hear what's going on in the business world and really see that there is nothing for me here. I like engines more than computers."

"So, what does all this have to do with your asking me to meet with you today? You hear about some kind of jobs for students graduating this year?"

"No, that's not my proposition. You ready?"

"I'm not sure … but go ahead."

"Well, I been aware of you since high school and noticed you in some of those big lecture classes we've had since we came here to college. I regularly see you in the restaurant and wondered if you are the one."

"The one for what?" she asks, paying a little more attention, not watching the birds skittering around across the way.

"To help me stay a Christian," Quentin continues now that he's gotten her full attention.

"What does that mean?"

"I always hear the guys talking about the girls, and they say you are approachable but not touchable. That you're probably still a virgin."

"I am, but what's that to you? I'm a Christian, too, and have committed to being a virgin until I get married."

"Well, I'm a Christian and a virgin and have made the same commitment. I mentioned there are no jobs around here for me, but my counselor told me to try the Air Force. I also am a conscientious objector but wish to serve the country that welcomed my ancestors so many years ago. We have had soldiers in every generation since. Now that the Vietnam War is over and there is no more conscription, all the branches of the military have to depend on volunteers to sign up. The Air Force really needs more techies like me."

"That's all well and good, but what does that have to do with me?"

"Well, I've heard you and your friends talk, and I know three critical things about you that may make you open to my proposition."

By this time, Glendella is a mix of curiosity and fear. What does this handsome Christian guy want from her? She's had some sniffers, guys trying to get her to do things, but with her Christian commitment and focus on schooling, she's done little dating or even thinking about marriage. Now, this guy's hinting at something.

"Well, Glendella, I also know you want to learn to play the keyboards, and you want to travel widely across the States and around the world if possible."

"That's true. But how you know all that about me?"

"Like I said, I've had my eye on you since high school, and when you and your crew are in the restaurant, I hear a lot. Folks somehow think we can hear nothing when we're clearing tables or topping up your drinks. Anyway, I talked to your Mom."

She swirls around and looks him directly in the eyes. Could this be true! "You talked to my Mom? About what?"

Hearing her turn, he swivels so he can see her as he responds, "About my proposition. She says she's been praying for you 'cause you seem more restless these past few weeks."

"Who wouldn't be restless? I'm graduating from college and have no prospects of a job. I can't keep living off my Mom. My dad's insurance pretty much paid for my college, and I've been living at home. I got a younger sister, you know. The rest of the insurance is for her." "Yeah, I know about Lillian. Anyway, you want to hear my proposition?"
"Sure, just give me the rest of the tea, and I'll sit back and listen. This better be good and quick. My bus comes in eight or nine minutes. I gotta get over there early."

"No problem. Here's the tea. And I also can drive you home. I got an old clunker parked around the corner."

Ride in the car with a stranger? No way! But it'll be okay to listen to him out here in the open.

"Well, Glendella, I've decided to join the Air Force. I already passed the test. They really want me, and I'm to report for basic training on June 15th."

"That's not much time. What're you going to be doing till then now that school is out?"

"Courting you, I hope."

"Courting me," she yelps. "You don't know me. I don't know you. You mean get married to you?" Then, she sits back and confesses, "I can't have children. I'm sterile. Coulda' been from that chemical plant where my dad worked. We don't know for sure about any of it. I just know that I'm infertile and can't be having no babies."

"I know you can't have children. That's a good thing. I'm looking for a wife. You see, I committed to the Lord not to drop Sanchez seeds all over the place. When I get married, I will be faithful, but I'll be in the Air Force, deployed who knows where. I want a wife with me, so I don't join the stereotypical pool of randy soldiers having sex with anybody, willing or not. I've had the feelings, but so far, the Lord has kept me strong enough to control those urges."

"So, what's your proposition? This obviously is not a proposal in the traditional sense."

"The proposition, Ms. Glendella is for you to marry me and get what you want. You want out of this town! You want to learn to play the keyboards, and you want to travel the world. If you accept my proposition, I will buy you one of those portable electric keyboards with earphones so you can practice anywhere we live and not disturb the neighbors as you learn and practice. As a military couple, we are likely to be sent to various places across the country and around the world. And, as often as possible, we will vacation in places on your "I want to go there, list."

"You kidding me, right? Hmmm." Glendella sits quietly for a while, then looks at her watch but doesn't move. Quentin sensitively does not rush her, sensing she is giving serious thought to his proposal. He also thinks she'll let him drive her home now that she knows he knows her Mom.

"Quentin, I don't know why this sounds tempting. I, too, have been praying about the opportunity to travel. I didn't think many guys would be interested in marrying me when they learned I wouldn't be able to have children. By the way, how did you know?" she jerks around to look at him again, "Did my mother tell you?"

"No, she merely confirmed what I'd overheard in the restaurant. It must have been the day you learned the news because your friends were commiserating with you rather loudly."

"Quinten, you talked to my mother about marrying me? This sounds like an arranged marriage kind of thing where the man talks to the parents before proposing to the woman."

"Putting it that way, Glendella, I'd say it has been arranged by God."

"Arranged by God. You think we're players on a chessboard! I'm my own woman with a God-planned destiny." Glendella pauses. Thoughts about her real situation with no job prospects and unwillingness to be a financial burden to her, Mom thinks that maybe God has had a hand in this after all. She then verbalizes,

"Oops! I guess I agree with you after all!" Glendella giggles nervously.

Quinten continues, "I do believe you are giving serious consideration to my proposition. I urge you to talk with your Mom, pray about it and let's start spending time together before I leave for basic training. Then we can write and call, as time permits, and then have a small wedding before I go to Texas for tech training. I promise to get you that electric keyboard and ask that you be my wife in every way."

*****

The two college graduates married, became a military couple, and traveled the world. Glendella learned to play keyboards because Quinten kept his promises and usually had music lessons lined up for her wherever they were stationed. She gained enough skill to become one of the accompanists at the chapels on the various bases they were stationed. She, too, kept reading, taking correspondence classes, then online courses.

She earned enough college credit with the CLEP exams but was never in a location long enough to earn an official degree. However, her scores earned in the College Level Examination Program looked impressive. She soon got security clearance and usually was able to find work on or near the bases. It was during Quinten's last assignment in Afghanistan that the bombs got him. She had been traveling with a tour group in Australia when she learned of his death on the news. That was a bombshell for her.

Over the years, the couple did fall in deep "like," and though they never claimed they loved one another, they respected each other and were content as a couple. Once her husband's physical remains were flown home, there was a memorial service for him. Captain Quinten Sanchez is now buried in Arlington Cemetery. Glendella has decided to make her home in town with her sister, who has just experienced her own bombshell. Thank the Lord the two sisters have each other.

*****

Lillian's phone rings. It is her sister calling back. "Hello, Glendella."

"Hey, Baby Sis. Are we still on for going to Nourish Your Curls Boutique next week to get some hair care products? I heard she's released her own line of products under the salon name."

"Definitely, yes. Um. Can I get back to you after Church tomorrow?

"Sure. What's up? You can't talk now? Okay, No biggie. We can talk after church tomorrow. I'm excited about your song."

"Thanks, Big Sis. See you tomorrow."

*****

"Glendella! Oh, my God!" Glendella's supposed to be accompanying me when I sing at church tomorrow. "Tomorrow! Dear God! "Just a Closer Walk with Thee." How can I sing that song with what I now know? That first verse is gonna make me cry. I know it!" The choir will start with the chorus, then I'm to sing the verses as a solo.

I am weak, but Thou art strong.
Jesus, keep me from all wrong.
I'll be satisfied as long,
As I walk, let me walk close to Thee.

39

Lillian Wonders

Until a couple of years ago, Lillian had been a merry-go-round, Christian. While still a teenager, she'd attended a fire and brimstone youth service. The preacher had described that hell awaited those who did not accept Christ as Savior. She and about a dozen other youth crept up to the altar, bowed their heads, and accepted the prayers of the deacons and deaconess who met them there.

She and Glendella had been raised in the Church. Active participation in church programs brought them satisfaction, even joy. Glendella, the older sister, had married a career military man and traveled with him worldwide. So, Lillian found a family in the church community. She gleefully rode the merry-go-round of the liturgical calendar: singing for Christmas and Easter programs, taking first Sunday communion, helping celebrate Mother's and Father's Day, and visiting the sick with her youth group, when young, and then as a college student, reserved time to serve in their Neighborhood Care Ministry.

When she first moved to this town after her internship, Lillian had joined in fellowship at Beth-El Community Church, an interdenominational congregation. Their Pastor, a Bible scholar, encouraged them to be light and salt as Christians. She understood the light and had to ask for explanations about being salt. He referred her to the writing of Skip Heitzig, who explains that salt preserves and adds flavor. She wanted to preserve her marriage and add flavor to entice Louis to remain her husband.

One Sunday, a couple of years ago, concluding a sermon series at their church, a guest speaker directed the congregants' attention to the formatting in the New International Version of the Bible. "Note the subtitle of this section of Matthew's Gospel. It's the BE-ATTITUDES. Jesus' sermon describes WHO we should BE, not just WHAT we should DO. Once we accept Him both as Savior and Lord, we'll begin to grow into the men and women He purposed us to be."

That sermon evoked recognition of her stagnant spiritual state. As a teenager, Lillian had been doing church work for insurance, not as an outgrowth of a relationship with her Savior. Reflecting on those early years of marriage and the first years of motherhood, Lillian saw little evidence of developing the attitudes of the Beatitudes.

You see, she had never accepted Christ as Lord. She had not recognized it was a relationship she needed to cultivate, not just religious rituals. New insight sent her to the altar and down on her knees to, once again, accept the fervent prayers of altar workers. She committed to rectifying her oversight. Since that service, she has become more conscientious. She's striving to nurture her relationship with God, not just stagnate in her walk as the bearer of insurance from Hell.

She works diligently with Christ-centering motivation. No longer revolving in busyness, she has been evolving, becoming rooted and grounded in Christ, her safeguard Savior and, also, her beloved Lord.

This evening, sitting alone in the living room, Lillian wonders, "Am I grounded enough? Will I be able to withstand the inevitable winds that are coming now that my husband and his best friend, Claude, are planning to live as a couple in the upstairs flat? How are the children going to deal with all this change? Louis is a man of his word. If he says he's moving, that's what he's going to do."

Lillian scoots out of her chair, rolls the newspaper, and puts it in the tall narrow basket they use for a trash receptacle in the TV room. She repeatedly wonders, "Why didn't I see this?" She thinks back on the Sundays she sang in the choir. At her church, the whole choir sings on the first Sunday, when the congregation celebrates communion. Small ensembles sing on the other Sundays. The youth often perform on fifth Sundays. What fun to see them up there singing familiar songs, the ones she cherished as a teenager, written by Kirk Franklin or recorded by the Higginsen's Youth Choir.

Now, as an adult, Lillian is up in the choir stand twice a month. On the first Sunday with the full choir and the third Sunday with the small gospel praise team, of which she is a part, she leads the worship service.

Shaking her head again, trying to settle the swirling thoughts, Lillian leaves the living room. She heads back to the master bedroom suite, undresses, and takes her ritual Saturday evening shower. When the kids were young, Saturday evenings were for getting ready for Sunday morning. Everyone chose what they would wear. The twins laid out ribbons or barrettes to match their Sunday go-to-meeting outfits. Each family member was expected to clean and shine their shoes. Often this just meant putting lotion on the leather shoes or Vaseline on the patent leather shoes Lillian and her daughters wore in the Spring and Summer.

Lou and his dad would choose color-coordinating slacks and shirts, and as he got older, Lou Jr. added odd-colored vests or jackets. Though teenagers now, all three youngsters still dress special for Sundays, but with less emphasis on church clothes and more on what's in style. They did have to keep in mind dad's caution, "If it's not for sale, don't advertise!" meaning the girls had to be careful about showing too much of what God had gifted them.

And on Saturday, everyone had to take a full bath! In their apartment, they had only one bathroom, so they had to take turns, get in and out, and not use up all the hot water! Louis, the thoughtful man that he is, would be last in line. He often squealed when the hot water ran out and could only take a cold shower. "Oh well," he'd say, "such is the life of a father."

Now that they have their own home with three places for Saturday evening ablutions, they must still be careful about too many taking Saturday night baths and/or showers in too short a time. Even with an automatic water heater, they often run out if someone selfishly stays under the shower too long.

Well, that won't be a problem tonight. No one else is in the house! "Does this mean my husband will go upstairs with Claude this evening? Oh, God! What are we gonna do when the kids get home tomorrow? Louis and I haven't talked about that. Well, I'm not ready. I'll take my shower and do my evening devotions. What'll the Scripture passage be today? Will I see things more clearly after my prayer time?"

Lillian takes a quick shower and shrugs into a long-sleeved nightgown. She continues to question her blindness as she ties a silk headscarf around her freshly washed and cream-conditioned hair. Her naturally curly, oh, okay, kinky hair tends to be dryer lately. She's learned that the leave-in conditioner soaks in better when she wraps her head. So, recently, she's been sleeping with her head tied in a scarf or wearing a nightcap. Either work, keeping her curls nicer and the pillow cleaner. Louis hasn't complained; in fact, he's complimented her on the colors. Hmmm.

Accepting the fact that he probably will not be in until later, if he comes in at all, Lillian takes out her colorful little square devotional booklet and turns to the page with today's date. She sits in the comfy corner chair near the window on the side, where she can smell the woodsy cedar fragrance of piney juniper trees. It's a relaxing fragrance. After all, she's been through this evening.

Ah, what is the devotional title? "Hurt Can Turn to Hate!" and the Scripture is, what? Oh, Leviticus 19:17-18. That's odd; most of the time, the writers in this devotional series use Scriptures from Psalms or the New Testament. The two-page daily devotionals end with challenging questions for readers to ponder as they consider how the Scripture applies to their lives. The readings often end with questions like, "What would Jesus do?

Still, knowing what the Bible says does not keep the questions from running through her mind. What about ME? Is my marriage a lie and a sham? Was I never loved? What am I going to do now? Our kids are teens. What about when they are grown and gone? I don't want to be left alone! I'm too old to marry again.

Then Lillian ponders the possible reactions of others. Am I the victim here? Or was I so anxious to be married with children that I ignored signs of a relationship between Louis and Claude? How could I NOT have known? Am I so blind or so stupid? Who else may have guessed all this? The confusing mix of stunned disbelief, anger, and sadness nearly engulfs her. It makes her feel like she needs another shower. Then she remembers that she is a child of God, and He's promised to help. Maybe the reading in this devotional will give her an idea.

Lillian starts reading and learns that hurt can turn to hate and that harboring hate can make one hurt others. Well, Louis has certainly hurt her with his revelation! Will that automatically make her start hating him and Claude? How can she? They'd been positive partners in her life for nearly two decades. How will what she learned today to change that? Will she be looking for ways to hurt them the way their news is hurting her?

Tears spill down onto her silky nightgown. Lillian struggles to process the news and anticipate the future. Her shoulders tighten and sweat pours from her armpits. "Oh, pew! I forgot to put on deodorant!

Lillian takes care of refreshing herself and, as she puts the stick deodorant back in the cabinet, notices the Tylenol PM that she used last year when she had slipped on the snowy driveway and injured her back. She was hurt then, and she hurts now. Maybe if she just takes one tablet, it'll help her fall asleep.

She grabs one of the water bottles she and Louis keep in the bathroom for rinsing after brushing their teeth. She fills her mouth with water, pops in the pill, and lets it float down her throat. Quickly screwing on the bottle cap, she returns to the bedroom to continue her nightly devotions and meditation. Somehow, taking a little time to read a short Scripture passage and a brief contemporary application, the affirmation statement and the brief prayer seems to help her relax after mommying all day.

Tonight, Lillian, actually, says the prayer aloud. She usually reads it silently and nods her head in consent to indicate to who knows who, "Yeah, that's a good one!" Tonight, speaking the words of the prayer helps to calm her spirit. She lays the bright-colored booklet on the nightstand next to her side of the bed. Her side.

"Oh no! Will this whole bed be mine alone from now on!" True, Lillian and Louis have not been very active sexually, but that's not the only thing they did in bed.

Sometimes they lay holding hands, praying, and giving thanks for being in the presence of the life partner who had made them a parent. She and Louis talked a lot in the privacy of their bedroom, lying coiled together in this comfy queen-sized bed. Tonight, she pulls back the spread and quilt and then plumps the pillow. She looks over to his side and then climbs in alone with her back to that side. This is not the first time she's slept by herself since she and Louis married seventeen years ago.

His job often involves him traveling on buying trips for the building crew he supervises and attending professional development workshops. That is one of the things he insisted on adding to his job contract. He budgets time for himself and his senior staff to attend a job-related conference yearly. Louis looks forward with excitement to meeting with others across the country who are employed in similar work settings or fill comparable roles. Lillian thinks her husband has stayed with this job for so long because he's been able to get away regularly.

Oh no! Maybe those trips were also getaways with Claude! Who knows? She never suspected, so she never asked. "Enough! I'm going to sleep. The kids won't be home 'til tomorrow after church. After church! I'm supposed to be singing tomorrow! Am I going to be able to get through that song? With Louis and Claude ushering at the back doors of the sanctuary, will I be able to get a note out at all?"

*****

While Louis grew up in a similar church, much of the protocol was new to Claude. The usher director at their church is old school. He has the usher staff trained to military precision. When on duty, both men and women are expected to stand at attention with their hands behind their backs. As congregants arrive, they are escorted by one of the two ushers at each of the three rear doors of the sanctuary. The ushers hold out gloved hands, palm up, to beckon and direct the person or group to vacant seats as close to the front as there is room.

Most families are accustomed to being seated as close to the front as possible so latecomers will not disturb those already there. Being an interdenominational congregation confuses some newcomers. Those from more established traditional denominations wonder, out loud, why there are no "assigned" seats with names of the old families emblazoned on brass name tags screwed to the back of the comfy, uncushioned wooden benches.

Their pastor, who invites all to call him by his first name, believes in equity and unity. "We're a family, headed by Christ. My role in the family is to pastor; I'm just a shepherd here to feed the flock and guide our church members to safety. But I'm no more or less important than anyone else who comes into the house of the Lord."

This was a little hard for Louis to understand. He was familiar with a more hierarchical church structure where the Bishop was treated as royalty. The relationships among the church family here are equitable, amiable, and supportive.

Louis and Claude often usher on the first and third Sundays. At Beth-El, the ushers have reserved seats in the rear to be on hand to attend to latecomers entering from the rear doors. So, once the Pastor reads the Scripture passage for the sermon and prays that God's Word will be heard and understood, the ushers close the center doors and walk with military precision to their allocated seats. Unless needed to escort out a restless child or adult needing assistance to the restrooms, the ushers remain alert but seated until it is the time at the end of service to collect the tithes and offering.

So, Lillian is accustomed to seeing her husband and Claude seated together, even during church services. How will things appear now? Will Pastor allow the two men to remain in this position once they come out of the closet and begin living together as a couple?

Tomorrow, Louis and Claude will be standing at their places, ushering at the back doors of our handsome sanctuary. At that time in the service, special music plays, and the sunbeams flow through the stained-glass windows along the left side of our church home. Lillian wonders, "Tomorrow, will those sunbeams be accusatory spotlights pointing out those who've betrayed me? But my sister, Glendella, will be there, too."

Louis Reflects Alone

Back in his flat, after talking with Claude, Louis returns to the room where he had revealed to his wife of seventeen years that he'd like to move upstairs and live with his lover. Being bisexual, having a male and female sex partner didn't seem wrong to him. After all, he is as God made him. He is the example of that verse in Genesis, male and female created he them.

Louis is still a family-oriented person committed to fathering his children and remaining loyal to his wife, Lillian, and his lover, Claude. He has not cheated on either of them since he began his relationship with them. He had just not told Lillian that Claude has been more than a college alum and "baby brother" to him all these years. Telling her that was harder than he thought because he knew how much Lillian respects Claude as the only Uncle their children have known.

Lillian's older sister, Glendella, did marry, but she and her husband had spent their entire married life in military service, and because she'd always wanted to travel the world, her husband, Quintin Sanchez, accepted any international assignments that came his way. The two had no children, so Glendella was free to travel with him. Consequently, Louis' kids only knew Uncle Quintin as a soldier in a picture and a signature on holiday gifts and birthday cards. Claude, on the other hand, has been here since they were each born. Claude has been their relative, period.

Because Louis and Lillian had moved here to work right out of college, they left their aging parents back home. Within five years, Lillian's mom, then a widow, died of rapidly spreading breast cancer, and his Mom, who has remarried, now lived on the West Coast. Thoughts of his childhood roll through his memory as he, too, looks at the photos on the ledge under the windows next to the chairs he and his wife had sat in a couple of hours earlier. Not yet ready to answer more questions, Louis brews another cup of tea and comes here to sit for a spell.

He picks up the picture taken at their small church wedding. Glendella had flown home to be her baby sister's maid of honor, and Claude was his best man. They looked handsome, with genuine smiles, resolved to support one another as their nuclear family expanded to include Louis and Claude on one hand and Lillian and Glendella on their side.

Sipping his tea, he notes again the range of skin tones in the picture. Thinking about what he'd told his wife tonight, he recalls his Mom's response when, while a college student, he had told her about his sexual orientation. What a day that was! It should have prepared him for this one. He takes another sip of tea and sits back, letting the memories roll like a film through his brain. He looks at a birthday picture and, also, of one of his Mothers. He doesn't look much like her at all.

*****

Louis inherited his blue-black skin from his father, Jamal, a Sudanese man who had come to the United States for college. Louis' grandfather, a minister, had met an Episcopal priest at one of those ecumenical gatherings popular in the 1970s. (Some called it the Fourth Great Awakening of the Protestant movement.) More church groups seemed open to collaborating on community outreach in his small town. That White priest had asked his Black brother in the Lord to host this orphaned Sudanese college student being sponsored by the Episcopal group.

As generous as they were, the Episcopalians also were sensitive to the social times. Though segregation in public spaces had been outlawed, very few towns had integrated communities in the north. The priest thought the young man from Africa may be more comfortable living with a black family, feeling less visibly different in the still relatively homogeneous black neighborhood; the minister agreed.

The three of them, the minister, his wife, and their teenage daughter, welcomed this brother of color to their home. Though their living space was tight, their hearts were expansive. In preparation for Jamal's arrival before the fall term started, they converted the third bedroom that had been dad's home office into a bedroom for Jamal.

This first-year college student had learned English at the Episcopal-sponsored school in his South Sudan homeland and, with a good ear, soon spoke American English with relative fluency. The minister, a part-time pastor of a storefront church, who worked during the week at the county office, arranged for Jamal to get a green card. To help offset the cost of his care, Jamal had picked up a job in one of the fast-food chains. This job gave him insight into the community and lots of practice speaking local dialects of American English. It also exposed him to various germs that soon took their toll.

Ruby Lynn, the teenage daughter, a PK, had been considered royalty among her peers. The teens in the neighborhood seldom invited this preacher's kid to typical teen gatherings. The boys knew not to even think of touching her or asking her out. She was lonely and warmly welcomed Jamal to the family, to her heart, and all too soon to her bed. Her parents, initially furious at the young people, insisted that they get married right away, just in case she was pregnant. The congregation members could count, and the pastor did not want to deal with the gossip he knew would ensue.

His wife had heard this kind of talk at the Wednesday afternoon sewing circle she hosted for the senior citizens making quilts for the homeless in their community. It didn't take much to imagine the tittle-tattle.

"How could a man supposin' to be so smart be so ig'nant?"

"You mean, Paaasta. He shoulda know'd bringin' a handsome young man to live in the house was just fire waitin' to burn."

"Girl, you know you sho is right. And that Jamal being a forener and everythin'. He probly been used to takin' what he want without thinkin' nothin' of it."

"Yeah. How he different from the men 'round here?"

The wedding of Jamal and Ruby Lynn was small, but the pastor's daughter did not remain that way for long. She was, in fact, having a baby.

Unfortunately, Jamal had contracted some ailment that led to the quick demise of his health. The sponsoring Episcopal group thought it may have been a delayed reaction to the series of shots Jamal had had to have before he was approved for immigration. He died just weeks after Louis was born. By that time, however, the family had worked through their distress about the rushed marriage and had even begun to celebrate that there would be a male to carry on the family name.

You see, they named the baby Louis after the minister. Jamal had also taken his wife's last name, Robertson, to seem more American. Still, they all agreed to keep Jamal as the baby's middle name to keep the connection to his Sudanese family heritage.

Louis thrived under the parenting of his grandfather and managed to matriculate into the state college. The church family helped him with college expenses. But alas, in his sophomore year, his aging grandfather and the Pastor died. On his death bed, the Pastor had recommended that the church family not carry on the ministry in the storefront church, which he had been pastoring for the past ten years.

Congregation members gravitated to other non-denominational fellowships nearer their homes. Money for college stopped coming in, but Louis did not drop out. His grades were solid enough for him to get into a federal work-study program. That's what led to the internship and eventual job here in town.

By the time he had started college, Louis had become a proud man who'd learned, under the tutelage of his grandfather, to honor women. Grampa did not want Louis to be responsible for another family and experience a forced marriage due to e teen's indiscretion. This behavior was not difficult for Louis because he didn't feel strongly attracted to women anyway.

Sometimes, at the Junior and Senior proms in high school, he felt moved when the slow dances came up, but his temperature seldom rose to the height he was tempted to ask for more than a dance. And yet, he experienced the same warmth when he was around young men. After living with these feelings since puberty and having read books like The Kiss of the Spiderwoman by Manuel Puig and City of Night by John Rechy, Louis finally acknowledged that he is gay.

*****

One evening, on a Saturday he did not have to work, he settles in the chair Grampa nearly wore out writing notes for his sermons. Louis turns to his Mother and begins,

"Mom, remember when you told me about James Baldwin and how much you admire his writing."

"Sure, Louis. He is known for his articulate advocacy of civil rights and often is interviewed on college campuses and on TV talk shows. What about James Baldwin?"

"He was gay!"

"I know, but what has that to do with your reading his book? You read *Fire Next Time* for senior English, didn't you? That was a powerful book about the issue of the civil rights movement that got a lot of us thinking about what we should be doing."

"I know, Mom. I also read *Giovanni's Room,* where he talks about him and his lover living in Paris."

"And, again, what has this to do with us? We're Christians. We don't talk about that kind of stuff."

"Mom. I'm gay!"

"You can't be! You're my son! I've raised you better than that!" "I'm coming out to you, Mom, so you'll understand me."

Mom had read James Baldwin's Giovanni's Room and recalled what had happened in 1969 at the Stonewall Club in New York City when the gay people there rioted. She could not imagine her son as one of them.

Mom is furious. Her eyes flit left and right as though looking to see if there is someone else in the room. She storms over and slams the door even though there is no one else in the house but them. But, you never know. Folks still see this as the pastor's house and don't always knock before coming inside. Before today, their easy access to the house didn't matter.

She turns to her handsome blue-black son, looking up at him from her diminutive five feet four inches, and with piercing eyes, shakes her pointed finger up in his face.

"We raised you to be a man. A man of God! What kind of nonsense is this?"

"It's not nonsense, Mom. It's the way I am. You've told me since I was a wee one that God has known me since you carried me inside your own body. What's that verse in Psalms?"

"Don't be quoting Scripture to me, young man. That verse in Psalms 139 is not about you! It's about King David!"

"That's not what Grampa said. He said the Bible refers to me, too. That's why it has been preserved. So, I can learn how to relate to the God who created me. I accepted Christ as my Savior; that means I am a child of God. Why can't you believe God would make somebody with feelings like mine?"

"God, don't make mess like this. Can you imagine what the church folks are gonna say if you come out and tell them that you are a homo? They'll probably start thinking you have been more than a counselor with the young boys you been working with in Sunday School. You ain't been messin' with them boys have you?"

"Mom! No! Of course not! I wouldn't do that!" Louis returns his mother's glare with fire flowing from his eyes. "Being a gay person does not mean I am a pedophile. Nor am I promiscuous. I have not acted on these sexual feelings the way you and Daddy did before you got married."

"Oh, Louis!" Mom retorts, shaking her head, ashamed of the thought of her son bringing that up now. "That is so low! Your Dad and I made a mistake. God has forgiven us for that. We got married and everything."

"Well, I certainly am glad for that. It would be pretty bad for me to be both blue-black and a b… you know the word I'm not saying." Then, Louis stops, ashamed of how he talks to his mother. Grampa had taught him to respect women. His mother is a woman. Maybe she has a closed mind, but she is a woman and deserves his respect. He steps over to her to put an arm around her shaking shoulders. She lets him.

"Mom, I'm sorry. That was a low blow. But I was really hoping you'd understand. I'm gay. God made me this way. I'm not going to start sleeping around. I'm going to wait until the Lord leads me to my partner for life. Heck, it may even be a woman I take for my wife."

Then, Mom twists, swirls, and escapes his apologizing arms. "Louis Jamal! This is more than I can handle right now. We were hoping you'd follow in Dad's footsteps and restart the ministry he'd begun here."

Most of the folks worshipping at the storefront church when Grampa was pastor have joined other fellowships. But Mom and the regulars expected Louis to go to the seminary, return, and restart the work right there.

"We have a lot of work to do in this community and reestablishing a neighborhood house of worship would give us a center to work from."

"That's your calling, Mom, not mine. Folks are okay with women being ministers nowadays. Why don't you get yourself ordained?"

"Well, maybe I will. Maybe I will do just that! I know, though, I'm not gonna be able to stay around here. The folks will laugh me out of town. Maybe I'll accept the proposal of Charles, that guy at work who's been sniffing around me since you started college. He knew I wasn't gonna sell this house till you got grown."

"You're going to get married again, Mom? I wouldn't know you as a married woman. You been the Pastor's daughter and my mother all these years!"

"I'll always be your mother, Louis Jamal. But I don't have the strength to put up with what's gonna come up if you come out. Think you can hold off 'til I leave?"

His mother starts pacing around the room, trying to figure out how she can leave town without being tainted by what she believes will come when the community learns her son is a gay man. "Yes. Louis. That's a good idea. I can go to seminary in Los Angeles. That's where Charles is moving this Fall. You know, real estate's been turning over fast here. We can sell the house, use some of the money to finish paying for your college, and the rest for me to go to seminary school."

"Yeah, Mom. I'm not in a hurry to make the next move now that I've acknowledged my sexuality to you. I gotta finish college before I can afford to do anything anyway. And you know, Mom, women sometimes seem attracted to me, too. They seem curious about my skin and often come rubbing up to me to feel it. Why do they think blue-black skin feels different from brown-orange skin? You ladies kill me, Mom."

"Louis, you mean you're attracted to women, too?"

"I can't say I'm attracted to women. I'm not repulsed by them the way some gay guys are that I've read about."
"What do you mean you've read about? Have you decided you're gay just because of something you've read? You don't believe everything in print or on social media, do you? Hey, Louis, you may not be gay at all!" Mom seems to be looking for any way to change the facts.

"No, Mom, I am. What I've read has just confirmed what I've been feeling for some time. I'm not running from who I am. I believe the Bible. God made me, and I'm here for a purpose. I'm going to keep attending church, reading my Bible, and confirming what that purpose is. I hope it's being a father. I really want to have children to carry on the heritage of my Sudanese father.

" He died so soon, and you didn't have more children with him. So, it's up to me."

"Oh, Louis. That would be a real treat to be a grandmother. My mother seemed to enjoy that role with you, especially when you were a baby. 'Come here, Sweetness,' she'd say, leaning down to pick you up and cuddle you tight to her chest. "Well, while I do remember, Gramma, I wish she'd been around as I was growing up. But God took her home before I got to middle school. I was hoping she'd stop calling me "Sweetness." Now, she never will call me anything, again."

"Louis, we're not going down that road today. I miss her and my dad so much. They'd help me deal with what you've told me today, but I have their teaching to guide my thinking. I think I'm going to leave town. I'm not strong enough to withstand what I know is coming."

*****

Now, Louis sets down his teacup and puts the picture back on the shelf, his eyes a little damp as he recalls selling their house. His mom married and moved Los Angeles within a few months of his revealing to her his sexual orientation. He prays fervently that he will not lose another family just because of who he is.

Returning to the kitchen, he rinses his cup and puts it into the dishwasher. He has no idea why he thinks the dishwasher can't clean dishes by itself. Oh well. He helps where he can. Now that he has come clean with his wife, he prays that God will honor his honesty and help him keep his family.

Claude Reflects Alone

Today, I do numbers. It's my job. They are clean. They are clarity. They are perfect for me.

In high school, it was mathematics. I was decent in my other subjects, but with math there was no middle ground. There was no gray area. The results were clear and couldn't be redefined. By the time I was admitted to calculus I had also secured a spot on the mathematics team. My teachers found my quiet confidence admirable. No gray – all black and white. But the grey area still existed long before I started taking Lillian and Louis' children to the restaurant. The grey area existed before Louis, and then Lillian, came into my life.

My aptitude in math put me in good position for my freshman year. It was springtime, my favorite time of the year, just like now, the month of May. I had been holding down several shifts per week at Sumner's restaurant when I met Andrew, another server there. Tall, quiet, and slender with a deep- throated chuckle and a deeper voice that would startle someone who didn't know him; he was so quiet. Andrew wasn't a college student like me. I think he must have been three or four years older, and he worked several different shifts. He was kind, keenly interested in me in a way that other boys hadn't been in high school.

Those six months, I felt our friendship grow. Our interactions seemed effortless, and he was always smiling when I worked alongside him. He made me feel funny, interesting. He would tease me about my calculous books and my accounting calculator. He called me Numbers.

"Numbers, when you're done studying tomorrow, why don't you come over after your shift and we'll have a few beers."

Crab apple blossoms dotted the pavement there on the south residential campus along the walkway from my car back to my dorm. It was the second time I had slept at Andrew's apartment. He wasn't helping me to stay focused on my grades. He only wanted to "mess around." So, I stopped spending time with Andrew. I made it through my second semester with another 3.65 GPA. The consistent focused approach worked, and my grade point average remained the same.

I also remember the sound of the keys jangling in my pocket as Andrew walked me to the car. A symphony of my shame. Society just didn't understand men with men. Nor did I. The red-winged blackbirds in the trees created a cacophony, the sounds playing off my nervous jingling.

Then came Frank. The first night he visited my dorm, the picture didn't work; time with another man wasn't what I thought it would be. I wouldn't eat for a full day after. But I didn't understand why. The grip on my throat felt real, like someone slowly squeezing out every, last, drop of my pain.

Frank was nice enough, but I wasn't sure I wanted to see him again. But then, as his Datsun pulled out of the student guest parking section, I suddenly felt so alone. Watching his brake lights flash before he turned left onto West Campus Drive, the lurch – not sure if it came from my throat or heart – left me feeling empty. Embarrassed and alone. Though alone doesn't quite capture the feeling.

I've always been alone. Dependable, quiet Claude.

With Andrew, it was as if I was offered a test. I could no longer avoid these feelings. When I was about twelve, like David Sedaris, I came into a secret and grew furtive. I, as Sedaris said, am gay. It's funny how that works. One moment you're a child and know only that there's something different about you, something that separates you from other boys. Then you get a little older and understand what that thing is.

This was it; these times with Andrew and Frank confirmed who I am. Like the act of accepting Christ made me a Christian, this act of another man in my bed meant I would cross into another? reality. The body can't lie, and there would be no turning back now. There was no way to bury this, like I had buried my head into the pillow. I had always buried everything; it was just easier that way.

At the end of the school year, I left the restaurant job to focus on accounting and the course load for my major. The numbers felt a bit safer, truer to who I am. I would go on for years and pretend the relationships hadn't happened. That both were mistakes. Just a phase. I would keep burying it because burying was easiest. Put it away and never see it again. Not worth the trouble. I didn't want that kind of life.

But I can't seem to hide it or make it go away, and now this is the burden I will bear. This is the burden I was to my parents. They never understood my sexual orientation. Now, my recompense. Will I lose my lover now?

Learn about GEMS

Lillian lies in bed reflecting on her earlier years as a wife and mom. One day, walking through their home watering the plants she'd received as an unexpected gift from her friend, Delphi, whom she and Louis had met on their one and only trip to Hawaii. Louis traveled regularly on shopping trips and to professional development events for his job and had earned airline miles.

Claude had consented to stay with the children, so for their tenth anniversary, Louis had treated his wife to a week on Maui in a timeshare he'd seen published on the bulletin board at work. It seems one of the employees was not going to use their week there this year and offered it to someone who worked in the building. Several folks had asked about it, but because Louis had been first, the woman met with Louis and Lillian and consented for them to sublet it for this special occasion.

While on the trip, Louis and Lillian had met Delphi who was there with her husband for an anniversary trip, too. The two couples ended up spending time together and during one of the ladies' days out, Delphi mentioned something that later became important to Lillian.

*****

"Lillian, would you like to go do one of those arts and crafts sessions they offer here. Our guys won't be interested. We can make something to take home for our families. My mom lives not far from me."

"Really, both my parents have passed on, but they lived on the other side of the state anyway. We didn't get to see them much once we left."

"You mean you and Louis are from the same town?"

"Oh, no! I mean me and my sister, Glendella. She's a military wife and has been living abroad most of her married life. No, Louis and I met on the job. We don't work for the same company, but in the same building. His family, too, lived on the opposite side of the state from where we live now. His dad died when Louis was just a few months old. Louis was raised by his mom and her Dad. His grandmother had one of those freak accidents while chaperoning their youth group at a roller-skating party. They were playing crack the whip, then after a crack, someone let go. His grandmother fell and cracked her back when she flew into one of the corners at the rink.

The kids saw her crumpled up, but since almost everyone had fallen a couple times that evening, they didn't think it was serious. Apparently, the roller rink owner thought so, too, and delayed calling in the medical team. By the time they got to her she'd nearly bled out.

During the surgery to repair the break, she learned she'd never walk again. So, she told them she didn't want to be a burden to the family or his ministry. Just let her go. Of course, it wasn't as quick as all that, but she did convince them to put her in one of those homes. At that time, we Black folks had limited access to quality care. Louis' Mom contracted something and died within a year."

"Really? That's a shame. So, Louis was raised by his mother and grandfather?" "Yes, and their congregation. His grandfather was pastor of a storefront church in their town. He wanted to remain in the community where most of these Black folks lived but didn't want to spend excess cash to build a sanctuary that would only be used a couple of days a week."

"That's interesting. Most pastors seem to want big fancy buildings to show off the power of their ministries. My folks worshiped in a small wood plank building in Mississippi. I didn't go much because I had no respect for the pastor."
"What do you mean, you had no respect for the pastor?

"Our pastor knew my grandfather was a pedophile but didn't call him on it because Pawpaw was an influential teacher in the community. My mama was a victim of his groping paws."

"Oh Delphi! How awful for you! Is that why you spend so much time at the gym clubs, burning off anger at your childhood experiences?"

The women had been walking at a pretty-fast clip for those unaccustomed to walking on the sand. They'd taken off their sandals and walking barefoot really gave the calves a workout. Delphi stopped and giggled as she realized the misunderstanding about GEMS club.

"At the gym? What do you mean? Oh, Girlfriend! GEMS is an acronym! I'm sorry. I guess I thought that everybody knows about it since one of the groups with that name, Girls Everywhere Meeting the Savior! group has been around for over fifty years. But I've adapted what I do in our town to include the programming of another GEMS group, Girls Educational and Mentoring Service which addresses issues of girls who've been sexually abused or trafficked.

"So, that makes more sense. That's why you've become a GEMS club leader."

"Yes, that's one of the reasons. Since I've become an adult, moved away from that toxic town, and married, Malcolm, a man with respect for women and the vows of marriage, I've come back to the Lord. Thankfully, He never left me after I became a Christian as a pre-teen. I just ignored Him for years.

I've become a GEMS leader because I believe in the purposes of both the GEMS clubs I knew about. The one, called Girls Everywhere Meeting the Savior! was for females in elementary through middle school. And the other Girls Educational and Mentoring Services was for young ladies 12-24 years old. Currently, our town is small, so we didn't need two different clubs when a combo club would do it. For this reason, I keep the non- denominational feature of the first but include speakers and activities that prepare girls to become strong, independent women who live out their lives based on Biblical principles. I started to meet with upper elementary and middle school girls from a variety of churches at a church near the park in my neighborhood. It's not far from a real busy church called Beth-El Community."

"Beth-El Community Church! I go to a busy church near a park in …. No! Don't tell me! You're from the same town as me and Louis! You know, Delphi, we got a pair of twin girls who are in fourth grade. Do you think this would be a good place for them? I was thinking of Pioneer Girls, you know like a Christian Girl Scout or Camp Fire Girls, but they don't have one in our town."

"Sure, why not? When we get back home, you three can come to one of our open meetings. If you think it's right for your girls, I'd be glad to have them join us."

*****

During their few days on Maui, Lillian gathered that Delphi and Malcolm were active in their home congregation and since the GEMS group was non-denominational, Lillian decided to check it out. The girls did like what they experienced at the open GEMS meeting and when they were in fifth grade, joined. Because most of the girls were about the same age when they started, Delphi adapted both meanings for GEMS and blended the two in her meetings.

Delphi has kept the girls who wish to stay once they get into high school. That transition from middle school to high school is tough for many students, male and female. The GEMS club members support one another at school where it can be easy to slip away from the teachings they received earlier. Once they've completed their freshman year in high school, however, most of the girls drop out because they've gotten active in sports, drama, and music at their school. Alvyra and Alysa have stayed and now Lillian is thankful she has Delphi, who understands some of the challenges her daughters are likely to face when they get side-eyes from people who believe bisexuals are to be scorned.

*****

As Lillian finishes watering the pothos plants, she smiles at what she learned about this indoor plant that has been thriving in their new house. In fact, they've snipped the vines and have this vibrant green plant growing in a pot in the master bedroom suite. Lillian learned on a website she'd consulted to learn how to care for the plant that the pothos is one of the best houseplants for reducing indoor pollutants. Maybe these plants will help keep the air clean in their home symbolically as well as botanically.

Meet the Teens

Next year, my parents tell me, Next Year.

When I turn sixteen next March, I, Alvyra Lynn Robertson, will be able to get a third piercing on my left lobe and I will be eligible for a driver's license, and I can date – "with close supervision." It's as if sixteen is this magical number in adolescence, an instantaneous rite of passage, where suddenly, *boom!* I am so much more mature than I was at fourteen years old. How does that work? I'm not sure about driving, but I am ready for the piercing and my crush will already be graduating by the time I am deemed old enough for a supervised date.

"It's only a year," my folks say.

"A year is still a long time for a teenager," I counter. "That's 1/15th of my life. That's another summer and fall and Christmas and New Year's. A year for you is nothing. It's only 1/40th of your life! You close your eyes, and you could sleep that long."

"After dealing with you kids, I think I will!" my mom pipes back. My Dad gestures, politely and firmly, as if to say, "Listen to your mother." Meanwhile, she is shaking her head and rolling her eyes as she picks up the kitchen towel for her routine morning OCD-Mom clean-up.

She isn't used to me being the talk-back child. For years, my twin sister Alysa fit that job description and even our older brother Louie had his impertinent seasons. He was a troublemaker in fifth grade and then he mellowed out until his junior year when he turned into a brooding, exhausted, and occasionally mouthy jerk. He seems to be enjoying junior year though and he's been super nice to Mom.

So perhaps I just want a turn at the sass-wheel. I know, it's childish, but I'm tired of being Miss Perfect and I'm tired of pretending we're the Perfect Family. Because we're not. We are far, far from that. Every family has its thing. I'm not sure yet what ours is, but things are feeling funny since we moved over here.

For now, I find consolation in baton twirling. You can tease me. Alysa does all the time. She spouts, "That's so retro!" and "It's not a sport!" and yet she's secretly jealous. Not because of the act itself, but because I am really good at twirling and people are paying attention. As far as "real sports," I started playing volleyball in the autumn season and basketball last winter. The coaches say I am a "solid team player" with potential for varsity (again *next year*), but twirling a baton is kind of like a rare, ninja skill. Some people have the dexterity, but few people have the patience to work on the tricks nor the flair for performance.

If this sounds like bragging, well, I'll say, I cannot get full credit for this talent. My Mom liked ballroom dancing in her high school gym classes and my Dad has some aptitude in juggling. What I now do combines what they did. As far as perseverance, I would tip my hat off to my Dad and the whole side of his family.

"The Robertsons are not quitters! We may not always be winners, but we are never quitters."

I also find it funny that onlookers see the baton twirling as a show because I feel most peaceful when I am throwing the baton in the air and circling and jumping to catch it. I *cannot-not* smile. So, when it's the dullest day of the year – the day after the two-day, not A-squared birthday, a cold- gray-end-of-winter Thursday afternoon – I feel bliss. I can glance out the window to the soft snowy clouds shading our lawn and the no longer dormant crab trees and I appreciate the country beauty of our home.

I toss the baton high before I spin and catch it with my left hand. The emerald, green tassels shimmer while I roll the baton between my fingers. When I look out the window for the second time, I spot an unlikely audience member sitting in the crook of the pine tree trunk. Handsome, vital, red-breasted. He cocks his head. There is no way he could see or understand what I am doing, but he approves.

"Thank you, Mr. Cardinal," I say with a chuckle.

Confidence surges. In four months, I will perform with our high school marching band at the GEMS Fourth of July Celebration. I can't remember if the high school graduates are walking before us, but I do know that the majorettes will be ahead of the band and, crazy as it sounds, I will be the first majorette in our team. No pressure (haha), but I also was the first 9th grader in the history of the school to have this honor.

*****

Louis Junior's high school coach recommended that those on the team who could get away, should sign up for the camp being held for baseball players on the State College campus. The season was over, and the college students were studying for finals, so the campus fields were open for the weekend. What a thrill it will be for Lou Jr. to play on the field where his heroes had played.

The coaches put the high schoolers into groups and the coaches rotate through stations where the teen athletes get focused instruction on hitting, throwing, and fielding and time to practice new strategies for different positions. Several coaches from local high schools have come to run some of the sessions. Probably to scope out the competition for the next season. Who knows? Whatever. It is challenging and fun. Louis sees some skillful players. He hopes they don't outshine him and suck up all the scholarships that may be offered here in their state.

Louis wants to play first base, but he just isn't flexible enough. He is tall enough and a good catcher and usually can anticipate when a runner is going to try to steal second base. But when the ball comes and he must tag the runner before getting back to first, Louis just can't seem to turn and twist fast enough. If he catches the ball, he often misses tagging the runner. If he tags the runner, he sometimes drops the ball. So, no out. So, no first baseman.

On the other hand, this morning when he was assigned to play outfield, he'd really shown. Louis is fleet and has a good eye. When a ball comes his way, he usually can tell where it's going and nods to his teammates who trust him to get into position rapidly and ready to catch those highflyers. It was during one of those sessions that the scout was watching.

During lunch that afternoon, Louis sees the scout approaching his table. He and some of his buds have finished eating and are chilling with cool bottles of water. Their coach always tells them to stay hydrated and they'd stay healthy. Anyway, the water is free, so they have all taken an extra bottle. The scout has a tablet in his hand. He is checking his notes when he nearly bumps into their table.

"Oops!" he says when he realizes how close he is. "Say guys! You are really looking good out there. So glad the rain is holding off and we didn't have to postpone the outdoor events." He looks down at his tablet, then gestures to Louis. "Say, you're Louis Robertson, aren't you?"

Louis gulps and nods, "Yes, Sir. That's me."

"Will you step outside with me for a moment? I have a few questions for you."

"Sure. Yes, Sir. Right away, Sir." Louis rises, hands his empty bottle to his table mate and follows the scout outside onto the grassy area across from the cafeteria. The grass is all smooshed from the feet of the players who have not honored the signs requesting that all use the sidewalks until afternoon. The morning dampness softens the grass. It stays stronger and looks greener when it has time to dry before being walked on.

It's afternoon now, so the two can walk, legally on the quad and over to one of the benches across the way. The scout gestures for Louis to have a seat. He does and the scout sits next to him and glances down at his tablet again.

"Well, Louis. I've been watching you this weekend and have been impressed by your energy. You seem attentive to the coaches and eager to try whatever they recommend. Yes, I noticed your bumbling at first base, but you didn't give up. You caught a few fouls that could have gotten away from a less attentive player."

"Thanks, Sir. I really want to play first base."

"Well, I wouldn't recruit you to play first base at our school."

Louis slumps.

"You look better in the outfield. You seldom miscalculated where the ball was coming and you caught most of them, no matter how hard they'd been hit. You're an outfielder!"

Louis jumps.

"Really! You think I could be recruited to play outfield at State? That would be so rad!"

"That decision is not mine, Louis. I'm just the scout. The coaches make those decisions. What I want to know is, are you college-ready?"

"What do you mean? You askin' about my grades? Well, I'm doing pretty good. I got a solid B average and I'm taking my second AP course. In fact, the exam is next week."

"Next week? You got exams next week and you're here at baseball camp? Is that wise?"

"My folks think so. They said I need a break 'cause I been hitting the books every night. And Dad knew there may be scouts here this weekend. I got two younger sisters, they're twins, just a year younger than me. My parents want us all to go to college so that would mean three of us in college at one time. We all gotta do what we can to get scholarships or low-cost grants if we wanna go to college right out of high school. That's what I wanna do. I wanna come to State, play ball, and graduate in four, maybe five years!"

"Sounds like wise parents. What do you want to study in college?"

Louis shrugs and tilts his head. "Oh, I don't know. Nothing particular right now. Mom says the first two years of college are pretty much the same for most majors. By the time I complete my required courses, I should have a clearer idea about what I want to major in. Mom says she wishes that the NCAA would support schools that have programs for athletes to have ten years to complete their academic work so they can take half-loads during their sports seasons. But, when scholar athletes get a pro contract, they concede their college scholarships to the next incoming group of college athletes. What do you think, Mr …? What is your name, Sir?"

"I'm Mr. Millbank's. I scout for the state colleges and recommend athletes for consideration as scholarship recipients. That's an interesting idea your Mom has, but we're not there yet."

"Well, Mr. Millbanks, would you recommend me?"

"Louis, you keep playing like you are now, learning to play the different positions, and keeping your grades up, you'll be a good candidate for any of the State Colleges. You seem to have a good head on your shoulders and supportive parents willing to let you "off" to play but not off from your studies. No matter what folks say, college athletes are recruited to get their degrees. Our state colleges are torn between having student athletes win championships and earn bachelor's degrees. As a scout, I try to focus on balancing the two. Doing what I can to bring in new recruits who are coachable athletes and teachable students."

"You sound like my Uncle Claude. He's always telling us to keep our eyes on the goal and for us the goal should be to get a good education at the least cost possible for our parents. You know, they've been making us save our own money for college since we were kids."

"Sounds like my kind of parents, Louis J. Robertson, Jr.! By the way, what does the "J" stand for?

"Oh, that "J" stands for Jamal. My granddad immigrated here from Sudan. I get to carry on the Sudanese name, but I got my mother's looks.

She's Iroquois-Gullah Geechee!"

"Really? You are a mix, aren't you! Well. I just wanted to let you know that you've impressed me, and I'll be passing along your name to coaches seeking an athlete who will be both coachable and teachable. With your physique, you may not be strong enough to play pro ball, but you are flexible enough to play different spots on a college team and maybe even help them win a championship during your time there. And, what's most impressive to me is that you seem to respect the adults in your family. That usually spills over to respect for coaches."

Louis blushes at this praise and the peachy color in his cheeks give him away. He bows his head to hide how thrilled he is to learn that this scout will recommend him for a scholarship. Mr. Millbanks taps something onto his tablet and stands to signal the meeting is over. He stretches out his hand and Louis responds with a firm handshake. Louis walks across the quadrangle with a little more cut in his strut and glide in his stride. Then, he stops. Maybe I'm jumping the gun. I got that AP History exam next week. I better pull out my notes and study till time for the next coaching session!

*****

Back in the master bedroom suite, Lillian is drifting off to sleep, but thoughts of her children keep her awake a little longer. Will the kids stand with her or with their Dad? What about Lou Jr.? Whose side will he take? She remembers, like it was yesterday, an incident when Lou Jr. called her on her treatment of him as a pre-teen.

*****

"Hey! Stop him!"

Behind me stood Louis holding up a pair of shoelaces. The merchant thought my middle-schooler was shoplifting! Security escorted our family out as though we were criminals. I was livid. I didn't ask questions — just drove straight home.

I'd taught my children better! My son couldn't be a thief. But, I hadn't defended him when we were at the Mall. Instead, I wondered if he really had been planning to walk out without paying for the shoelaces.

Once home, I reprimanded him. "Go to your room! Get your Bible! Read Proverbs! Consider your behavior! Ask God's forgiveness!"

As a Christian, what was my responsibility? Downstairs, I picked up my Bible and read Proverbs 22:16 from the NIV.
"Start children off on the way they should go, and even when they are old, they will not turn from it."

I was right! Lou Jr. had to learn how brown boys would be perceived, and act accordingly. But why did that man think my son was stealing?

"Mom?" he had tip-toed back down the short hall and peeped into the living room.

"What! Did you read those verses I told you to read? Have you asked for God's forgiveness?"

"Mom?" His voice begged me to listen. "Mom. I wasn't stealing. I was just gonna ask if we could buy them."

"What? Oh, son! I didn't ask! I jumped to conclusions, too! Lord, what have I done?"

"You gotta tell him?" "Who?"

"The guy at the mall."

*****

Lillian, back to the present, recalls and connects the two incidents. My son called me on it. I had let a merchant call my boy a thief. I had not stood up for him. Yes, I eventually apologized to Lou Jr., called the Mall, and got the issue resolved. But still... What should I do now? Will Lou Jr. expect me to do the same for his father? Support him or line up against him? Whose side would the kids take? The girls are their daddy's darlings, and they revel in his love for them. Should I step away and let Lou Jr. and the girls deal with what's coming or should I stand with the man who has been my husband for seventeen years? God, help me!

Lillian senses the peace of the presence of the Holy Spirit. She relaxes and soon whatever is in that Tylenol PM courses through her body. Probably because of the combination of the Holy Presence and the mild sedative she's taken, she soon drifts off to sleep. When Lillian awakens the next morning, there is Louis, lying spooned against her back; he's sound asleep. Maybe he's decided to stay after all!

Beth-El Community Church

Over the past ten years or so, a variety of industries have boomed with a myriad of companies setting up plants and offices that attracted college graduates from almost every specialty. Locals were finding jobs in the plants in the supply chain servicing the new companies with needed resources and labor. Hundreds of new families representing multiple denominations arrived, many seeking a place to worship. A few families who'd met in Welcome Wagon events began to meet informally, rotating from home to home.

Within just a couple of years, it became clear they were outgrowing the limited space in their houses. Since most attendees were committed to fellowshipping regularly, they contacted the seminary in the next town which directed them to some of their graduates. Several accepted invitations to come meet and share their testimonies and philosophies of pastoring. The group chose one of the more experienced graduates who had a new family with children just starting school. He and his wife were seeking to make their home in the area, too. Not long after, the businessmen in the worship group said it was time to buy and build. They did just that.

The families who had met initially in their homes knew that wherever they gathered, God would be there in their midst because they are His children, and the Holy Spirit resides in them. When they felt led and had saved enough money to purchase the land to build this sanctuary, they registered their property in the name Beth-El which means "a house of God." They included the word "community" to remind them and those driving by or seeking a church home that all are welcome to this community of believers and seekers after the truth in God's Word.

These practical planners worked with an architect to build a home for the congregation with mixed-use space. The only place with fixed use was the pulpit. No stationary pews. Instead, they purchased comfortable stackable benches and chairs that could be moved around to serve different uses of the sanctuary area.

The church now has a fellowship space that serves as the foyer to the building and the kitchen is in the basement, but has a pulley elevator to move food, dishes, and utensils up when needed. There are just single-stall restrooms for men and for women on the first floor, and in the basement, full three-stall facilities for men and women, with showers. Four classrooms are along the walls and in the center, open space for small gatherings.

For accommodations, the planners included a mobile chair lift as well. So those who need to access the lower level can do so with ease. Of course, the kids and teens would be tempted to use it even if they don't need it. That's why the architect advised, and the planners conceded, that the church should purchase a sturdy, durable lift chair. May as well be safe than sorry.

While families were willing to get up in time to be at church for worship service at 9:30, few would come that early for Sunday School. Once the church board consented to flip the meeting times, folks stayed after for a time of snacks and fellowship, then paraded to the music played over the loudspeakers reminding the snackers to march out of the fellowship hall and to their classes. The kids and teens chatter down the steps and into the spaces set aside for age-level Sunday School meetings.

The adults have breakout groups based on quarterly topics. One group gathers in the back, a second in the front of the sanctuary, and a third small group meets in the side chairs of the choir stand. During the fellowship time, the ushers will have rolled in room dividers that help the adults stay focused and provide white boards for teachers who wish to use them. Being more mature and not as easily distracted, the adults keep their voices down and somehow their teachers are able to hold their attention for the fifty minutes.

The kids and teens meet in the lower level. The big open space between the classrooms along one wall, the bathrooms at one end and the kitchen at the other end, provides space for whole group gatherings. At youth events, multiple ages of teens meet there for games and general presentations before retreating to breakout rooms for age-appropriate discussions based on Biblical applications for living life.

Over time, the congregation has grown and become known as a welcoming home for Christians of any faith who are interested in growing in the Lord. There have been three pastors, who each brought different skills, but all have been teacher/preacher Bible scholars who respect the fact that "life is a journey and though we're on the same path, we are not in the same lanes." The members are encouraged to grow in the gifts of the Lord and honor those of others.

The first pastors used transparencies on overhead projectors to add visual components to their sermons. More recently, both the choir directors and Pastor switched to using computers to show slides that encourage congregant attention and participation with graphics on slides with the lyrics and to show sermon texts and images that clarify some complex concepts. Most importantly, their pastors have encouraged them to live Christ-like lives. When in doubt, rather than refer to traditions, check the Scriptures to learn, "What would Jesus do?"

Rev. Sylvester Jackson, the current pastor, is known to be an open man and a patient listener. So, it's not surprising that Lillian goes to him for help and counseling after Louis admits to her that he is gay. Little does she know that Pastor Jackson is struggling with his own personal life and faith journey. He wants to comfort Lillian and help save her marriage. However, he is not willing to do so at the cost of Louis being able to live into his truth. What a quandary for a pastor.

FIRST WEEK

She has not forgotten Louis' confession. Nor has she forgotten the nightly devotion. She eases out of bed, heart heavy, but she still wants to be the first in the bathroom to complete morning ablutions and fix? her hair in time for church. Their morning service starts at 9:30 and Sunday School classes for kids, teens and adults meet after the time of praise and worship, prayer, and the preaching of the Word. When the new pastor made that change, Sunday School attendance tripled in the first year.

Soon Lillian is washed and in her zip-up housecoat. She's added lipstick and a light brushing of eyebrow darkener. After breakfast, she will don a comfortable outfit that will not be too warm under the traditional robes the choir wears on first Sundays. Lillian slips out into the kitchen to brew the coffee and prepare a light breakfast. "Louis came back to me!" She marvels at the thought and tries to act like nothing unusual occurred yesterday evening. "Maybe I'll be able to focus on the service and sing my solo after all. She hums as the words float through her head. "I am weak, but thou art strong! Jesus, keep me from all wrong."

She can be as strong a person as Louis. He's hidden his true feelings for years. She can do so for a couple of hours. She hopes. Then, she hears the shower running and her chest tightens. Maybe she can't hide. Thankfully, she remembered to use a little extra antiperspirant this morning. Hey, a woman needs all the help she can get.

*****

Louis stands in the shower, glad that Lillian had left him some hot water. Well, that is not really a problem this morning because the kids are gone! No water hogs in the house today. For some reason, when arranging to buy this house, he and Claude had forgotten to check the capacity of the water heater before they closed the deal. Nor had they thought of it when they were remodeling the bathroom the sisters now share. Oh well, the family had been used to sharing before moving here, so they just kept it up. The kids took their showers on Saturday evening, then on Sunday mornings washed extra carefully in their face bowls using less water. So, really, there was enough for him and his wife. His wife! Yes, Lillian is his wife, and he hopes she remains married to him when he moves upstairs with Claude.

He had not even mentioned divorce when he decided to reveal to Lillian his bisexual orientation. What would really change other than where he slept more often? He'd still be the father of their three children! He'd been partners with Claude for almost two decades. So, things should not change all that much now that he has come out and stopped living a double life. It's a wonder he hasn't developed an ulcer with all the hiding of his true feelings for Claude. He knew how society would respond, especially some in the church communities

.

Ah, he smells the coffee brewing. He and Lillian splurge on Sunday mornings and drink Gevalia Kenya Special Reserve coffee. Other days, they make do with whatever store brand is on sale when they go grocery shopping. The Kenya coffee reminds him of his early years with his grandfather who sprang for East African blends in honor of Louis' Sudanese father. Yes, the marriage of his parents had been sanctioned to save her good name. Their prompt marriage was to avoid embarrassment for the pastor whose daughter was impregnated by the Sudanese immigrant they'd agreed to house while he was in college.

Grampa had accepted the fact and did not seem to hold it against any of the three once Louis was born. The two teenagers had become one and then he was born and made them three. Once his father died, they still were three. Just a different combination. His grandfather was a dealer in facts. His only child became pregnant, married, and soon was widowed. The fact was Louis needed a father, and Grampa stepped in and raised Louis like the son this pastor had never had.

*****

Louis finishes shaving, dabs on the creamy hair stuff Lillian has him using now that she learned about some natural hair care from the Nourish Your Curls store down in the village. He brushes his close-cut hair and dresses in the formal attire their ushering team wears on the first Sundays. Navy blue suits with white shirts and light blue ties. Can't forget the white gloves and just a light spritz of the Acqua Di Gio. The kids had sprung for this Giorgio Armani Eau De Toilette on his last birthday. Louis makes up the bed, checks to see that he's hung the bath towels neatly, so they'll dry smoothly, takes a deep breath, and strides into the kitchen.

By now, Lillian has scrambled a couple of eggs and toasted some wheat bread. He drinks his coffee black, but she always adds double cream. They used to tease each other that they drink coffee the color of their skin! Neither adds sugar or saccharin. They teased each other too, and explained to dubious waiters, "Yeah, we eat our sugar as jelly on toast instead of drinking it in our coffee." Since they'd met in the café of the building where they still work, the couple has had fun sharing meals and telling stories about the culinary choices they make.

*****

This morning, neither say anything. Both bow their heads, reach out for the hands of their mate, and silently give thanks for their meal. That's something they've done since they started going to that church. And they do the same, now, as a family. Always give thanks, before the food gets cold. The five of them say out loud together, "Thank you, God, for this food!" Then they eat it.

On the way to church this first Sunday morning in May, Lillian and Louis do little talking. Because she sings in the choir that warms up before service and Louis is an usher, they arrive early, so it is not surprising there are few cars in the parking lot when they roll into their customary parking space. The couple sits for a few minutes to pull themselves together.

Lillian turns to her husband, "Thanks for coming home last night. I wasn't sure you would. How's Claude?"

"Claude will be okay. He knows you and the kids are my first priority. That's not going to change. He just wants to be inside more than outside from now on. He knows I can't move up there with him until after we talk to the children. Claude and I wanted you to know first."

"Thanks, I guess," Lillian snips, not sure whether she is glad she has more time to work through this issue or sad that it is Claude who seems to be deciding the next steps.

"Well, you know, at school, the AP exams are coming up the next two weeks," Louis says as he removes the keys and swings the mirror around to check his tie.

"Yeah, I know. That's why I'm glad all three of the kids got away this weekend to get a break from all that AP prep they've been doing for school. This will be the girls first time doing those long, written exams. That World History class has been given them quite a go this school year. Because Lou Jr. had experience with APs last year, taking the US History exam won't be such a surprise or challenge for him. He's always liked history."

"Lillian, Honey," Louis turns to draw her attention from her primping in the passenger-side mirror. "Let's hold off telling them until after AP exams. No use raising issues they can do nothing about right now. You know how those advanced placement exams can be. Most of the kids are anxiety ridden, especially the first time they take'em. If we want Louis to get that college scholarship, he's gonna have to keep his grades up. You know it's the junior year grades that go on those college applications."

"Yeah, I know, Louis. That's something to consider. The kids are really gonna have lots to deal with once they know about you and Claude."

"It's not just me and Claude, Lil. It's all of us. We are family."

Lillian considers this reveal date in silence. If they don't tell the kids for two more weeks, she will have time to process what she's learned. Though she tends to be one to face issues head-on, she must admit the delay is a relief. It will give the three adults time to consider the ramifications of the inevitable changes yet to come. Even if the changes are just visual (as in superficial?) folks seeing different things going on at their house, on the job, at church, they are still changes.

"Okay. That sounds like a good plan. No news is good news, so they say. So, when the kids ask, 'Hey Mom and Dad, how was your weekend?' we can turn the tables and ask them about theirs. You know how Louis likes to brag about his agility in the outfield when he's playing baseball."

Louis, too, is relieved. He hadn't been sure Lillian would accept this postponement. But then, too, he was used to shielding his children from all kinds of news. This, too, can wait. But then, there is Claude. Lillian remembers, too.

"What about Claude? Is he coming for dinner today? I'm not sure I can handle him at our table now that I know about you two."

"Hon, if he doesn't come for first Sunday dinner, the kids will wonder why. Are you ready to tell them?"

"No, not me. This is gonna be harder than I thought! Oh, God!"

Noticing other cars pulling into parking spaces next to and behind them, Lillian and Louis cut the conversation. They bow their heads as they do before entering the church building. They pray that God will be with them as they fill their roles in the Sunday morning service. They pray silently, each adding the prayer that God will sustain them the next couple of weeks as they process the changes that are sure to occur when they tell their teens about their Dad's sexual orientation. As if on cue, they each reach for their respective door handles, take a deep breath, paste on a smile, and exit to greet the people getting out of the cars next to them.

Church Choir Director Imagines

Getting my mind ready for First Sunday services that include the celebration of communion, I hum, "There is room at the cross, for you." Our services start in about twenty minutes. As I am slicking my bronze ponytail back, I reminisce on how far I have come, not geographically, but spiritually. You see, I haven't always lived my life for God. Sometimes, it's surreal that I made it out even though people may think otherwise. Thankfully, my love of music led me to a choir concert where I heard the Word of the Lord. Oh, the power of music.

85

Our church is a little informal most weeks, but, for first Sundays, the choir wears robes, and white stoles. I have on a white button-up collar shirt with gold color cuff links, white dress pants, and my white Stacy Adam shoes. My Black classmates from St. Louis told me about them. I love the feel and am okay with the price. I have lost some weight, so this morning, I decided to wear a sequence vest and dabbed on some cologne. For service, though, I will remove the vest and hang it on the hanger from which I take my robe. Glad we have a nice mirror in there. I'll put back on the vest after service.

When I enter the choir room, I see Lillian looks a little dazed. She's earlier than the rest of the members. Maybe she's a little nervous. This will be her first time singing a solo with the choir. I never understood why she's held back. Lillian has a unique and beautiful voice.

This morning, she stands, perspiring a bit, staring at herself in the mirror the former director insisted on during the last remodel of the choir room. Almost like a dance room, we have mirrors along one wall so members can see themselves vocalizing. It's good to see how we look and sound before ministering in the sanctuary.

"Good morning Sister Lillian," I approach quietly. Lillian is mumbling. I rest my hand on her shoulders; "Everything is fine. You will do just great." I suggest, "Let's go over some range exercises before the others arrive."

Lillian nods her head in agreement but pushes my hand away.

"Repeat after me, " La, la , la , la , la . La, la, la , la. Hold for five seconds at the end."

She begins but sounds shaky. I encourage her to start again. Water wells in her eyes..

"We have been practicing for a month. You're ready for this. Ah, how about a little lemon tea with some honey? That'll clear your throat and help you relax. Anything else? "No, Brother Jesse. Yes. I want my husband back." Then she just tilts into me and cries uncontrollably into my chest. While I'm not exactly sure what she means, I can imagine. I've seen him with Claude. Oh Louis, how can you do this to Lillian, to your family, to our church? The shame, the embarrassment.

"There, there, Sister Lillian. Whatever you're going through, God knows all, and God sees all. Let's take it to God in prayer. You have the strength to keep going, despite what others may think. For the glory of the Lord, will rise among us. Let your voice sing praises.

Remember praise is what makes the enemy flee. Praise will allow us to get through these circumstances. I need you to praise Him, Lillian. Through our worship, we will praise onward to victory."

Lillian nods against my shoulder, sniffles a bit, then looks up with some relief.

"Oh, thank you, Brother Jesse. I needed that. I've been acting like I have to carry my burdens on my own. I've got you and my brothers and sisters in the choir!"

Now, with stiffened arms, to keep us apart, I hold her shoulders and help her stand up straight, I give her a reassuring smile. Then, reach back and pull a tissue from the box on the counter and hand it to her.

"I'll get some tea from the kitchen. They have a microwave down there. It'll just take a sec'." I need to get out of there. Folks coming in may think something's going on between me and this Sister. There isn't, but you know how folks jump to conclusions.

Oh, God! I hope she doesn't choke up during her solo. I say a quiet prayer and plead the blood of Jesus over Lillian and her circumstances, whatever they are. Please God, help her to seek you for understanding, direction, and comfort. In Jesus Name, Amen. More choir members arrive. I observe Lillian from afar, sipping her tea. She appears to have gathered herself, so I invite the choir to warm up today, singing "Oh Happy Day" as they pull their robes from the hangers, slip them on and adjust their white satiny stoles so the ends are even in front.

By the time we get to the chorus of the song, everyone is robed. I instruct them to sway side to side without moving their feet. Lillian begins "Oh happy day". The choir then chimes in and repeats the words Lillian sings like the Edwin Hawkins choir sings it.

Happy day, happy day,
When Jesus washed my sins away!
He taught me how to watch and pray,
And live rejoicing every day;
Happy day, happy day,
When Jesus washed my sins away!

As we continue to sing, Lillian's voice becomes steadier, the notes clearer, and not shaky like before. You would've never known she had been sobbing uncontrollably just a few moments ago. That prayer and tea have done wonders.

Lillian slips up into falsetto range, singing countertenor, "When Jesus washed, He washed my sins away!!"

The choir comes in singing, "Oh Happy Day!!!" By now, we are clapping, swaying, and feeling the power of God in the choir room. I smile hugely! Thank You, Jesus!!! We are ready for first Sunday services. I peek out the door of the choir room that's located to the front left side of the pulpit, opposite the pastor's sanctuary office.

The church family are filling the sanctuary that seats 200 people. The dim overhead lighting and the fluorescent white and blue lights from the pulpit show the range of attire worn by Beth-El parishioners. The older ladies wear hats and gloves and male counterparts don suits and ties. Influenced by the times, millennials dress in a wide range of casual to high fashion. All are welcome. We come to worship God, not to parade our fashions.

Tall candles flicker on the communion table. Against a pristine, linen tablecloth, Wooden, handcrafted communion trays hold the tiny cups of grape juice. Hanging a foot below the left and right edge of the communion table, white, flowy scarves drape over the loaves of bread we will be sharing during the sacrament.

Our church edifice is modern, but many of our practices are not. One of the old traditions I love is the choir marches in from the rear down the center aisle. We'd always done it like that back home, and when I became choir director a year ago, I started that here. That's another feature I like about Beth El Community Church. It's interdenominational and open to alternative styles of worship. As long as the focus remains on God, we're encouraged to do it.

Some of the practices are general across sects, some are unique to certain cultures, and some folks of various races find that experiencing the new has made attending our church a learning experience while reinforcing basic Bible principles. Sunday service is about praise and worship, prayer and being fed the Word, through song and praise dance, and preaching by our preacher/teacher.

The choir members line up at the back of the church ready for the processional. I nod to the organist who begins playing "Holy, Holy, Holy." Her brunette hair piles along the collar of her robe and flicks when she reaches in to adjust the organ stops. Our drummer adds an African beat and the ushers step aside as the sopranos lead in single file, followed by the altos.

I whisper to Lillian, "You're ready. Your song comes right after the pastoral prayer this morning. Everything will be fine. It's a happy day.' She looks at me with reassuring eyes, then darts a look over my shoulder. I slowly turn and see that her husband Louis and Claude are engaging in conversation while Louis is fixing his bow tie. It's clear that Claude is letting him know it's not straight because he now is repositioning Louis' tie for him. I think to myself, "if you don't get a mirror."

I turn and see Lillian fighting back tears. I remember what Lillian said back in the choir room. It dawns on me that something is not right about this. What can I say now? Quick. Um. I have to think of something quick. I do not need my soloist to run off right before service. I lean in and whisper, "Sister Lillian, remember what I said, God knows all. God sees all. Worship will make the enemy flee. Let's praise Him in advance because He is about to do a work in you."

The Twins Arrive and Wonder

One of the GEMS Club leaders drops the sisters off at the church. They are a wee bit late and arrive just about the time the pastor has invited members to come to the front of the sanctuary for the pastoral prayer. He, and the two previous pastors have taught that "we all stand in need of prayer," and that one should never be reticent to come stand around the altar during pastoral prayer.

This somber portion of the service follows the vivacious opening songs of praise and worship. The ushers at the back door hold up their white-gloved hands to remind those arriving late to stand quietly until after the prayer. The choir is softly singing the chorus,

> It's me, it's me, it's me,
> O Lord, Standing in the need of prayer
> Not my sister, nor my brother,
> but it's me, O Lord,
> Standing in the need of prayer.

The girls notice that their parents are gathered at the altar for family prayer. Mom is on the left side of the line; Dad is in the middle, and wait? Is that Uncle Claude on the right end? It's not unusual for one or the other to be up there from time to time. But, this morning, all three have gone forward for prayer! That's odd.

Lillian stands with her head bowed, swaying to the rhythm, listening to the congregation singing the familiar hymn. Then she stops. "Oh, God!" she thinks, "In two weeks we have to tell the kids about their Dad and Claude." The third verse of the song takes on deeper meaning. 'Not my father, nor my mother, but it's me O Lord, standing in the need of prayer!"

Pastor, standing with his open palms toward heaven, has asked the parishioners in the family prayer line to hold hands with the persons on their left and right, reminding them that they all are God's family.. Waiting behind the altar line, the prayer warriors raise their hands. One sister steps closer and places a gentle arm across Lillian's shoulder. Lillian stiffens, then relaxes in the warmth of a soft double pat and hint of a squeeze on her upper arm.

Way over to the right, one of the deacons puts his hand on Claude's shoulder. He probably glams on to the second verse, "Not the deacon, nor the preacher, but it's me O Lord, standing in the need of prayer!" Claude had come later to this congregation and is still getting used to the rhythm of the church service. He finds it comforting to join the members of the church family who gather with such confidence that God will answer their prayers.

Louis stands in the center, feeling awkward. He can smell the mixture of fragrance from the candles on the communion table and the cologne of the brother standing to his left or maybe it's the perfume of the woman on his right. It doesn't really matter. He extends his hands to clasp that of the persons on his left and right.

His bows his head and doesn't notice that none of the elders have come to stand with him today. Louis probably is singing the fourth verse of that song. "Not the stranger, nor my neighbor, but it's me, O Lord, standing in the need of prayer!"

It was tough deciding to go stand with others at the altar because he is not sure what he's praying about other than to seek Spiritual guidance for him, his wife, and his lover. Their decision to tell the kids about the plans for him to move upstairs with Claude will require courage. Louis wants the extended family circle to remain whole. Family is all to him.

*****

The girls turn, each making eye contact with her sibling. They raise their shoulders in unison, shake, and then bow their heads, each wondering what her twin is thinking. The song ends, and the prayer begins.

*****

The organist plays softly, supporting, careful not to overwhelm the voice of the praying pastor. The musician continues to play after the prayer as the folks standing in the front return to their seats. The ushers now seat Alvyra and Alysa and others who arrived during the pastoral prayer time and had been standing in the foyer. Announcement time.

The church secretary steps up to the microphone, welcomes visitors, then mentions the names of people who have had birthdays this past week, and reminds everyone of times for meetings and services this week, and upcoming events like men's baseball and plans for vacation Bible school. She leaves the pulpit and eyes turn to Lillian. The program schedule projected from the tech booth in the rear of the sanctuary onto the wall hung screen to the left of the cross on the wall behind the pulpit, proclaims that Lillian will be the soloist for the special music selection this morning.

Glendella has reached the organ and replaces the person who regularly accompanies the choir. She slips onto the bench, leans in to adjust the organ stops, and begins playing the introduction. The music flows out, in much the same way that Ralph Ellison describes in a synesthetic line in his novel, *Invisible Man*. "A high cascade of sound bubbled from the organ, spreading, thick and clinging, over the chapel, slowly surging." The choir director signals for the singers to stand and Lillian wiggles out from the alto section to stand in front of the mike.

Louis is so proud of his wife and her gift of music. Her rich contralto voice has been a boon to their family since the very beginning. She's taught their son and daughters most of the traditional children's songs of the church. Even as teens, they can be heard humming or singing as they do chores around the house. Since all three attended a middle school that offers choral music classes, the girls learned to sing in harmony. That's a treat, too. But now, his attention is on his wife. She jiggles her choir robe and smooths down the stole. The choir changes their stole colors to reflect the liturgical seasons.

The stoles are white now; this is the color from Resurrection Sunday until they exchange them for red on Pentecost Sunday. Their church is interdenominational with leaders who realize that colors are a way of emphasizing symbolically the life and ministry of Christ. So, today, now that Lillian's white stole is straight and Glendella has played the introduction, the choir begins singing the chorus of "Just A Closer Walk with Thee." The choir members' shoulders sway two beats to the left and two beats to the right in four/four time to the rhythm of the song:

> Just a closer walk with thee.
> Grant it, Jesus, is my plea.
> Daily walking close to thee.
> Let it be, dear Lord, let it be.

They repeat the chorus with a little more vigor and the director nods to Lillian. She sings solo:

> I am weak, but Thou art strong.
> Jesus, keep me from all wrong.
> I'll be satisfied as long,
> As I walk, let me walk close to Thee.

Claude, now standing on duty at the doors on the right side of the church, listens to the words of this familiar Christian hymn wondering why the words strike him so differently today. He had gone up for prayer to have the strength to wait before sharing with his dear nieces and nephew that their father and he plan to move in together.

In the row of seats ahead of Claude, the wee ones have gotten restless, and a grandmother passes them each a wrapped peppermint candy. The rustling distracts Claude for a moment, but by now, Lillian is singing the second verse of the song. He drags his attention back from the thought of getting a peppermint himself, to consider the lyrics of the song.

> When my feeble life is o'er,
> Time for me will be no more,
> Guide me gently, safely o'er
> To Thy kingdom's shore, to Thy shore.

That has been Claude's fervent prayer since he recommitted himself to Christ at this very church. He had not been a regular church attender since he moved from home to college. Once his aged parents passed, he'd not been back to his hometown at all. At college, he sometimes went to Campus Crusade meetings with buddies in the dorm, but he had not given much attention to end-of-life thoughts.

According to their website, "Campus Crusade for Christ is a worldwide, Christian evangelism and discipleship organization, founded by Bill and Vonette Bright in 1951." Claude admired the students who attended regularly. But college was an academic challenge for him, so he limited his extra-curricular activities to almost none.

He knew Christ died for the sins of all, but that was about it. He was not "sinning," so he was not worried about end-of-life recompense. It did annoy him, sometimes, hearing the students keeping score of those they had witnessed to (whatever that meant) as though they were comparing the "stars they would get in their crowns."

Who needed a crown? Claude needed tuition. He conscientiously kept his focus on the end-of-semester exams and re-upping his scholarship. He was in one of the work-study programs that could be renewed if he kept up his grades. Co-workers at Sumner's, like Andrew, sometimes distracted him. But that was two decades ago. Today, Lillian's song strikes him in a new way. Brother Jesse signals Lillian to sing the first verse again. She slows the tempo and wails in a jazzy sort of way. Glendella plays the piano chords.

Then the director signals the choir to begin stepping from left to right in rhythm with the chorus. He turns to face the congregation and invites them to sing along. The lower range voices begin singing along with the sounds of the bass foot pedals of the organ that is playing a counter rhythm in double the time of the soloist who now is singing a countertenor.

> Just a closer walk with thee,
> Just a closer walk with thee
> Grant it, Jesus is my plea. Grant it,
> Jesus is my plea.
> Daily walking close to thee,
> Daily walking close to thee

Lillian, now singing alone, begins a slower pace and almost a moaning plea the congregation feels deeply,

> Let it be…………….. dear Lord…………………. let it be.

She stands unmoving, for a dramatic ten or fifteen seconds with both hands raised to the Lord, then turns and walks back to her seat. The choir remains standing until Lillian is back in place, and the choir director with hands turned down, signals for them all to be seated.

Glendella remains at the organ, playing the hymn as Pastor Jackson approaches the pulpit and sets his iPad on the tilted lectern top. He swipes up the tablet screen and spreads his fingers to enlarge the view, and then looks up at the congregants sitting pensively in the pews. He, too, can feel the Spirit and does not hurry to speak. Instead, he stands until the organist reaches the closing measure of the song

The pastor, then, invites the congregation to stand with him as he reads the Scripture text for today's sermon. The congregation can see on the wall screen that he is preaching from Joshua 1:9 in the NIV Bible. Have I not commanded you? Be strong and courageous. Do not be afraid; do not be discouraged, for the Lord your God will be with you wherever you go." After reading and praying that the Lord would speak through him in ways the congregation can understand and apply in their own lives, Pastor signals for Glendella to retire to her seat.

She sidles over to an end seat in the choir stand, and Pastor begins the sermon of the morning. He usually begins his teaching/preaching with an Old Testament Scripture and concludes with one from the New Testament. He does the same this morning drawing attention to the pledge recorded in Matthew 28:18 where Christ promised that He would be with the disciples till the end of the ages.

*****

Not surprising, each of the family members has heard something different in the sermon. The twins and other high schoolers, think about their upcoming exams and wonder if this Scripture can be applied to the anxiety they are feeling.

Alysa has struggled to keep up with the reading for World History because she often becomes distracted and wants to write poems about the people instead of sticking to the objective facts connected with historical incidents. Alvyra, who is struggling memorizing theorems for Geometry, works hard to keep up with the minutia their history teacher expects them to recall for use on these heavy- weighted advanced placement exams.

*****

The students at their school get a bump on their grade point average (GPA) if they take honors' courses and pass the exams with at least a score of three. Students' transcripts look more impressive in the college application packet if they show the exams with a 4 or 5 scores. And, some colleges even give incoming students college credit for required courses, if their AP scores are higher than three.

Their Dad encourages all three children to do their best in each of their classes, but he assures each of his offspring that he will do what he can to supplement their costs for attending college.

But the key is "supplement." When each of them reached twelve years old, their parents opened an account at the local bank in the child's name. The parents promised to match what the kids saved. For as long as they can remember, Lou Jr., Alysa and Alvyra have been taught to pay tithes out of any income, even birthday presents, and to save at least 10% of whatever income they receive. In the early years, the savings went into old-fashioned piggy banks that Uncle Claude had gotten for each of the kids. From 10% of their allowance, to 10% for babysitting, running errands for neighbors in their apartment building or cutting the grass or shoveling snow now that they lived in a house on the cul-de-sac. Tithe 10% and save at least 10%. That is the house rule!

*****

Money, money, money.

Pastor has finished the morning sermon. This is the time he invites the congregants to stand while he prays that all who hear will let the message "marinate" and contact him if they have any questions. Then, he asks the ushers to prepare to collect the morning tithes and offerings.

Their pastor is not a beggar. He teaches them that it is an expectation for all to tithe and an honor to be able to give more. God will bless all that is given with a cheerful heart. For the most part, because few in the church family feel pressure, the majority tithe faithfully and eagerly donate time or money for special projects.

But, alas, this is the first Sunday and they celebrate communion before collecting the morning offering. In honor of Christ and in tradition, the church family celebrates the ordinance. However, to honor the different faith practices, the pastor serves communion a different way each month. It's just symbolic, he reminds them. The key is what they are celebrating! The death and resurrection of Jesus Christ, our Lord and Savior, who gave His life to save us all. We are the Family of God, celebrating this fact.

Different each month, but always on the first Sunday. Some months, they are served from a single chalice and pull a bit of bread from a single loaf. Another month, the deaconesses prepare miniature cups of grape juice and arrange them in the round slots of their fancy communion trays with crosses on the top and then cover the trays of juice and broken bread with white strips of lace.

During the ceremony, as the organist plays, chosen deacons take their places in a military stance at each end of the communion table. The pastor ceremonially removes the draping, folds it, and hands it to one of the deaconesses seated in the front row. He cleanses his hands in the white China bowl one of the deacons holds. After the pastor dries his hands, he raises the loaf of bread heavenward, blesses it, then breaks it into small clumps and returns it to the golden platter in the center between the two trays of cupped juice.

Next, he raises one of these trays of drinks and says a short prayer before handing each deacon a golden container of juice cups and inviting the congregation to come. On the other months, they make do with pre-packaged cups of juice with paper-thin bread-like wafers under sticky plastic pullbacks.

During Lent, they go traditional and have minimally fermented mustum? wine and matzah crackers. The year Lou Jr. was four years old, the pastor at that time introduced the congregation to Maundy Thursday celebration with a Seder Supper, a reenactment of the Passover Supper described in the Old Testament and observed by Christ and his disciples the night before he was crucified.

Louis, as the youngest male present, got to ask the main traditional question: "Why does this night differ from all other nights?" Though the congregation does not celebrate Seder every year, they do include foot washing followed by a candlelight service and a silent communion observance on Good Fridays before Resurrection Sunday.

*****

Today, the organist plays "Nothing But the Blood of Jesus" and "Because He Lives!." Louis, Claude, and the other ushers now beckon the congregation with open- palmed gloved hands. They direct parishioners on each side of the main aisle to proceed from the rear of the sanctuary, up the center aisle to come take a cup from the golden tray and a crumb of bread from the center plate and return to their seats. Ushers in the front direct the congregants to turn left or right and return to their seats by way of the side aisles where the celebrants remain standing until all are served.

Once all have bread and wine, the pastor pantomimes the raising of the bread in the right hand and quotes a scripture reminding them that Christ gave His life, it wasn't taken from Him. Then they all eat the bread. Pastor raises the chalice or cup of wine or grape juice, and they drink it at the same time Then they burst into song. It's a joyous occasion. On the first Sunday, joy is in the air.. Most are delighted they have something to give…after all, Christ has given the ultimate sacrifice for them.

*****

Lillian noted when her girls arrived, but she was distracted by last night's news and anxious about the solo. . She didn't even remember to make eye contact with Alysa or Alyra. This probably puzzled the girls, but they looked at each other, raised their shoulders and shook their heads, as they followed the gesturing usher to two open seats.

Now Lillian must put the morning sermon into practice and be strong. The church family gathers in the fellowship hall for light snacks before heading to Sunday School class. Lou will miss his class this morning because he won't return home from baseball camp until dinner time today. He texted both parents that one of the scouts did seek him out to talk about Louis' plans for college. That's all Lillian knows for now. Now… Whew!!!

She joins the choir members in the side office where they hang their choir robes. Her fellow singers express appreciation for her dramatic interpretation of the traditional hymn.

"You sounded like CeCe Winans out there! Girl, those lyrics truly spoke to my heart today!"

Another singer bumbles up and gives Lillian a full-body hug. "Yeah, Sister. And after pastor's sermon! I think I can make it this week. We got a lot going on in our family. What with Mother Millie taken sick and all."

Others, reaching around Lillian to hang up their robes, add their thanks and comments about the encouragement they feel because of her song and the Scripture texts for today's sermon, "Be strong and courageous" and "I will be with you."

Lillian hopes the same will be true for her, too…Strong, courageous, and accompanied by the Spirit of the Christ whom they just celebrated in communion.

Claude stands in the corner of the fellowship hall talking with one of the men from the church baseball team. They have a game this week and are hoping Claude will sub for one of the regulars. The church can't play without a full roster. Though he is not really a jock, Claude has played enough ball with Louis senior and junior that he knows he won't let down the team, but probably won't help more than filling a spot in the outfield.

Playing ball will give him something out of the house to do this week while Lillian and Louis figure out the best time and place to talk to the teens. At first, it seemed like a good idea to wait a couple of weeks until after the AP exams, but now waiting seems like a bad idea.

"Well, Bro, we certainly hope you're going join us this week. We have a decent record for so early in the season. We didn't want to have to forfeit a game. See you Thursday?" It is interesting the way the men and women of the church pick up the slang words of their African American brothers and sisters. At least, here Bro also means "Brother in the Lord," so it didn't matter who was saying it.

"Sure, guys. I'll be there. Where do you play? What position you do want me playing?
"Oh yeah. We play over at the park there not far from you guys' new house. How're you doing over there, by the way? We heard you got a real nice place with lots of space. Maybe you guys can host the end-of-the-season barbeque. If we do well next week, we may be celebrating a winning season. What you say, Claude? Think you can catch a ball hit into right field?"

"Yeah, man. I'll do what I can!" Claude has consented to play and to wait; he is a man of his word. So, he'll play ball and wait to see what unfolds during the game on the field and in the game of his life. Maybe that is what the message of the song and sermon is for him today. He is weak when it comes to his family.

Still, he knows that when in the past he has asked for help from the Lord, he has received it. He expects to experience that same courage and companionship of the Spirit this week out on the field and up in the house. The guys stand gazing as if they've not heard his answer.

"Okay, guys! I said, yes. I'll be there and I'll do my best not to embarrass you guys too much. Awright! Let it go for now. You hear the organ. It's time to head in for Sunday School." The guys give him the fist bump and walk over to the table where they put their coffee cups and throw their crumpled napkins in the trash can. Claude is on the clean-up team for today, He's extra careful, so there will be fewer missed shots to pick up later.

The kitchen committee serves a variety of snacks including fruit trays, crumbly cookies, and sticky donut holes. They try to select foods easy to serve in single servings. They take time to slice the fruits, sprinkle them with lemon juice to keep them looking fresh, and arrange them attractively on spacious trays. Claude cocks his head to the side and nods. Yes, it's time to move on.

The organist plays "Onward Christian Soldiers" as a signal that snack time is over. The kids and teens stride in tempo downstairs to their grade/age level classes and the adults march back into the sanctuary for their special topic classes in spaces now created by whiteboards Louis and a couple of the other ushers have rolled in.

*****

After Sunday School, Alysa and Alvyra clump upstairs and grab their backpacks and sleeping bags they had chucked into the front coat closet when they arrived late from their GEMS overnighter. They squish their things into the trunk Dad had opened with the thumb button on his car key holder. Pooped from staying up much later than usual, the girls nearly doze off during the short ride back home.

Alas, they hear the crankling of the garage door rising and leap out to grab their bags to race inside to be the first into the shower. Overnights are fun, but there seldom is enough time or space for more than a simple washup in lukewarm water before going to bed or when getting up for breakfast in the morning.

This morning, Lillian had not thought to take out anything to cook for dinner, so she decided to place an order through KFC and asked Claude to pick it up on the way home. (Kentucky Fried Chicken is Sone of the few restaurants that is open on Sundays.)

It's impossible not have Uncle Claude in their lives and it's going be challenging to keep a secret. They have a couple more weeks. She'll ask Louis to do it this time. But he tells her Claude already has planned to grill burgers out back since the weather is nice. He'd mentioned that plan while they were adjusting their ties before going to usher at their assigned doors at church this morning. They decide not to waste money on KFC if Claude already has food ready to grill.

She will have time to season up some frozen vegetables and mix and bake some corn muffins. She has a couple of first of the season tomatoes in the fridge that she'll slice for color for the week.

Her mom always said, "You must have meat, a starchy something, and a vegetable to have a well- rounded meal. A tossed salad is good, too, but not necessary. Add cornbread and something for color and you be all set." Today, for dessert, Lillian will thaw that half dozen remaining chocolate chip cookies she and the girls had made the last time Louis was out of town..

She had a hunk of gingerbread for Claude. Why is she always planning for Claude? Why, oh why? Well, today is Sunday family day and, so far, Sunday has always included Uncle Claude.

The Couple is Back to Work

Lillian makes it through that first Sunday. The first Sunday of the rest of her life as the wife of an admitted bisexual man. Now that the three of them, Louis, Claude, and she have decided to hold off telling their teens about their dad and Claude, Lillian thought the weight would be lifted. But, that morning, while showering and getting ready for work she wonders if she should be tested for HIV. She knows from articles about women's health that over 50% of women with HIV are women of color, mostly those who self- identify as Black. She may look light, but her genes include those of her indigenous and Gullah ancestors. She could be one of the 50% with HIV who don't even know it!

She's not been feeling ill, but when she gets back into her bedroom, she picks up her tablet and does a quick search. She goes to the site of the United States Department of Health and Human Services to check the symptoms and treatments of HIV. She learns that having intercourse with a man who is mating with another male without using condoms makes her a candidate for the infection. While she is sure that Louis and Claude have been careful, she'd better check. Louis has already left for work, so she can't ask him now. She keeps reading.

Lillian switches to the site for Healthline and reviews the symptoms of women with HIV and checks her health against the issues on the list. Nope, no sore throat, muscle aches, night sweats, or flu-like symptoms, but she has had a recent skin rash. "Wonder if that could be a sign? Of course, it could be that new facial cream I've been using. Better have this checked out." She turns off the tablet, "I'll check the CDC site during my break and if I'm still worried, I'll call my doctor. Centers for Disease Control and Prevention using has pretty easy to navigate websites. I better get going!" Lillian grabs her purse and a lightweight blazer. It is only May, and it may be cool this morning.

Now, dressed in her modest office attire, she calls out, "Hey, kids! You guys ready? I'll drop you off at the bus stop if you want me to."

"No, Mom! Thanks, anyway. We'll walk. We got time. It's not late. You know Dad always tells us to leave in time to be late. We're leaving now," calls out, Alvyra, the oldest of her twin daughters. She is already standing at the side door. "Come on Alysa! We can't be late. The guys are gonna be waiting for us at the bus stop. Oops!" She looks around when she feels her mom's eyes on her.

"What guys?" Lillian demands. Her girls are now fifteen years old and sophomores in high school, but she's not ready for them to be dating. School, then college, then marriage. And no messing around in between!

"Um, Mom. These are the guys who're gonna be helping us with the GEMS set-up for the Fourth of July. Ms. Delphi told us to plan ahead. So, we texted the guys from the overnight to see who we could have signed up to help with the heavy lifting. We're strong girls, but not too proud to get help from cute guys." Alvyra teases back at Mom.

By this time, Alysa has finished her box of juice, dumps it in the trash, and grabs her backpack. "Bye, Mom!" she says giving Lillian a quickie hug while winking over her shoulder to her twin grinning at the door. "Let's go, Sis. Lou Jr.'s already gone. Now that it's warmer, he started getting' out of here so early!"

"Yeah," her twin adds, "cause he can jog to school and be there on time. These athletes kill me! But some of them really are cute. Oops!" She ducks her head and chuckles. A soft shimmer of blush turns her cheeks a warm peachy color. She's the twin who looks most like their mom.

Alysa is the younger twin sometimes wishes she were Blasian. Being Black-Asian, she thinks will make her more different from her sister. Alysa loves art, all types, but particularly visual art. The weirder, the better. Recently, Alysa is supremely annoyed that Alvyra is now interested in art as well and wants to be competitive. Alysa is more extroverted, but equally academic. She had no interest in Alvyra's crush until she learns of his interest in her, the emo twin. Now Alysa is interested! Conflict ensues between the siblings!

The door slams as the girls scuttle out the door. In minutes they're around at the stop where the school bus picks up the teens over at the next cul-de-sac from where the Robertsons live.

*****

On the drive to work that Monday morning, Lillian gives thanks that she still has a good job. Once the children had been born, she'd not had to take much time off from work to stay home to care for her wee ones. Three children under three years old would have been quite a chore, though not a bore for a woman who loved to read as much as she did. Still, she was glad she could return to work knowing reliable childcare was so near and affordable.

It had helped that the daughter of the owner of their business office building was pregnant the same year Lillian became pregnant with the twins. She had been working part-time, just coming into the office once a week and arranged to be there for the annual business meeting of the clients renting building office space.

The two soon-to-be moms convinced the board to convert an unrented suite of offices on the first floor into a childcare center for infants up to 3 1/2 years old. From home, Lillian had conducted research on what was required to have a licensed facility in their office building. She knew that sanitation would be a key concern, but that would be no problem with Louis the head of the building care crew. The janitorial staff was one of the many care teams under his leadership.

Once they received board approval, the two expectant moms called the local college about hiring recent graduates to work with the experienced childcare director the board had hired through an online search. The new director led the interviews of likely candidates, and the three-member team chose one student with a medical certificate and one with a degree in early childhood education.

The suite chosen for the childcare center had its own pair of restrooms and was next door to the café where Lillian and Louis had met. This location proved to be convenient because the kitchen manager consented to assist with food preparation. The childcare center would have a countertop toaster and microwave ovens. The owner's daughter offered to donate the mini fridge she had used in college.

Thanks to modern technology for virtual meetings and portable laptops secured with encryption software, Lillian could do much of her work from home. Had she not become pregnant with twins, she would have returned to work right after her parental leave expired. But alas, she was to be birthing two more within the next year! But having an onsite childcare center where she and Louis both could stop in and see the wee ones made it emotionally and economically feasible to return to her job. The fee for using the facilities lined up with what they would have had to pay for home care. Although she could easily work from home, she was acutely aware of how convenient it would be for other mothers working in this building in their companies who didn't have that luxury. Also, management would benefit from less call-ins.

*****

Last week, when Lillian had shared this tory with her neighbor, Andrea, she could hardly believe it. "Wow, that's some story. What a blessing, indeed."

"Yeah, while my department chair, Virginia was willing to have me work from home a short time, I didn't want to press for too much accommodation from a company who'd hired and paid me so well."

"Ah, Girl Friend, I'm sure you were worth it."

"But I didn't want to press the boundaries of their goodwill. Drawing from both our incomes, Louie and I found it affordable to return to work after I'd weaned the twins?"

*****

Now, with Louis' plan to move upstairs, who knows how much she'll have to pick up in expenses now as their family life veers in a new direction?

Lillian turns into the parking garage, flashes her ID card at the security man, and rolls into her assigned parking spot. It's not far from the elevator she takes to her fifth-floor office. She notices him across the way; Louis is conferring with the crew responsible for the landscaping around the grassy lawn the office folks use during the warmer weather. It's May and most of the bulb flowers are starting to wilt. The team will be putting in annuals with flowers already in blossom. The goal is to keep the place looking nice so folks working in the building can take a nature break without leaving the grounds, becoming distracted, and getting back to work late. A reason for everything!

Lillian smiles and waves. Not at Louis. No! She waves at the woman in the hijab that he is talking to. Rizwana, a recent graduate from the agricultural college across the state, has just been working there for a short time. Lillian regularly goes out of her way to welcome newbies because she's not forgotten what it was like when she, a woman of color, first started here, right out of college. Her warm welcome back then is one of the reasons she has stayed these twenty years.

Before exiting the car, she pulls down the mirror, checks her hair and the collar of her creamy white blouse and adjusts the string of chunky wooden beads on the necklace her daughter has made for her. Lillian noticed when Alysa noticed this morning. One of the joys of motherhood! Wearing original jewelry that only costs her pride when folks at work look askew at Lillian's sometimes odd accessory choices. Now, most of the coworkers, just smile, nod, lean in, and say, "Oh, another one, huh? Lemme see."

This morning, the necklace reminds her she must hang together. The family needs her to be strong as they work out the inherent ramifications of her new knowledge. Now, she's gotta get through the workday. Lillian pastes on her smile, pulls her purse and slender briefcase from the passenger seat, locks the door on her lime green Honda Civic, and marches to the elevator. Thankfully, no one else is on it, so she can relax a few more minutes. The folks on her floor are going to expect a beam of sunshine when she arrives.

Forcing her little light to shine when her batteries are spent seems phony. Lord, why does that song keep running through my mind this morning? "This Little Light of Mine"? Why does the pastor keep preaching about being the light of Christ so others will be drawn to the Savior? Christ, you're gonna have to shine through me 'cause I'm not really feeling it today.

Lillian's Department Chair Makes Offer

As is my Monday morning routine, I make the rounds and touch base with the staff who report to me. I like to see how their weekends have gone. Lillian, usually full of life after Sunday services at her church, especially on weekends she sings, looks a little odd. Usually, one who gets all excited to be working with numbers, today, she appears dazed and distraught. She doesn't appear to be in any shape to concentrate on her work. I ask her chirpily, "What's up?"

At first, she tries to deny anything is wrong, but I let her know I don't believe it. She whimpers a bit, then blurts while gesturing air quotes, what her "husband" had unloaded on her Saturday night.

"Oh, Lillian! You must feel awful." Lil has never expressed sentimental utterances of Louis. It always felt to me as if hers is a marriage of two friends for the goal of childbearing. I need to verify that before I articulate our families' somewhat akin situation. I have a meeting scheduled with the VP of Finance in twenty minutes, but I know Lil needs an understanding ear right now.

"Sit tight, Lil, I'll go get us some coffee. Double cream, right?" I leave my office to get us both decafs. Neither of us needs more stimulation. I phone the VP's assistant from the break room.

"Hey, Chuck. Something's come up. Will you check his schedule for a slot this afternoon? I can come by right after lunch. Sure. Okay. Thanks. See you then." I'm glad for this time to talk with Lillian. You see, I have my own story of sexuality.

Growing up with my sister, we had observed my Mother's roller coaster of emotions. One day when she was in a low ebb, her coir-colored hair, looking wispy and dry, our Mom told me and my sister about the bombshell announcement she had gotten from her fraternal twin. It was decades ago, but Mom was still reeling. I am hoping I can help Lil avoid going down quite so many "rabbit holes." Holding the two cups of hot coffee, I back into the office and push the door closed with my foot.

As I hand the mug of hot coffee to Lil, I ask, "How did you and Lou meet?" She shares that they began as acquaintances from simply seeing each other around the building. "And love blossomed?" I smile.

Well," she replies, then blows across the top of her coffee, more as a reason to slow down revealing more of her life, then continues, "we both wanted to have kids, so we decided to get married and start a family." My mind races to carefully craft the next part of the inquisition.

It probably feels strange to Lillian to be asked such personal questions by her department chair. Lil appears to be so distraught, and probably not processing info; just simply answering my questions. I pause a bit and sip my own still-hot coffee. Lil looks defeated, almost blank, an odd expression on a woman usually so confident and chipper. Tears intermittently dribble from her eyes; they appear odd stuck there on her cheeks, as though they don't have enough energy to move further. They're not rolling down as gravity usually pulls tears from weeping eyes.

Lil tilts her head slightly, her eyes focusing on something outside the window. A bird flits by. Then Lil continues. "I guess I thought that was love, or at least enough of a basis for marriage." Now looking at me directly, she declares, "I feel like a fool!" Tears now tumble onto her cream and black blouse. Anticipating the need, I had strategically placed a tissue box within reach for both of us. She seems to require prompting to even recognize the need for a tissue, so I pull one from the box and hand it to her, then place my hand on her arm hoping the touch will assure her she is not alone

Lillian isn't audibly sobbing, but the tear ducts are on full throttle. She sits up straighter in her chair, stares into my eyes, and apologizes. "I'm sorry, Virginia. I know you have work to do and here I am keeping you here telling my sob stories. Thanks for the tissues."

"There's no need to apologize. We're women who've known each other for some time now. We share and support one another. Right? I'm glad you honor our friendship at that level," I reply pulling out another tissue and handing it to her. Neatnik that I am, I lean around the corner of the desk to grab the wastebasket to put in the floor space between our sets of feet. I realize I am not just mouthing the words of a compassionate office boss. I truly hope she allows me to help her navigate the quagmire of her emotions and the next chapter of her life. She looks at me, smiles a little, and without her words, I sense these current tears are tears of appreciation.

"No more questions, Lil, but I'd like to share something with you." She looks a little surprised. You see, though Lil has worked in our office for years, we've not really had many heart to hearts. She does her job and I do mine. Today, I see that my job is to recount for her a story that may help her see that she may hurt a while, but with the support of caring friends, of whom I see I must be one, she'll make it.

"You see, Lillian, my mother had some tough rows to hoe when she learned deep secrets about her twin sister."

"You got twins in your family, too! That does bring us a little closer, Virginia. What happened with the twins in your family?"

"Well, it is not quite the same as yours, but I believe hearing my story may help you in some small way. I'm not trying to cut you off. I simply think you can use a little break. I'm not minimizing what you are going through, either. Lillian, please just accept what I am about to share at face value, Don't read anything into it. Folks tend to do that way too often."

"Okay, Virginia. I'll listen and sip the rest of this tasty coffee. You put in just the right amount of cream." She wiggles her shoulders as though releasing some tension, crosses her ankles, and settles back into the chair. I begin.

"When my Mom realized she was pregnant, she joyfully shared the news with her fraternal twin sister that she and my Father were expecting me. My mother and her twin had grown up sharing everything, from favorite foods to clothing, music to school subjects; and sharing dislikes equally. They even got married within a year of each other! They'd graduated from college with the same degrees and had pledged the same sorority. So, Mother couldn't envision they could have been any closer even if they had been identical twins. She was so wrong! Devastated at what she learned from her twin that day.

After sharing the news of my conception with her twin, Mother said she'd love for the two of them to raise their families with kids approximately the same age. So, she just blurted, 'Why don't you and your husband try to get pregnant!' Her twin declined, saying they weren't planning on having any children.

"No kids? ... But we're twins. ... We do things together!"

After a few more teases, my Aunt announced, 'I'm gay!" Tears on Lil's face stop flowing, and her bottom jaw drops like she can't believe what I am revealing is true. We sit in silence for a moment before I continue.

"My aunt told my mother, "I only got "married" for public perception, tax, and insurance purposes. My "partner" and her partner's "husband" are in fact two same-gendered partnerships. Yes, we live next door to each other in a duplex, but we built an indoor passageway between our two units.' You see, Lillian, sad as your story is, others have lived with similar situations."

I went on to tell Lil that my mother initially felt livid that her twin kept such a secret from her and like blurted, "How could you!." My Aunt held up her hand in Mom's face and exclaimed "This is exactly why I have lived my closeted life. If my own twin can't understand and accept me, how can I expect anyone else to?'

"My Mother immediately felt shame" I told Lil. "Mom started to question everything between them. "I ask Lil if this rings true for her and Lou. Her eyes widen and she nods in the affirmative. Then, shakes her head in disbelief

"So, I'm not the only one to have had this happen? Whatever 'this' is?" Lil asks. I assure her she is not. Then go on to inform her I had become aware of just how 'underground/closeted' gays are through studies I had undertaken in college to try to understand my own family dynamics.

"As a society, Americans are very much behind the times in our understanding of gender identification and subsequent acceptance." I told Lil there were resources I had that I'd bring for her since I hoped to "help" her normalize Lou's newly discovered orientation. She looks at me like I am talking in a foreign language. "Yes" I go on, "Lou has spent his entire life not feeling normal, and as a child of Jesus, we all need to accept each other as God created us. I'm hoping to pass along some resources to help you get through your shock."

I continue and tell her "there are predictable stages she will need to traverse; five stages identified by many in the field of human studies. "Girlfriend, you are going to feel like your emotions are on a wild roller coaster ride, and you aren't going to be able to stop the ride until you DO go through the stages." "It sounds like you're on Lou's side" Lil accuses gently but with a puzzled look. Shaking my head from side to side, I tell her that I don't see the situation as having "sides,"

"It is a situation with many lives involved in a new reality" I offer. "Lil, my suggestion is that you try to "sit" in Lou's secret for a bit. Just imagine what it has been for him and Claude to have "pretended" for their entire lives to be something they are not!"

"Well, Virginia. I'm gonna need both patience and prayers. For the past two or three years, I've been spending a little more time each day doing daily devotions. Some of the Scriptures I've been reading are starting to make more sense to me. That one in Isaiah was one of the key verses last week. You know, the one about *They that wait on the Lord shall renew their strength. They shall mount up on wings like eagles.* Well, that's what I'd like to do right now. Mount up on wings like an eagle and get out of here. But I got a family. My kids are gonna be even more shocked than I've been.."

"You're right, there, Lil. There's really no escaping when you have a family. My Aunt asked my Mother to do this as they discussed their new reality, and my Mother told me she knows that was an impossible ask, but that it helped her 'get out of her own angry head' long enough to have some clarity."

Lil asks, "How can there possibly be any clarity in this muddy mess?"

"Lil, this is going to require understanding and some coordination, if you and Lou are going to proceed "together," it will be easier on the kids as well as the both of you, do you agree?"

117

"That seems logical," Lil concedes, "but I don't see that in the cards. My mind is so jumbled whenever I think about it, or even look or think of Lou right now!"

"No doubt about that. Um Lil, where are the two of you in regard to telling the kids?"

"Well. We haven't decided exactly when, just not yet. I told Lou we are not telling the kids anything until my own 'fog' clears. Since he wants to be with Claude, that he should spend the night upstairs. I didn't care to look at him. The kids won't think it strange because they're accustomed to seeing him and their Uncle Claude working on projects together and they'll think they're just working late. "

"Well, my dear, you don't even realize it, but you have already begun that coordination phase with the way you handled last night; kudos to you! Don't minimize your capacity to 'get through this.' You know what? I have a DVD I think will help. My cousin is in film production at the National Geographic Channel. They're working on this piece with Katie Couric tentatively called: *Gender Revolution: A Journey with Katie Couric.* It's not due to be shown for a couple of years because there's still some mastering to be done. But, my cousin knows about my aunt, so she sent me a preview copy here, instead of to my home."

"Really?" Lil asks somewhat surprised that I'd suggest such a thing because we are not supposed to use computers for personal purposes.

"Yeah, Girl Friend. You're not in any frame of mind to work today, so we'll call it mental health work. You're taller than me. Will you get the DVD off the shelf there in my coat closet?"

"Okay, Sure. You think I'll be okay watching a show in my office. How long is it?"

"I'm not sure, but yes, it's okay." I say pointing her to the closet door on the left wall.

"Right?

"Yeah, on the right side. See it?"

"This it?" Lillian asks slipping out an unmarked DVD case and turning it over, looking for the title.

That's when I realize I am hiding, too. I keep the DVD in my office, but in an unmarked container. The label inside makes it clear the topic of the Couric show and when Lillian pulls it out, she just sighs.

"That Katie Couric presentation goes WAY beyond what applies to your situation, but my hope for you is that it expands your awareness of the diversity of humankind. Lil, you are in no shape to concentrate on work, so what do you think? Just come back in here this afternoon. I got a meeting with the VP. You can tell anyone who asks the truth. You're doing something I've asked you to do."

Lil doesn't look eager, but she admits she doesn't really feel she can concentrate on work, so she agrees to watch the documentary. I let her know it is a little long but am glad she'll watch it today before she returns to the quagmire at home. "Let's see how you feel about that after watching the piece."

*****

That evening, when I got home, I pulled three books from my bookshelf to take in tomorrow. I hope she'll be open to reading as she tries to clear up her "fog."

The next day, I clear my office for the morning and invite Lil to come to see me... just in case. When Lil arrives, she appears much calmer. She sits down and once again locking eyes, she admits, "That Couric presentation sure opened my eyes. I have always felt I was aware of things happening around me, that piece pretty much squelched that notion!

When I came to work yesterday, I was having my own little pity party, now I have some of that "Catholic Guilt" going even though I'm not Catholic. Thank you for suggesting and allowing me to "get schooled!"

"Glad it helps clarify some things for you, Lillian. I won't ask you how things went at home last night. But I am glad you felt strong enough to return to work today. You did pretty well after lunch and got most of the stuff on your list ticked off. That meeting with the VP went pretty well, too. He can be a real kick, sometimes, with his silly jokes. Huh? Oh. Yeah. Why'd I call you in?"

"Yes, Virginia., I did wonder. But first, please know that watching that DVD by Couric and hearing of your Aunt has assured me I can really use your help right now."

"How about we catch something at one of the food trucks, and head to the park," I ask. She returns to her office, and I stay in mine till lunchtime. Glad the weather is a little nicer and we can sit and eat outside.

*****

While at lunch, Virginia, thinks of an idea that may work for the Robertson family. When she'd prayed about what she should do, the idea that came seemed wild at first. Then, just right. Share what you have. "You know, Lillian. It may be good for you and the family to get away for a weekend. How about a weekend at Letchworth?"

120

"You gotta be kiddin'. We can't afford that right now."

"No, I'm mean, how about accepting a gift?"

"A gift? I'm not following you, Virginia."

"Oh, you haven't heard! Our family inherited our grandparents stone cottage near Letchworth State Park in upstate New York. Since we've fixed it up, when family's not using it, we rent it."

"That's fine, but we can't rent anything like that right now."

"My Honey and I are having our children join us there next weekend for Mother's Day, but you guys can use it the next weekend." As expected, Lillian is a little surprised, but with a mouth burning from the spicey pulled chicken sandwich she got at the food truck, she says nothing, but "Hunh?"

"The cottage is really where my grandparent's used to live. It has four bedrooms. We rent it out as a VRBO, you know vacation rental by owner, but we don't start that till school's out. How 'bout you guys taking the third weekend in May. All you must do is leave it clean, 'cause my sister and her family will be using it Memorial Day weekend."

"Really, Virginia? You'd let us stay in your family home for the weekend? But, you know, it may be tough to get away 'cause I sing with the praise team at my church on the third Sundays. Oh heck. I'll just let Sister Mamie; our ensemble leader know. I'll send her a text. Besides, it'll be good for the kids. They'll be done with AP exams by then and ready to unwind. Let me get back to you."

"Sure. No problem. I'll confirm with my family."

"That weekend probably will work okay for me, Virginia, but I'm not sure what plans my husband has. He and Claude may have golf that Saturday. But, to get up to Letchworth may be just the thing. We've done day trips up there, but never overnight that close to the park. Sure, your family won't mind us using it?

"Nah! They know I wouldn't loan it out to anyone we couldn't trust. Anyway, I keep the books and take care of reservations for rentals. It's my decision. I'll just let them know that our Letchworth cottage will be booked the third weekend in May."

"Oh, what a blessing! It'll be good to get away. We haven't told the kids, yet. Maybe we can do it that weekend. Telling them in a neutral place may be less stressful afterward for us all. Then, we can go "walk it off" up by the waterfalls. That's one of our favorite places in that state park."

Claude Suspects

Two weeks ago, Claude and Louis were working in the backyard as they often did after work. Now that the days are longer on Daylight Savings Time, the two can meet outside in neutral space.

*****

"She saw us," Claude exclaims to Louis as he turns on the pilot light and glances at the buns waiting to be toasted on the upper section of the gas grill. They both are engulfed in their projects, silently working in the same space but not entirely occupying it either. "Either she knows and it's time to tell her, or she doesn't know and it's time we tell her."

"No, she didn't see us, nor does she know," Louis, Sr., emphatically mumbles as he wipes down the table for what seems like a third time. He's still not looking at me, and he's curt and to the point. I've worked with accountants, and I've worked with Louis, and he can be a man of very few words when he wants to be. He can be quite direct, too. She saw my hand cover his. Hours after, I could see the quiet, steely yet seething look in her eyes like the time Alyssa came home from the youth group meeting and didn't greet her mom. The taut mouth. The anger and disappointment. Or like that time the baseball coach had grabbed Lou Jr.'s arm, a bit too hard.. It was seeing her eyes shut tight. The lips flat. The rigidity in her back. That made it clear. Lillian's anger. It reminds me of my mother's.

Louis Sr. tends to avoid tension. Perhaps I do, too – okay, well I know that's true - and maybe that's why we still work together somehow, after all these years. We are masters of the unspoken, the innuendo. The quiet glance, the unspoken word, and the burial of the hatchet. Never to be spoken of again, as if it didn't even happen. The facade works for us and always has.

Or so it seems.

Our conversation, in this moment, runs brief and direct, as one might expect. Moment by moment, frame by frame. The strain of this is bearing its weight on us, conversations feel pained, grievances not muttered, just taken in stride, as though time has started driving deeper trenches into the common field we tend carefully. Quietly. The rows must stay aligned.

What have we been sowing?

After our brief exchange, I go back upstairs to my kitchen to get the burger patties to put on the grill and get ready to assemble the food tray since Lou Jr. will be home soon. His father is now wiping down the chairs, as if we're about to host a family meeting, not a Saturday evening family dinner. I look up at the south bedroom window where Alvyra is taking her third AP practice test. I'm grateful, in this moment, for the line-up of juniper trees between our house and the neighbors so my partner and I can continue this discussion.

"Louis, we have to tell them soon," I say as I move the patties from the plate to the grill. "We can't go on like this. I've made peace with our situation, but it's time we make peace with your family."

"Claude, I know what you want me to do, but I can't do it now. The girls have too much on their plate and Lou Jr. is in spring practice, The plates are too full."

"There will never be a good time to tell them," I remind him. We've gone through this before. It's a song and dance.

"What do you want me to do then, Claude?" His whisper has turned into a growl.

"Lillian has to be told, Louis. We can't do this to her anymore. It's the on/off button with you."

"What do you mean?"

"You've made peace with the pivot. Going back and forth between the two of us, and it's not honest. That's where you will lose the children."

"Don't bring my children into this."

"How can I not?" The possessive pronoun "my" stung a bit. At this point, they feel like mine, too. Lillian has called me *family* repeatedly in the neighborhood and in front of our church members. I'm *Uncle*, after all.

"This isn't all on me. We agreed to do this. You can't change the rules now."

"But Lillian hasn't agreed. I know we made certain sacrifices and agreements, but my relationship with God, my relationship with your children— it's evolving. People evolve, Louis."

"What are yyou saying then, Claude?"

"I'm saying it's killing me and your family."

"What's killing you? Let's not be overly dramatic. You're doing just fine."

"Don't say that Lou, my love. As a Christian., the lie is killing me and my spirit."

"Well, I'm sure your spirit remains intact, despite all this."

There he goes again with the flip of the switch. On and off. Hot and cold. Black and white.

I can't live within these confines anymore, and he knows it. The structure, as he intended it, couldn't be sustained anyway. Now the cracks are giving way. The weight of the world on this relationship and reality is becoming too much of a burden. I see it in the way he slouches and moves his body through the world. He's slowing. This secret has aged him, detached him from his children in a way.

And I can't nag him. He has a wife for that.

Lillian and Louis Walk and Talk

Wednesday, after dinner, once the teens are settled in their rooms doing homework, Lillian and Louis take a walk around the neighborhood. They want to be seen, but not heard, so they keep moving. As they walk, they note the fragile blossoms in pinks, light purples, and white of the lilac bushes that their neighbors have interspersed in the landscaping, some as trees and others as shrubs. The sweet aroma floating by as the breeze rustles the leafy limbs reminds the couple of one more reason they are thankful to have bought a home in this area of town. But now there is a stink in their house, and they have to deal with it.

Earlier today, Lillian had gone online to search for a marriage counselor in the next town that they could meet with more privately than if they sought counsel at the office down in the village. Most of the sites said pretty much the same thing, so when she found a list of questions that seemed to show up on most of the blogs she viewed, she saved the link. She'd sent that link by email to Louis during lunch that day and asked him to consider the responses and to talk about them during a walk after dinner.

Thankfully, he agreed. One of the common questions asks the couple to verbalize the problem for which they seek counsel. That's obvious so Louis and Lillian skip that one and move on down the list. They seek to verbalize to one another how they are feeling right now and to visualize what the road ahead looks like for them and the family.

Louis asks, "Lillian, now that you know about me and Claude, what do you think will be different?"

"That's what's really confusing me, Louis. We've been traveling parallel lanes for our whole marriage, and I never noticed. What's the matter with me?"

"I don't think there's anything the matter with you other than you're surprised to learn about this parallel lane. I don't see how things have to be different other than my spending more time with Claude without wondering what you will think. You seemed to be satisfied with the way things have gone so far."

"I know, Louis. But have you?"

"Well, for the most part, yes, I have. You've been a good wife to me in that you seem to appreciate me as the co-head of our household, father of our children, and brother in the Lord. What more could a man ask of a wife who married him to become a mother?"

"Louis, I didn't marry you just to have an onsite sperm donor! I wanted to be a wife, too! You know, share a home, have children, attend social functions with a handsome man at my side. True, you've been all that to me. That's why I don't understand why I'm so upset."

As they walk along the sideway, nearing the exit to the cul-de-sac, they nod and wave to neighbors, the Mekonnens, sitting on their wrap-around porch. But the couple does not stop.

"I don't know why you're upset, either. You know after the twins were born, you decided to have that tubal ligation. That seemed to reduce your seeking after sex with me."

"Yeah, after having the two girls, added to our one son, the three of them seemed to be enough children, so having my tubes tied meant I wouldn't have to worry about taking birth control pills for the next twenty-thirty years until I hit menopause. That seemed like a good idea at the time. The gynecologist did let us know that sex drive sometimes is diminished even if one continues to monthly menstrual cycles. But I was so busy being a mom of three kids under three years old, that I didn't notice much change. You seemed to be satisfied, and now I know why."

"You're right there, Lillian. Being bisexual means, I was being fulfilled sexually with both you and Claude. The fact that he has been an integral part of our family, he has not been jealous of you. Being three adult orphans, we've been family for each other."

"Yeah, but what about the kids? They're not going to understand your being obviously gay. Do you and Claude have to live together to continue your relationship? I don't know how I'd feel about that with what I now know, but what about the kids?"

"I don't know. I think they'll understand. This is the twenty-first century!"

"Yeah, Louie. But what about our neighbors? What about the church?"

"I don't worry about our neighbors. We are independent citizens of the United States and are not answerable to any neighbors. Let them think what they want!"

"What about the church?"

"That's a big one. Do you think we should talk with Pastor Jackson before we tell the kids?"

"I don't know, Louie? What do you think he will say? What will he be askin' us to do? You don't think they'll make me leave the choir? Singin' is what's getting me through this."

"Well, let's talk with Claude. It's the three of us in this, Lillian. The only thing I think is the issue is that people may not accept that God made me this way. I didn't choose to be bisexual. I've just been able to live this way because the Lord led me to Claude and to you. I do not sleep around. We three have been going along pretty well all these years."

"But Louis. You are just telling me! I'm still in shock that I didn't even suspect anything earlier. Am I really that blind? How did I not know you love Claude in that way?"

By this time, the couple has circled the block from their cul-de-sac past the park and are on their way back home. Home? Whose home? Who will be living where? Neither says very much as they pass by the signpost where the kids catch the bus to school. Will their schoolmates treat them differently when they see Claude and Louis living more openly as a couple? What about the neighbors who've been so welcoming since the Robertsons have joined the families on this street? What's it to them?

Louis Hears Radio Sermonette

Loud hip-hop music blasts when Louis starts the car the next morning. His son had driven the car to run an errand for his mom last evening. Louis reaches for the dialer to get back to his regular music station. As he scrolls, Louis catches the voice of a minister from his hometown. Yes! It's Rev. Zusman. Grampa used to do community outreach projects with him. So, Louis stops scrolling.

Let's keep it real, talk about it, straighten it out,
Let's stop minimizing, playing it down, laughing about it
Let's tell the truth about. Infidelity, adultery, cheating, fling etc.
If it is not the worst thing that can happen to a marriage,
a relationship what is?

The opening invectives make Louis slow down a bit to turn the volume back up. He's at the street corner but forgets to signal. The car behind him honks, Louis nods an apology, pushes down his turn signal and enters the traffic flow.

What is the Old Man preaching now? That minister was always one to use the latest media to, what he called, "Get the Word out." What's the Word he's getting out today? Now that Louis is on the street that takes him in five to seven minutes directly to the expressway downtown, he gives his attention to the words flowing from his dashboard.

What can break a heart and trust quickest
can shut down and destroy communication,
bring about anger, rage, low self-esteem,
upset family dynamics, change relationships,
change personalities for life,
change the home for life,
change a person's outlook on life
change a person's relationship with God and the church
change a person's circle of friends
change where you live, sleep, and eat
bring the loss of a job, home children,
bank account and respect?

These are tough questions. Where's Rev. Zusman going with this? More importantly, why am I hearing this message this morning? I know I've been praying, asking God for directions as Claude and I begin our life together more publicly. Is this what I have to consider?

What can cause more pain, shame,
 insecurity, guilt, fear, secrecy, separation, and hopelessness?
Not only is there a reason God said don't do it,
there are unimaginable reasons why He said don't cheat,
don't commit adultery.
So, the next time someone says,
 or we rationalize
it's not the worst thing that can happen in my marriage
in this relationship, ask yourself what is?

That's what I've been doing. For weeks now. What's the answer, Rev. Zusman? What's going to happen to my family now that I'm expanding it to publicly include my partner?

Let's keep it real.
Let's straighten out.
If you are in a fling, physically, mentally etc.
immediately get out just like you got in.

Don't try to count the cost
because the devil and our sin nature,
along with our impulsive emotions
won't show us the full price tag and hidden costs

Let's keep it real.
Drop it /them like it's hot
Let it / them go.
It will result in not a love, but lust TKO!

131

*****

Not surprisingly, this sermonette stays on his mind as Louis turns the button on the radio to the quiet classical station. He needs some soft music in the background. He's got to think about what he has just heard. Is Zusman talking about anyone in a sexual relationship with someone other than their spouse? What about people like him, Louis, who is bisexual?

Maybe he'll call Reverend Zusman and ask. Grampa respected this minister of the gospel and maybe this brother in the Lord can help Louis figure out why he is wondering about something he thinks is okay. After all, following the model of a minister he had grown up with, Louis is living out his God-driven purpose as a confirmed Christian man committed to being the breadwinner and father, husband, and faithful friend.

Delphi's Back Story and Lillian's Front Story

Delphi Louise Stephens, the leader of the GEMS club the Robertson sisters attend, invites her good friend, Lillian, over for lunch. But that is just a ruse to get her there to talk about her daughters and their sudden change in behavior…..and the reason, why. As she awaits the visit, she reflects on the time they met on Maui.

*****

About ten years ago, we met the Robertsons at our timeshare on the island in Hawaii. Malcolm, my tall, not so muscular, but firm bodied, slim and, oh, so, handsome husband, and I had just bought our first timeshare at Maui Lea in Kihei. It was at the welcome party during which the manager offered a traditional Hawaiian brunch. That day it was hula dancers with a solo vocalist playing ukulele. I fancied myself a pretty good hula dancer and did not hesitate to join in when invited by the crew.

132

Malcolm and I arrived dressed in our swimsuits and matching cover-ups, because we intended to spend the rest of the afternoon in the pool and then the jacuzzi. My honey grabbed a table out of the sun, and we sat sipping on Mai Tais and nibbling on the simple brunch spread provided when Lillian and Louis, timidly, approached and Lillian asked,

"Are these seats taken?" She was wearing sunglasses, and sandals, and a multicolored mu-mu that hid her hefty girth very well, She also had on a fresh flower lei made at one of the many workshops the timeshare managers offered to guests. Louis had opted for tan shorts, a red shirt that suited his small frame and very dark complexion. He wore rubber flip-flops and a straw hat; the kind that fringed at the end, and around his neck hung a puka shell necklace. I recall fondly how truly they were dressed for the occasion.

"Why, no. Please join us," Malcolm replied, directing them to the two empty chairs at our table. It was no wonder they sought us out. We were the only other Black couple at the party. But the most fascinating part was that we discovered that we were from the same town and lived only a few miles apart! For the rest of the trip, we spent a lot of time together exploring what the island had to offer

. That evening, while he and I were in our timeshare, preparing for the farewell luah, Malcolm blurted, "That Louis is as funny as a two-dollar bill!" We were going to meet the Robertsons there, in Wailua, one of the ritzy spots in Kaua'i County,. We'd opted to go in separate cars, because Malcom wanted to spend some time alone with me just walking the beach on our last night there. I loved that about him.

"Why do you say that?" I asked, puzzled. "Funny, how?"

"Well, not funny, "Ha-Ha;" if you get my drift." Malcolm winked and grinned that silly grin that I loved so much. "I told him that I wanted to walk on the beach with you on our last night and he asked if he and Lillian could tag along! Haven't you noticed? They are never alone with each other even when they are not with us."

"Well, yes, I had, but I chugged it up to not feeling comfortable in a new place so far from home. Everyone is not as adventurous as we are, you know." I offered.

"You may be right, but my Spidey-sense" says it's something else." Malcolm chided using a term from the comic book superhero Spiderman, a term generally used to mean a vague but strong sense of something being wrong.

"He may not be a "man's man," but he seems attentive enough to Lillian, don't you think?" I countered.

"Mark my word, there's something off with those two. But, like my mama used to say, 'It's their business and none of mine!'" Malcolm says, grabbing me and giving me a long loving kiss. "Can't go there, Delphi."

Funny, we never spoke of it again. But, today that time a decade ago on Maui with my Malcolm when we first met the Robertsons is all coming back to me as I sit waiting for Lillian to join me for lunch.. How I miss that dear man.

Malcolm and I married so young. I was 19 and he was 21, but he was ambitious and determined to make life better for his family than his parents had made for him. "Young Gifted, and Black" was his theme song and he intended to live up to it no matter what. Well, over the years. Malcolm reached the level just one step down from the vice presidency of the company and was still aiming high when it all came crashing to an end. He was killed in a car crash two years ago. And I'm, still, trying to get my feet planted firmly on the ground. But this revelation about Louis and Claude opened old wounds I thought were long healed and forgotten.

Delphi Louise Latimore Stevens, I was born on the day my great-grandmother died. That's how I got my name! It was to honor great-grandma, Delphi Matti Louise Houston. "We come from a long line of sexually abused women, and yet, persevered through it all." That's what my mom, Lydia Latimore, said about the lives of the women who shaped our lives. They were some strong women. "You know beauty is a curse to Black women! That's what my grandma-Matti used to say."

Great-grandma Matti was what folk called "high yellow" in the southern town in which she was raised. Black men drooled over her, and White men tried to "get in dem pants." Matti was the daughter of a slave woman named Matilda who had been a concubine for her master. She bore him ten children and when times got hard right before the Civil War broke out he sold off five of their children. Grandma Matti was the youngest and the prettiest if color was the only criteria.

Matti used her looks to get by 'cause men would lavish her with gifts. But she paid a heavy price for them; making love was just a term she never understood. She wouldn't call herself a prostitute, but she wasn't "easy" nor "cheap." She married the blackest man she knew and bore him sixteen children. Times were hard, but together they kept the family above water.

Grandma-Louisa was the youngest; fair-skinned with what" in Mississippi they call "good hair. She was raped at the age of fifteen and later, when she was twenty-two years old, she met and married my grandpa. He was a teacher and highly respected in the Black community. He was also an incestuous pedophile who had pestered my mom from age seven to fourteen years old,

Mama, tall and chocolate brown with big boobs and tight butt, was the middle child with all that entails. Mama didn't talk about him or her childhood much, but she had fancied herself a lesbian at one point in her life. Because of what her dad had done, she hated men and found solace in the arms of other females. Then when she was 20-years old she met Daddy at a revival she had gone to on a humbug. It was like a lightning bolt struck her heart! She fell hard for him, a preacher! That's when she found the Lord and left her other lifestyle behind. That's also, why to this very day she has little tolerance for homosexuals. I am the oldest of their four children whom they raised together in a loving home in which the LORD was the head. Still, I rebelled.

"What a fool I was!" At the age of 15, my parents' lifestyle seemed so bland and unexciting. Nothing they did or said made much sense to me. I remember hating when mama assessed my friends and found them lacking and began to hang out with kids from the "wrong side of the tracks" as they say down home.

"That girl is not your friend," Mama warned me about Carmen Jenkins, a classmate with whom I had begun spending a lot of time on and off school grounds. One day Carmen enticed me to sneak out to go to a party on the far west side of town, the "bad" part as mom had put it. It sounded adventurous, so I went, surprised at how easy it was to sneak out of the house while my parents were watching the television.

Later that same night, reality came crashing down. Carmen took me to a party of college frat guys, pledges -- ten horny, drunk guys who proceeded to gang- rape me then left me weeping with my eyes closed. A big brother named James, came in and covered me up. 'You gonna call the cops?" I was too embarrassed and replied, "NO!: Then begged, "Please, just take me home!"

It was easy enough to sneak back into the house. I waited until James had driven off to climb the trellis to my brother's window and knocked. He let me in as I, ashamedly, had done for him on many occasions/ No questions asked.

*****

While in college, I learned from a soror about GEMS and in the library one day, searched the web about the acronym and its link to neighborhood girls' groups. Amazing! One group is a quasi-STEM program with the E and M meaning Engineering and Math. I found two others, though, that seemed something to which I could invest my gifts and passions. A couple of years later, I proposed that our home church launch a GEMS group. Ours draws guidance from the national groups designed especially for traumatized females ages 12-24 years old and the other that nurtures younger girls to embrace a relationship with the Savior. Our church leadership team consented to share our facilities and fund programming for girls starting when they are young and remaining with them through their teen years.

Now, as a GEMS leader, I and my team are here to help other girls get through the awful actions of the worst humanity. Doing so brings some solace to my spirit. But I did not have a GEMS leader. After that night I prayed for forgiveness for my disobedience and returned my life to Christ. The Word got me through what a psychiatrist would not because I would never share that experience with anyone, except with Malcolm. the love of my life. But now, he is gone and someone's knocking on my door. The rain has stopped, but the cloudy sky is evening grey, casting a pall over this mid-May afternoon.

Glendella Learns and Leaves

Thursday, Glendella has had it. Something is going on with her Baby Sister, but Lillian hasn't told her what. Glendella has been trying to be patient, so she hasn't called.. Since they've lived apart for so many years, she probably has her own go-to-friends she talks to when she's upset. And her sister's a married woman with her own family. Glendella drinks her morning coffee but ignores the news playing on the TV she has in the kitchen. She's into those cooking shows and often watches and cooks along with the TV hosts. The phone rings. She turns down the TV when she picks up her cell phone. It's her sister.

"Hey, baby sis, are you ready to come to Nourish Your Curls in the village? Wanna meet me there? I can walk from my apartment."

"Yes, I'm ready, but I don't feel like driving. Will you pick me up? I can take a break from work. I'm working from home, but have an afternoon ZOOM meeting with my team at 1:30."

"Pick you up? You want me to drive all the way over there when I can walk from my house. I just want you to be there when Karen describes her new products and see what she says about the different kinks and curls we Black folks have on our heads."

"I know, Glen, it's inconvenient, but will you come get me. We need to talk."

I arrive at Lillian's house and she's sitting on her front steps. How perplexing to see her looking like a teenager on time out. I roll up in the driveway, lean over and call through the passenger side window. "Okay, Lillian. What's going on? Is there something you want to talk about before we leave?" By this time, my baby sister has walked to the car and is opening the door to get in.

"Just drive, I will tell you later."

"Ok, you know you can tell me anything, no judgement."

For some reason, I just don't pick up on the vibes and, once Lillian has clicked her seatbelt, I start the five-minute drive back to the village shopping strip. "Oh, since you are not ready to talk, Let me. I am so excited to try Nourish Your Curls new haircare line. I love and hate that I am a product junky, but she always has great product recommendations that work for me. Are you going to buy anything for Louis?"

"Not today, I'll let you enjoy your shopping."

"Hey, we are here. You're coming in, right? You don't have to buy anything."

"No, I am going to stay inside the car and wait."

Finally, I'm tuning in and sense there's something serious here. "Okay, but when I get back you must tell me what is wrong. We are not going back home until you tell me what is bothering you. You know I don't like when my baby sis is not happy." She nods but doesn't look at me like she normally would when I call her baby sister.

I exit the car and go into Nourish Your Curls store in a bigger hurry to get out.

139

Karen rises from the back desk. From there, she has a good view of the store, can work on her business stuff and see clients come in as they arrive. She meets me about half-way along the spacious single aisle in her bright yellow walled store. Though she has everything out, it's not crowded looking. I never feel closed in when shopping at Nourish Your Curls.

"Hello, Glendella, Welcome back!" That's another thing about this store owner. She remembers your name.

"I am doing good. I saw on your Facebook page that you've launched your own line of hair products. Wanna tell me about them. I am here to see if your new line can work for my hair."

"Well, glad to know those posts are being viewed on that media platform. Yes, I do have my own line and they can work individually or together with others I sell here."

"Okay, give me the spiel quickly. I trust your recommendation. But my sister's out in the car. Something is on her mind, and I want to get back right away."

"Well, Let's start with Nourish Your Curl: Curl Smoothie. It has a soft hold and is not heavy or greasy; it won't weight your hair down."

"Sounds good. I'll take a bottle. How about Louis, my sister Lillian's husband? He wears his hair short. I want to get him something. He's a big wheel at one of the downtown office buildings and he likes to look good for his job. Neat, but proudly African."

"I would recommend Nourish Your Curls Buttercream because I remember his hair being more of a kinky texture. The Buttercream will moisturize and soften his fro and it can be used every day if needed."

"Um. Let me have two of each product. Thank you."

As she rings up the purchases and bags them in her nice, monogramed bags, she gives the typical, but authentic response, "Thank you for being a loyal customer. See you soon."

"Oh, can my sister, Lillian, use the same products? Her hair's a little looser curl. Remember?"

"Yes, you both can use the Smoothie. Lillian picked up a sample last week. Ask her how it's working."

"Sure. I will. Thanks so much. See you next time." Bidding farewell, I hurry back to the car, hand Lillian the bags, and sit, but do not start the engine.

"Okay, Lillian. Are you ready to talk now?"

"Yes, "I think I am ready."

My baby sister unloads! And it's a big one. "Wait, stop, tell me this is not true. Sis, do you want me to go talk to him and give him a piece of my mind and more. I can't believe this. This is so wrong on so many levels." I bang my fists on the steering wheel.

"I always wondered why his best friend had to be around all the time and even moved in the same house when you bought that two flat house over there. I know it is an independent living space, but really, it looked odd. I've always wondered why he never has a girlfriend ever with him.

Lillian shakes her head. "I don't know why I didn't notice that, too."

"Girl, you are better than me because you would be calling the ambulance for him after I am done with beating his butt. This is unreal. If I was in your shoes, I would have to divorce him and kick him and Claude out. Yes, he will be paying just not living in our house. What are you going to do? You know I am here to support you and the kids 100 percent."

"Yeah, I know, Glen. I'm gonna need you. Louis has not mentioned a divorce. I'm not sure what I'd do if he asked. I just know, I can't keep living with what I now know."

"What do you mean, you can't keep living? You're not thinkin…"

"I don't know what I'm thinking. I just wanna go home now. Take me home. My kids are gonna be home soon. I don't want them to worry. They were looking at me funny at dinner yesterday."

"Well, Sis. You know the next thing I have to say is, 'God's got you! He would not allow anything in your life that with His guidance you can't manage. Remember your song. Remember Pastor's sermon. Remember, most of all that I'm your big sister and I'm gonna be here for you. Let's go see Pastor, now."

*****

After meeting with Lillian, sitting outside when she spoke to Pastor Jackson, and reflecting on the plans Louis has revealed, Glendella does what she does when she needs to get away and think. Take a road trip! She decides to go on the next weekend. That'll have her on the road for Mother's Day. That's a good thing. She's never borne children of her own and her own Mom passed away some time ago. Mother's Day is a bittersweet day for people like her who are childless and motherless.

142

A couple days later, while shopping at the Christian bookstore, looking for a CD to play while driving to Michigan to visit the Meijer Gardens and Sculpture Park, Glendella hears a song over the loudspeakers. It is a female singer who sounds like she recorded multiple tracks of herself singing harmony and counter-rhythms. The words are both clear and new. The vocalist seems to be telling stories of experiences with the Lord. Hmmm.

Maybe this will be a good CD for Glendella to buy for herself and Lillian. They can learn one of the songs to offer as special music in the August Family and Friends Day service their church holds on the fourth Sunday in August. It's just early May, so the sisters will have plenty of time to listen, choose and then learn the song. While they both are musicians, neither really reads music all that well. Instead, they play and sing what they feel. And Glendella is feeling the songs she's hearing in this store today.

"Excuse me, Ma'am," Glendella says softly to a woman restocking the shelves with new books. "Do you know who that is singing?"

"Sure. That's Ms. Rochelle. Her CD just came out and everyone is raving about the lyrics. Almost everyone who comes in seems to connect with one or two of the songs they hear while shopping. Which one caught you?"

"Hmmm. It's both the music and the lyrics. The accompaniments are a little different from what one usually hears on gospel albums, but they seem to work."

"Well? Do you wanna get a CD? They're right over there by the entryway. The boss is featuring Ms. Rochelle this month. You can check out at the counter next to the exhibit. Gotta get back to work here," she says picking up another handful of books and slipping them into the space on the shelf she has just cleared.

"Thanks, and I will," Glendella acknowledges, gets the CD, and stands in line to checkout.

*****

To this day, the songs continue to resonate in her soul because she stuck the disc in her car player and listened to Ms. Rochelle sing the rest of the ride home. Now she's thinking about the song to suggest her sister Lillian reflect on while they are trying to hold on. This weekend, she, and her husband plan to drive up to Letchworth State Park. The kids think it's just a respite from exams and prep for the final weeks of school.

Little do they know the other reason is to have space to come to terms with the fact that their father is bisexual and wants to move in with his lover whom the teens know and love as Uncle Claude. Nothing like planning a praise song. Glendella is confident that the Lord is going to rescue her sister. With God by their side, as the pastor's sermon declared is promised in both the Old and New Testament Scriptures, Christians can live victorious lives.

YOU RESCUED ME

You rescued me
Did I do this to myself
Did I really walk away
I was so confused
Did what I wanted to do
I did not know
I could have been destroyed
But you protected me
When I couldn't see
Didn't know what I was doing
when I walked away
I heard you pray
But still, you rescued me

(Rochelle Jones 2010)

144

As Glendella reflects on the lyrics of this song, she realizes the words speak to her about her experience meeting and marrying Quentin Sanchez. Not many men she'd known back then would have been content married to an infertile woman. Most men wanted to be fathers. Thank the Lord, Quentin just wanted a wife, homemaker, and traveling companion, someone to come home to after his days on duty as an airman stationed on various bases around the globe.

The Air Force had sent them to Iceland, Germany, Kenya, and March Air Force Base in Riverside, California. She'd considered walking out on the marriage when he got his first assignment to Afghanistan. But she'd hung tight. He returned with symptoms of some kind of infection but recovered enough to accept one more assignment before retirement. Unfortunately, that did it. He became one of the fatalities in the questionable war.

Now, her sister is in a questionable relationship and internal war with her thoughts. Will she stay or will she go. "Today," Glendella says, "I'm going!"

Lou Junior Questions Mom

Thursday, while Lillian stands in front of the dryer waiting for the cycle to end and she can take out a load of light clothes for her and Louis, her son walks out from his basement bedroom and puts his arm around her shoulders. She stiffens at first, then relaxes.

"Mom, what's the matter?"

"What do you mean, Louie? I'm fine. How're you doing this week?Ready for that exam tomorrow?"

"No changing the subject. What's going on with you and Dad?"

"Me and Dad? We're doing okay. Just trying to work out some things for the family."

"What things? I noticed Sunday, when I came home that every time me or one of my sisters asked you about your weekend, you looked at Dad. But it didn't look like a look of something you had done that was fun. Even Uncle Claude seemed a little tense. What happened this weekend, Mom?"

"Well, you have been observant. We were so excited to learn the news of the scout who came to talk to you about playing ball for them at State College! What was it that he told you?"

Louis, once again, is deflected from Lillian's issue and gets all excited about his memories of baseball camp.

Her son relates much of the details of the memorable weekend to his mother, then pulls her back on topic.

"Mom, what is going on? Me and the girls see how you and Dad have been avoiding each other since Sunday. Yeah, you may be in the same room, but the ambiance feels different. I asked the girls if they'd noticed anything. The only thing they said was that all three, you, Dad, and Uncle Claude all went up for pastoral prayer during service Sunday. That usually puts folks in a good mood, but you three haven't been. What happened while we were gone?"

"Louis, I'm not ready to talk about this now. Our family has some serious decisions to make and when we're ready we'll have a family meeting to discuss them. Okay. You gotta trust your parents on this one."

"Okay, Mom. You want us to be praying about this, too? Our Sunday School teacher always tells us to pray for guidance. You know he made us memorize the verses from Proverbs 3:5-6 about trusting in the Lord and not leaning on our own understanding. Well, I certainly don't understand what's going on, so I guess this will be a time to pray for that."

"You got that right, Louis! I don't understand either, so I'll definitely be praying for guidance, too."

"Ding, Ding, Ding!" Talk about timing!

The dryer timer signals the clothes are ready and Lillian leans down to open the door and remove the load of now dry clothes. How disconcerting to be pulling out Louis' jockey undershorts intermingled with her silky panties. Lillian doesn't even want to think about it! How different will things be when her husband moves upstairs! Well, it'll be less laundry for one thing. But less family time with her husband, too. Is that what she wants?

Louis Calls Radio Minister

By Friday, Louis decides to call Rev. Zusman, that minister he'd known as a teen and had recently heard speaking on the radio. Rev. Zusman, had worked with Louis' grandfather on community education projects in their neighboring towns. The talk on the radio about being faithful in marriage is making Louis wonder if the teacher also is preaching about bisexual men, like himself, who are married to a woman and in an active love relationship with a man.

During lunch, Louis goes out to the parking garage to sit in his car, for privacy. He parks near one of the openings in the multi-level facility and can easily get a signal, so he pulls out his cellphone to search for a contact number for Rev. Zusman. He now is Dr. Zusman and is shown wearing his clerical color in the same beige as his browny blonde hair. He doesn't look like his's greyed much over time. Louis sees that Dr. Zusman is now a professor at the seminary and has an email address listed on his page. There also is a phone number. Louis bows his head to pray and ask for guidance. God, do I really want an answer that says I must stop my relationship with Claude? Can we still be friends if we do not engage in sex?

Louis taps in the numbers. Then after three rings, he hears, "Hello, this is Dr. Zusman's office. He's not available right now, but if you'll leave a message and number where he can reach you, he'll call you during his next break." Whew! I don't have to talk now, but I have made the first move. Okay, I'll leave a message.

"Hello, Rev. Zusman. This is Louis Jamal Robertson. You worked with my grandfather on those neighborhood education projects in the early 1990s. Do you remember me? Anyway, I heard your message on the radio earlier this week, you know the one about marriages. I have some questions. Hey, you know what? I'll just text you my email address and we can arrange to meet on SKYPE. It would be great to see you again. I see your email address on your website where I got this phone number. See you soon."

Am I being a wuss to not just ask the question? Do I really want to know the answer?

*****

Dr. Zusman replies to Louis and sends along a link for a SKYPE meeting the very next day. He must have figured Louis would be free because he set it during the same time Louis had called. It was his lunchtime and so Louis had no reason not to confirm the meeting and take his lunch and computer tablet with him out to his car.

"Why if it isn't Louis Jamal! Young man, you really haven't changed much. Still slim as ever with that shiny blue-black skin. You're wearing your hair a little shorter and it even looks a little curlier. What are you doing differently?"

"Dr. Zusman, thanks for consenting to meet with me. About my hair. My wife, Lillian is having me use some kind of creamy lotion that gives my hair a little shine and a looser curl. Who knows? It smells a little herby, but she likes it. The things we do for our wives."

"Louis, to help me recall you, I went online and saw your family website. You've got three kids now? The girls…how old are they? They look really close in age. Could they be twins? Folks probably ask that all the time. Wow, how time flies. I remember when you were the age of Louis, Jr. That's his name, right? Does he carry your middle name, too?"

"Yes, we're keeping Jamal going in honor of my Dad. I never got to know him 'cause he died when I was a baby. But Grampa taught us it's important to maintain connections with our heritage through our names. So, yes, my son is Louis Jamal."

"You know I also saw another man in almost all of the family gatherings. A white man. Who is that red head?"

"Oh, that's Claude. My partner."

"Your business partner? That's great! What business are you in, now. Louis? Your grandfather would be so proud of you to have your own business."

"No, Dr. Zusman. No. he's not my business partner. He's my lover."
"Your lover! I thought you said you are married. How can you be
married and have a lover showing up in all your family photos?"

"That's what I'm calling you about, Dr. Zusman. I'm bisexual and we've just told my wife that Claude, that's his name, and I have been partners since before I married her."

"Hold on, Louis. You mean to tell me; you found a woman willing to marry you when she knows you are a homosexual."

"Not quite. Rev. Z. She didn't know about that. You see, I'd met Lillian at work. We were getting into our late twenties; she wasn't married yet and wanted to be married with a family. I couldn't have children with Claude. I liked Lillian, we attend the same church, so she and I decided to get married and start a family.

"Claude has always been "in the picture" as you saw, but not in the way Lillian understood. She just thought we were all good friends because we work in the same building downtown, were new to town about the same time, and all are committed Christians. Claude's become Uncle Claude for my children, too."

"What do you mean, you're all committed Christians and living like this?"
"That's the issue, Rev. Z. I'm bisexual and am faithful to my wife and to my lover. I was not promiscuous before entering a relationship with Claude and had not been with any other woman before marrying Lillian."

150

"So, why are you calling me, Louis? You seem to have all the answers figured out."

"But that's it. I don't. Claude would like us to stop living parallel lives, so I told Lillian about him and me the other day. She had a hissy! I don't see how things will be all that different because Claude lives upstairs from us in the two-flat home we bought last year. I'd just spend more time with him, openly. We're tired of hiding the relationship from the people we love."

"Love! How can you love your wife and be cheating on her all this time!" Dr. Zusman nearly loses his cool at the thought of his minister mentor's grandson in such a fix!

"That's why I'm calling you Rev. Zee. I'm puzzled. God made me bisexual. I've been faithful to both my partners. How can this be adultery as you described in your sermon? The main thing is that Claude and I haven't been transparent because we know how society frowns on same gender-relationships. It wasn't that we were trying to hide something from God. We know God is omniscient and omnipresent. In fact, Claude and I often pray together thanking God for bringing us together in a relationship in which we three, he, my wife and I, and even the kids get along so well.

"Further, Claude started attending our church with us and was best man at our wedding! We've continued to serve in the congregation where we are getting solid Bible teaching."

"How are you getting solid Bible teaching and you don't realize the state of your souls?"

151

"What do you mean? Our pastor teaches us to be light and salt, to be caring parents, reliable businesspersons, generous givers, and all the same stuff my grandpa taught. I haven't heard one sermon that I could not imagine Grampa preaching if he'd been our pastor. That's why we chose to join in fellowship with this non-denominational congregation, Beth-El Community Church."

"Is that where you all go? To Beth-El Community Church? I know the pastor there. We've met at state ministerial meetings. Does he know about you, Lillian, and Claude?"

"I've not told him. I don't know about Lillian. She may try to speak to him now that she knows about the different level of relationship between me and Claude."

"Well, Louis. The fact that you've sought me out suggests you have some questions about the way forward. You've come out of the closet, so to speak, now you must face the church family and community and deal with their responses. As I tell my seminary students, don't try to get between a pastor and his flock. If someone has a Pastor, one they trust and respect, encourage them to make an appointment to meet with their own shepherd. Louis, I don't understand this bisexual stuff, but I do know about being monogamous. The Bible tells us that the two shall become as one. There's nothing in there about becoming three."

"So, what am I supposed to do? I love my wife, my lover, and my children. They are my family!"

"Louis, this is something you're going to have to get worked out in your personal relationship with God. He'll guide you, I'm confident of that. Please know that I will keep you in my prayers and urge you to definitely speak with your pastor. He'll help you "see the light" so you can walk in the light."

"Buzz. Beep. Buzzz"

"That's my timer, Rev. Zee. I mean, Dr. Zusman. I have to get back to work. Thanks for meeting with me. It was great to see you and to talk with someone who may not understand my situation, but who does understand God. I will make an appointment to talk with my pastor next week. Have a good afternoon."

"You, too, Louis. I'm honored that you reached out to me as a man of God whom you trust. Your grandfather would be proud that you are seeking God's answer to this dilemma."

"Bye, now!" Louis clicks the screen. "Lord, that "Show me the way," sermon that Grandpa often preached is making more and more sense to me. Psalms 143 may not have been written by King David. Some writers say the descriptions of their interactions could mean he was in a homosexual relationship with Jonathan. True or not, I certainly understand how it could have been that way." Louis' tablet screen fades, but his complications don't.

SECOND WEEK

They've made it through the week with the amazing grace of the Lord! It has to be God's Spirit, otherwise each of the adults would have crushed someone or crumbled themselves. Hiding in plain sight is taking much more energy than any anticipated when Claude, along with Lillian and Louis agreed not to tell their teens about their father's sexual orientation and plans to move to the upstairs flat to live with his lover.

This morning, as the teens tumble out of the back seats of the car to go greet their buddies standing outside the front of the sanctuary, Lillian and Louis stay a little longer in the car. It's the second Sunday, which means neither has a role in the service this morning. On second Sundays they usually sit together on the left side of the fifth row. No, there are no assigned seats in their sanctuary, but the same folks tend to sit in about the same places each week,

When the children were younger, the family took up the whole row. Usually, Louis would sit in the space nearest the center aisle, and Lillian in the space nearest the side aisle. The three young ones would be seated between them, with Lou Jr. next to his dad. As the children grew older, the parents would have Lou sit between the sisters to keep them from tickling and giggling during the service. Now, that all three are teens, they usually sit with their friends further back in the sanctuary. They know they still must behave because God's got His eye on them and so have the ushers.

This week, Lillian and Louis chat a few minutes before exiting the car to enter the house of worship. Their walk to talk over marriage counselor questions has been revealing to them both. They both are surprised at the openness of the other. "Just one more week, Lil. We'll have this settled and we can move on."

"You think we'll be ready?"

"Well, we won't know for sure till we do it. Our kids are smart. They understand these things better than we probably did at their age." The couple continues chatting superficially, then stop.

Organ music seeps through the one inch opening of the slightly lowered car window. As the pre-service hymn, the organist has begun playing "Count Your Blessings." Lillian, wishing to refocus her mind away from current stresses and onto the upcoming service, begins bobbing her head, then softly singing the first verse.

> When upon life's billows you are tempest tossed,
> When you are discouraged, thinking all is lost,
> Count your many blessings, name them one by one,
> And it will surprise you what the Lord hath done.

Talk about surprise! This whole week has been filled with them; few of them all that pleasant. But! But they'd made it through week one. They are still a family. Louis turns, looks at his wife, and smiles as they both check their mirrors before getting out of the car. They know the refrain and mouth the words as they reach for the handles, open their doors, close them, pause, listening for the click of the locks when Louis presses the key fob. He walks around the car, and now holding hands, the couple strides up to the front door of the sanctuary, struggling to ready their hearts to give thanks for the blessings they know they may lose if they are not careful, remaining open to what the Lord is telling them to do.

> Count your blessings, name them one by one;
> Count your blessings, see what God hath done;
> Count your blessings, name them one by one
> ;Count your blessings, see what God hath done.

Louis' and Lillian's smiles let the other know they know they are in avoidance mode for this morning. Neither denies that the time is coming when they must meet with the children and make plans for the future.(is plans sufficient?) But they've agreed to hold off telling them until after the three complete the round of Advanced Placement Exams. Lou had his exam Friday, and the girls are scheduled to take theirs this coming Thursday. It has not been difficult for the parents to avoid talking about personal issues with them because the children all are focused on schoolwork.

*****

So far, since starting school, the twins have had different teachers for most of their classes. Louis and Lillian agreed early on to give the girls space to grow into their own destinies. The fact that they were wombmates did not mean they would be interested in the same ideas or be good at the same skills. From their first year in school, when Lillian took the girls to register them for Kindergarten, she asked the principal to add to their records that it was the parents' wish that the girls not be placed in the same classes when there was an option.

So far, the school population has been large enough that there usually are two or more sections of the required classes. Alysa and Alvyra generally have had their own spaces to grow without the constant comparison of being in the same classroom all day and the same bedroom all night. The fact that the girls have been in the same courses, often with different teachers has been a mixed blessing. When the sisters do homework, the assignments often are different, so there is little sharing of answers.

Having different teachers for the same classes, however, also has expanded their learning. The girls often compare and argue about what they are assigned. Explaining their teachers' rationales helps the whole family see that though the teachers may approach the content matter in different ways, the results have been positive. All three of the children have remained eager to learn and have maintained B averages so far.

So far is the issue now. In what ways will having a change in living arrangements at home impact their children as students? With just three more weeks of class and the first high school dances with dates for the girls. Dates! O, Lord! Will the guys who asked the girls to the End of the Year Dance renege on those invitations?

This afternoon, the girls are going to quiz each other on the factoids from their World History class. But they are going to do it in writing. Each one is writing a quiz for the other to take. Their mom taught them this. She knows when you write a quiz or test you are reviewing. You have to decide what is important and identify facts the responder must include in the answer to show they know. And, to avoid undue arguments, the quiz writer has to have the page numbers that show the answers available to substantiate their claims about what is the correct answer. Clever Mom!

To help them focus this weekend, Lillian had the girls download a World Map and place it in the center of a PowerPoint slide. Then, the girls have had to create slides with this map that show social, economic, and political issues on each continent that they recall. Then, they are to use font colors to show what country seems to dominate the events. The girls have noticed that the world map looks different when viewed on a European website, an Asian website, or a North American website. That's been insightful for the girls, too, as they consider that whoever is telling the history, usually is the hero of that history. And, they have come to see the interdependency of the different countries in terms of food, technology, and transportation of goods.

News reports are starting to make sense to them. This World History class and the increased reflection on the world maps have raised their consciousness and concerns about supply chains. More than ever, these sophomores are coming to understand the power moves between nations and how they relate to the delivery of goods on boats, ships, and docks, and who controls the traffic flowing through waterways like the Suez and the Panama Canals.

Lillian imagines the girls are counting their blessings this morning that they have access to a variety of international products at prices they often can afford. At least she hopes that's where their minds are this morning.

*****

The organ music changes just as Louis is opening the door for Lillian to step through wearing her pasted-on smile. What's the song? Ah! "Faith of Our Mothers."

> Faith of our mothers, living still,
> In cradle song and bedtime prayer;
> In nursery lore and fireside love,
> Thy presence still pervades the air:
> Faith of our mothers, living faith!
> We will be true to thee to death.

Today is Mother's Day! Flowing across the screen hung on the front to the right of the giant cross behind the pulpit are photos of the women who attend the church. What a lovely range of races now fellowship at Beth-El. Mother's Day? The kids hadn't said a thing this morning.

Louis and Lillian have been so weighted under other issues that they'd been watching little TV, so they hadn't noticed the ads that generally are running 24/7 the week before this national celebration! By the time the couple reaches their fifth-row seat, the photos stopped scrolling, and now a picture of an open Bible fills the screen as the youth group marches down the center aisle singing the next two stanzas of this traditional hymn.

Faith of our mothers, loving faith,
Fount of our childhood's trust and grace,
Oh, may thy consecration prove
Source of a finer, nobler race:
Faith of our mothers, living faith,
We will be true to thee till death.

By the time the youth have sung verse one, the line leaders have reached the first row. The teens stop. Alternating from front to back so that half are facing the left and half are facing the right, the teens sing directly to those standing on their side. Some even make eye contact with those observing and nodding their heads..

Faith of our mothers, guiding faith,
 For youthful longing, youthful doubt,
How blurred our vision, blind our way,
Thy providential care without:
Faith of our mothers, guiding faith,
We will be true to thee till death.

The picture of the Bible fades as the young folks again face the pulpit and march up to assemble in the two front rows of the choir stand. The words of the final verse scroll onto the screen and Sister Millicent, the choir director for second Sunday, invites the congregation to sing along.

Faith of our mothers, Christian faith,
Is truth beyond our stumbling creeds,
Still serve the home and save the Church,
And breathe thy spirit through our deeds:
Faith of our mothers, Christian faith!
We will be true to thee till death.

Tears wet the cheeks of most of the adults standing in the pews awaiting the pastor to lead them in the opening prayer. Each verse of the opening song includes a phrase that "spoke or poke" each of them. Lillian recalls her mother reading the Bible and telling Glendella and her that the Holy Book contains answers to any of their questions. It was their mom who started them reading the little devotional booklets their church provided quarterly. Mom had even told them she did the extra reading that led her to read the whole Bible through in a year, year after year.

*****

With the tears come the memory of one of the last times Lillian and Glendella were home together with their Mom.

"Do you know, girls, since I've been home with this unrelieved cancer this is the sixth year I've done this. You know, read a selection from the Old Testament and one from the New every day. And every day, something new comes through to me. I still am reading those Christian fiction novels Andrea's mom and I used to read when you girls were young."

"You mean when you used to take us to story time at the library? That was fun, wasn't it, Glendella. Remember the African American Read-Ins when the librarians would read picture books by authors of color. They said some group called the National Council of Teachers of English recommended that schools and libraries do that every February. Then the library started doing that kind of focused reading for other special cultural and racial celebrations."

"Yeah, I remember," piped in Glendella. "Wasn't it fun to see the illustrations? One of my favorites was *To Everything There is a Season!* That husband-and-wife team, Leo and Dianne Dillon did the illustrations for that one. It was cool to see them imitating the artistic styles of so many different cultures to illustrate a single chapter in the Bible."

"My favorite was *Heaven's All Star Jazz Band* by Don Carter. I think he wrote and illustrated that one. I never knew so many of us were that famous."

"Yes, my dears," mother butts in. "That's why we took you to the library at least once a week. Not just to get Andrea and her two wiggle worms out of the house so their dad could sleep, but also because we liked getting books for ourselves. We both had intended to go back to college when you all were older. But that didn't happen for either of us. Once Dad was earning enough for us to move out of that trailer and nearer to town, I started volunteering at your school. You know." Mom said shaking her head," they liked my work in the office enough to offer me a job subbing.

"Wow! Did I learn a lot trying to teach, ha! Not teach! Trying not to waste class time when those teachers took off for one reason or another. I certainly gained lots of respect for those who had to come in and work with you all every day. Period after period, week after week, year after year, another group of students with different skills and interests having to be taught the same content and skills by the end of the term. Subbing was enough for me! I was glad to get back into the office."

*****

Louis is not surprised that pastor's sermon "Missing Mothers – Now and Later" has struck him so personally this year. This holiday celebration is a mixed blessing. Listeners rejoice that they have fond memories and mourn that they'll be making no new ones. But it is the sermon text from the fourth chapter of Paul's letter to the Philippians that he thinks about most as he stands with the congregants during Fellowship Time following the service. Amazing how many remain for class on the holiday. Few are rushing out for afternoon gatherings.

6Do not be anxious about anything, but in every situation, by prayer and petition, with thanksgiving, present your requests to God. 7 And the peace of God, which transcends all understanding, will guard your hearts and your minds in Christ Jesus.

Louis basically lost his Mother when she married a man who moved them both to Los Angeles where he had a new job and she decided to attend seminary. Louis had hoped that Mom could come to terms with the fact that he is bisexual, married with a family and pleased that he is successful on his job. She sees photos of Claude in most of the family celebrations they faithfully send to her, but probably has not figured out his relationship with the family.

Ruby Lynn is still his mother! How frequently childhood memories with Mom arise as he notes the way he and Lillian plan holiday celebrations for their children. So many of the same rituals. Mother's Day, of course, is toughest, even for a full-grown man, because he is reminded that another year has gone by, and his mother has not met his wife or children in person. When he and Lillian had flown to Hawaii for their anniversary stay in the timeshare on Maui, he'd planned to arrange a visit during the overnight stay in LA on the outbound or return trip, but Mother had not been ready to see him, yet.

164

True, her husband, Charles, had convinced her to SKYPE with the family during the Christmas holidays last year, but that's not the same. Seeing someone and being with someone is just not the same.

The pastor's sermon on about not being anxious makes Louis think, too, about his wife, the mother of his children. How's she going to manage when he moves upstairs with Claude. Maybe they should not change their living arrangements, yet. There are more intricacies to this plan than he considered when he agreed so readily to make the move and to tell his wife about it.

Rev. Jackson, in the sermon earlier, kept going back to the fact that in every situation, Christians should pray for guidance. The guidance Louis had received about the current status of his family was to tell Lillian the truth, the whole truth, and nothing but the truth. Louis has done that but has not yet experienced the peace that the Scripture promises. When's that gonna come?

*****

After Sunday School the Robertson family does not hang around long chatting. In fact, most of the families with teens scuttle out and quickly leave for whatever they do after church. Louis and Lillian already have been advised by their three that they'd be ZOOMING with classmates reviewing for assignments this week.

Lou Jr. has a group project that requires some tech work for the multi-modal presentation in his US history class during the closing week of school. The teacher has assigned an end-of-the-year group project as the final assessment since the students will already have taken the AP exam. He wants to see how the students can apply what they are learning in United States History to current events in this metropolitan area and state. The assignment prompt usually has been general enough for the students to present interestingly unique perspectives based on factual information

For example, this year, Lou's group is doing a heritage presentation. They plan to show how specific historical events reflect the family history of the five people in their group. Their research question is: "What happened in the United States that brought our families to this country, to this state, or to this town?" Louis is responsible for arranging the graphics another group member has located online that represent the historical events. Each student has gotten family permission to share photos of two generations of family members. Another student has arranged those photos in chronological order to be interspersed with the historical event graphics.

Akeem, the musician in their group, volunteered to find music to play in the background either to suggest the mood of the historical event or the time of the event by playing pop music from that decade. Since the students in the group all are about the same age, the music popular when their parents were young is pretty much the same.

The main differences the students are noticing are the cultural celebrations of their families. The historical events are common, but the impact of these has been different. That's the role of each contributor. Each group member has to write and record a one-minute narration to go with one of the five historical events their group will present. The time limit the teacher has given for each group is six and a half to seven minutes. This allows time for the introduction, the five-minute narrations, and some kind of closing overview and or call to action.

Their teacher is ingenious. He has had his US History students working on this project for almost a month! Doing so has been his way of having students do a review of key events of the past four hundred years of United States history since 1619! Hey, when they think they're getting a jump on a heavy-weight assignment by using class time to prep, the students usually stay engaged.

Pastor Reflects on Meeting

When he moved to town to become shepherd at Beth-El, Pastor Jackson had brought his Schwinn Exercycle. He didn't really have room in his house for it, so he has it set up in the back corner of his office, behind a folding screen. Each day, he takes time to ride for 35-40 minutes while listening to playlists of Christian songs. Depending on his mood or his need, he may listen to classical hymns, country and western, or contemporary gospel. Because the church is inter-denominational, he strives to stay tuned to the various songs that may be well-known in one and unknown in another sect.

Thankfully, his two choir directors are both trained musicians, can read music well, and both can sing arias from operas and Southern Gospel from both Nashville Country Music charts and Louisiana soul music. One is a professor at the local institution of higher learning and often brings in students from the college to sing solos on more complex choral pieces. Some of these young musicians have chosen to remain after graduation and now fellowship with the Beth-El congregation.

For the most part, the two music directors tend to split up the styles and focus on singing all kinds, but not every week. For example, First Sundays usually have traditional Protestant hymns during Communion, and four-part choral music on second Sundays. Third Sundays, usually feature Southern Gospel music sung by a select ensemble of those who sing by ear and harmonize and improvise with ease. It was interesting, this past First Sunday that the choir director chose Lillian to sing, "Just a Closer Walk with Thee" and she slipped off into improvising that third verse. Somehow, though, it opened the way for him to preach the sermon the Lord gave him to share.

Now, he's waiting to meet with Lillian, one of the long-time members who for some reason asked for an early afternoon meeting on a Monday. He, like many pastors, usually reserves Mondays as his day off. But the tremor in her voice sounded like this was not an ordinary pastor/congregant meeting. She was coming with her sister, Glendella, later this afternoon at about three o'clock.

That's good, because Pastor Jackson makes it a practice not to meet with females without his wife nearby; she also is his secretary. She is off on Mondays, too and is home working on some project for the Women's Ministry group she co-chairs. She'd kicked him out of the house after the kids left for school, so he had run some errands, and decided to do his riding this afternoon. He slipped a Phillip Keversen CD of Piano and Strings music disc into the CD player and put on his headphones. He wasn't a fast rider and seldom even broke a sweat, so he wasn't worried about being musty when the ladies arrived for the appointment.

The first song on the CD is "Blessed Assurance" and later comes "What a Friend We Have in Jesus." No matter what it is the ladies are coming to talk about, Pastor Jackson is confident that meditating on one or both of these songs will help him prepare to listen and advise as needed. How right he is!

*****

"Click, clack…Click, clac… Click, cla…"

Lillian's footsteps slowly disappear down the hallway.

Pastor Jackson slumps down into his large, black leather chair behind his equally large, mahogany desk, trying desperately to sink into the fading sound of her heels as she walks away. She is gone, but the conversation and the emotions that it brought with it, still hang heavily in the air: anger, betrayal, fear, shame, anxiety, uncertainty.

The last two, anxiety and uncertainty, are the feelings that hang most palpably in the air, in part because they may belong more to Pastor Jackson than to Lillian. She didn't seem anxious or uncertain at all. She knew exactly what happened and what she needed to do. She had come to terms with it and what it meant. Pastor Jackson, however, not so much.

It's late, but he loads a coffee pod into his Keurig, fills the reservoir with water, and pushes the large blinking "K" in the middle.

"Swish."

His cup of coffee starts to brew immediately, filling the office with the scent of cinnamon and a Haitian breeze.

He thinks, "It ain't rum, but it will have to do." He stopped keeping a flask at the office after the custodian found it one morning. Jackson had mistakenly left it on the desk.

"Okay... How are we going to handle this one?" As he begins to try to silence his anxiety and uncertainty, his office phone rings, interrupting his thought process. Annoyed, he puts the phone on "Do Not Disturb." He thinks, "The old preachers were right... If you want to get anything done... Don't come to the church office to do it!"

"Hmph...," he opines, "Gone are the days when Pastors had studies. Now, like other 'professionals,' we have offices where emails get sent, phone calls returned, meetings are held, and things are managed."

169

"Managed… How in the heck am I going to manage this?" He sits with his cup of coffee, running his long, brown fingers along the rim.

A few months ago, when he spoke with the church Board of Directors about being more "Open and Affirming" and "welcoming" to the LBGTQIA+ community, he had hoped to first lead the congregation in an honest, healthy dialogue about faith, human sexuality, and hospitality, to create a safe space for same-gender-loving people to worship, and to turn the church into a model of inclusion and acceptance" (while also increasing attendance and Sunday giving, both had taken a dip over the last three years).

"However," he thinks, "after that conversation with Lillian… this thing between Louis and Claude. When it gets out? The sheer scandal. The secrecy of it all. The perceived violation of the sanctity of their marriage. (Though how sacred could their marriage really have been if it was based on a lie?) What a way to have to start this conversation? Church folks can be opinionated.

"This could stall, if not stop, everything.

"What will people think? What if Louis and Claude want to continue to worship here? What if they want to get married? Join the Marriage Ministry? I should probably say something to Deacon Thomas. Whatever happens, she and I need to be on the same page about this."

Then he thinks, "What if Lillian and her teens want to continue to worship here?"

He feels tightness in his throat as he realizes that, if they all decide to stay, he would have to somehow manage his relationship with them all, in the same place, at the same time, while also trying to convince the church to be more welcoming and affirming of same-gender loving couples.

"Talk about threading a needle? Had it not been such a well-known couple and family…" he thinks. "Had they not seemed so happy all the time… Had they not literally looked like the paragon of Christian marriage…

"One of them could just disappear, right? I mean people disappear in churches all the time."

Reassuring himself, he says aloud, "This might not be so bad. Managed. How can this be managed?"

Pastor Jackson realizes that he is doing the very thing he hates, the very thing he rails against. Still having not taken one sip of coffee, he stops himself mid-thought.

The problem with the professionalization of the pastorate is that the pastor begins to think more like a manager and less like a shepherd. He is thinking in the way he promised himself, the ancestors, and God that he would not.

He wonders, "How long have I been…"

He stops himself again, "No time for that. No time for introspective navel-gazing." Managers generally don't have time for that.

"There are real people involved here. This is not something to be managed. This is a situation with people who need to be shepherded through a crisis. They need resources. They need counseling." Never once does he think that they need prayer or wholeness, or authenticity, or peace, or grace, or love. Just resources and counseling.

"Perhaps, I should give Louis a call… and maybe Claude. Should I speak with the two of them together? Should I speak with Lillian again? Should I try to speak with all three of them together? What about the kids? They will need counseling, too. I better give the youth minister a 'heads up.' She just finished seminary. This will be some good 'real life' ministry experience for her."

Leaving his coffee un-sipped on his desk, Pastor Jackson gets up from his overly large chair, turns off the lights, closes the door, and leaves his office satisfied that he has put together a plan to "pastor" instead of "manage" as he begins walking down the hall, glad to see that Lillian's sister, Glendella is waiting for her in the car.

"Click, clack…Click, clac… Click, cla…"

> Nobody knows the trouble I've seen;
> Nobody knows but Jesus.
> Nobody knows the trouble I've seen,
> Glory hallelujah.
>
> Sometimes I'm up, sometimes I'm down,
> Oh, yes, Lord!
> Sometimes I'm almost to the ground,
> Oh, yes, Lord!

*****

Later that week, after talking with Dr. Zusman, Louis had called and met with Pastor Jackson. Now, he understands that the Brother does not believe being an active bisexual man is unChristian. In fact, based on his understanding of Scripture he is living out "his purpose" as a child of God, loyal friend, husband, and father. He quotes Scripture relating to being made in the image of God, being shaped in his mother's womb, and having accepted Christ as Savior as a youth, and confirmed in the Episcopal church when he was sixteen years old.

He has been a husband and father to his children in a responsible way. Until this revelation, he has not neglected or abandoned his family, nor does he plan to do so now. Sitting under the ministry of the series of pastors in this inter-denominational church, Louis feels confirmed as he checks his conscience about being a consistent man of God living, loving, and sharing in the compassionate care for others. He believes he is being all these, even to Claude. Now, once he learned of Claude's strong feelings, he has begun to rethink just his living arrangements. That for Louis would be the loving thing to do.

Although you see me going 'long so,
Oh, yes, Lord!
I have my troubles here below,
Oh, yes, Lord!

Teacher Saw Something

Two months ago. Ash Wednesday. All day students had stared at the smudge of gray across her forehead. She'd had to get up an hour earlier than her typical 6:00 am alarm in order to get to Mass before school. Now she is fighting exhaustion, willing herself to get through the stack of essays on her desk. And she still has to prepare tomorrow's lesson.

173

The rap on the door is tenuous – so faint that at first she isn't even sure she'd heard it. Then it opens just a crack.

"Mrs. McBride?" A whisper-soft voice.

The teacher raises her head from the grading and looks at the student. "May I come in?"

Alvyra. One of the Robertson girls. At the beginning of the year, she'd had such trouble distinguishing one twin from the other. They were assigned to different class periods and their looks are not identical. But both are tall and athletic, both girls play the clarinet and are trying out for marching band. Alysa and Alvyra, Alvyra and Alysa. But as the year wore on, she'd begun to notice subtle differences. The way Alvyra pulls on her ear when she is speaking. The way she shifts from foot to foot when she is standing in line. The way she often defers to her sister.

*****

Tori McBride's first instinct is to wish she had locked her classroom door. She does not have time for an interruption, especially not this late in the day. She repeats this morning's Ash Wednesday prayer in her mind, "*Give me the grace to enter the space of these days with anticipation of our meeting. And, when I open my soul to your presence, let your loving-kindness flow over me and seep into my heart,*" then, willing herself to smile, the teacher warmly answers the student,.

"Why, yes dear. Of course, you can come in. What can I do for you?" Tori shuffles the papers on her desk, certain now that her grading rhythm is ruined, and she'll have to reread the paper she has just finished.

174

"I just wanted to return this book," Alvyra says, pulling it from her backpack and making her way to the bookshelves that stretch along the sidewall, beneath the bank of windows.

A few thoughts race through Tori McBride's mind as Alvyra reshelves the book. Why didn't she return it in class today, or why not wait until tomorrow? And where is her sister? They sometimes walked as if Velcroed together. But Tori admits she's seen less of that lately.

Alvyra stands as still as a stone, staring straight ahead at the shelves stuffed with well-worn copies by Baldwin and Morrison, Jason Reynolds and John Green, Steinbeck and Harper Lee, Tupac and Elizabeth Acevedo, Jacqueline Woodson and Matt de la Peña, Celeste Ng and Jane Austen.

Mrs. McBride has an insatiable love of literature, contemporary and classic, and a contagious excitement about "the human condition." Every week she adds a new title or two, first reading a few pages aloud, then asking the class to imagine what challenges the character will have to overcome by the end of the book. She always says there is no problem that can't be solved if you just look inside the pages of a book for the answer. For her that also means the Bible. But she dare not say that in this public school.

"Alvyra? Is something the matter, dear?"

Alvyra answers without turning around to face her teacher who is slowly rising from her desk. "No, just looking for that book you told us about today. You know, the one about those boys who, um, who liked each other."

"Oh dear, that one was gone before the third period!" Mrs. McBride laughs as she nears the spot where Alvyra stands so still and stiff, "All three copies are checked out already."

"Ok," Alvyra turns and begins walking toward the door.

Tori could have just let her go then so she could get on with the grading and the lesson planning before heading home for a glass of wine with her cat curled on her lap. It would be nice to watch a rerun of something soothing. She could have easily done that. But Tori McBride knew that you couldn't be a teacher for nearly forty years at the same school in the same classroom without being able to see the understory. Her sixth sense was never wrong. Never.

She leans in a bit. "Did I ever show you my signed copy of..." But before the teacher can finish her sentence, Alvyra Robertson bolts out the door.

Tori stands stunned in front of the bookshelves, wondering what just happened. She is too unsettled now to finish her grading or plan tomorrow's lessons. "I guess it's going to be another early day tomorrow," she tells herself, sighing, as she crosses the floor to her desk. She jams the graded papers in one folder, the remaining ungraded ones in another, turns off her computer, and heads out to the parking lot.

On the drive home, worry prickling her scalp, she runs through this late afternoon interaction with Alvyra. Alvyra who is seldom without her sister. Alvyra who has never once come by after school. Alvyra who's never been the least bit impolite, who would never turn and leave without so much as a thank you or a goodbye. Alvyra whose tastes run to the Bronte Sisters and Jane Austen now asking for a book like that.

Without even thinking, the puzzled teacher finds herself pulling into parking lot of the grocery store across from the freeway entrance. She always does this, it seems. A bad habit left over from her college days. Looking for something delicious to comfort herself when working out a problem. She'd planned a meager meal tonight to begin her Lenten fast. But now she finds herself filling her basket with lasagna and garlic bread and coffee ice cream. She tosses in a head of broccoli and a few apples as a counterbalance before getting in line.

"Did you find everything all right?" the teenage clerk asks in a monotone as he slides the purchases across his code reader. Tori is too distracted to answer, too focused on the two men at the self-check-out across the aisle, their backs to her, swaying together to the piped-in music booming from the store speakers. One man with his hand on the other's shoulder. Their quiet intimacy as they work together – one sliding the groceries over the glass scanner, the other loading the plastic bag.

She mindlessly inserts her credit card, staring across the aisle. Her sixth sense rearing again, her scalp tingling. There is something so familiar about this scene.

"It's beeping." the clerk says, tapping the machine, and bringing her back to reality. "And ma'am, you've got something gross on your forehead."

Give me grace, Tori prays as she drifts through the grocery's automatic door, toting a paper sack filled with guilty pleasure. *Something gross – for goodness' sake!*

"Mrs. McBride?" a deep rich baritone follows her out the door.

Tori looks at him quizzically, waiting for the recognition she is sure will come. Over the years she's taught so many children and their children, and now she is even starting to see a grandchild or two. It can be wonderful and unnerving at the same time. She takes in his kind, deep brown eyes. They look so familiar, but she can't quite place him.

"You have my daughters," he offered, touching her lightly on the arm. "They love your class."

She kept staring. Skin as dark as night. Crinkly, twinkly eyes. Who did he remind her of?

177

"We met at the art fair last month." Click. "Louis Robertson, Alysa and Alvyra's father." Click. Click.

"Oh, yes, of course, Mr. Robertson. Of course. Lovely girls. Just lovely."

"Here, let me help you with that," he says, reaching for her grocery bag. "I'll walk you to your car."

The conversation lasts as they walk twice around the jam-packed parking lot. "I can't believe I forgot where I parked!" she laughs nervously as they pass by the storefront the second time with Tori anxiously pressing the alert button on her key fob. Finally, with a sigh of relief, she hears the familiar wheep-wheep of her car's recognition.

"This is me," she says opening the passenger door for him to deposit her groceries, the ice cream surely turning to a slushy puddle by now, but he just keeps standing there talking. Sharing. His daughters. His ball-playing, college-bound son. His sweet wife. Such a family man. Such a godly man. She is grateful for this unexpected connection, feeling it is somehow pre- ordained. Or at least an interesting coincidence.

"I'm a worrier," he says finally, settling the groceries on the floor of the front seat and closing the car door. "A man worries about his baby girls, you know. Can't help it." He taps on the roof of the car, and sucks in a big gulp of air. "So, if you ever see…" his voice trails off then. "Just look out for my girls for me, okay?"

A car horn beeps as Tori slides into the front seat and starts the engine. As she puts her car in drive, he strolls away. There is something so familiar…

She watches as he opens the door to a car in the next row, its engine running, the red-headed driver reaching up to give him a high five as Mr. Robertson climbs in.

Click.

Focus in a flash. The two men who'd been swaying together in the grocery aisle are now driving out of the parking lot together, their car loaded with secrets.

*****

Tori can't sleep. She'd left the ungraded essays in their folder in her school bag when she got home, turned on her laptop, pulled up an old lesson plan from last year, and resigned herself to the fact that tomorrow was going to be one of those days where she just taught on autopilot, something she hated doing. No matter how many times she'd taught Toni Morrison's *Beloved*, she always approached it with new eyes. That's what kept her excited, kept her teaching alive. But tomorrow she'd focus on flashbacks and memories. Tomorrow she'd talk about ghosts.

Now she tosses and turns, replaying the scene after school with Alvyra, the encounter in the market with Mr. Robertson, and the disconcerting understanding that she'd witnessed something she hadn't meant to be privy to. Or maybe she had been directed there on purpose by something larger than herself. Lord, what is it? She pulls out the devotion book she read at night during Lent. Today, the first day, the passage came from Proverbs 20:12. She reads in her New International Version of the Bible, "Ears that hear and eyes that see— the Lord has made them both."

She plays out different explanations in her mind, working to connect the dots. Had Alvyra wanted to tell her something, but lost her nerve? Did she have questions she'd hoped she'd find answers for in the pages of that book? Or is Tori simply piecing together a story of her own, stitching together unrelated scenes into a narrative-driven by curiosity and conjecture? She shifts to snuggle the softly purring cat beside her, and offers up a silent prayer, asking for the grace to understand, and the wisdom to act in accordance with His will.

She drifts off to sleep with this song playing on her bedside radio.

> Open my eyes that I may see
> glimpses of truth thou hast for me.
> Place in my hands the wonderful key
> that shall unclasp and set me free.
> Silently now I wait for thee,
> ready, my God, thy will to see.
> Open my eyes, illumine me, Spirit divine!
>
> Open my ears that I may hear
> voices of truth thou sendest clear,
> and while the wave notes fall on my ear,
> ev'rything false will disappear.
> Silently now I wait for thee,
> ready, my God, thy will to see.
> Open my ears, illumine me, Spirit divine!

Louis Meets with CEO

Louis's Chief Executive Officer, Melvin, is a take it or leave it kind of guy. If you do your work well, he takes you on and supports you as best he can. If you're sloppy or undependable, he invites you to leave, "Right now." When he thinks about the relationship between his building supervisor, the man to whom his security, parking garage, landscapers, and janitorial team leaders report, Melvin wonders how this news will impact the workers in this building. Though he's not one to worry, Melvin does invite Louis in for a chat. He buzzes him on the Motorola pager all the top staff must have on them during work hours.

"Beep. Beep. Beep."

When his pager rings, Louis knows to answer right away. It could be an emergency and he's responsible for keeping things running smoothly in this eight-story business office building. He pulls the beeper from his waist and notes that the phone number is that of Melvin, so he heads over to the nearest wall phone and calls.

"Ring-ring-ring."

Melvin picks up the phone right away confident it is Louis.

"Yes! Is this you, Louis?"

"Yes. This is Louis. Something the matter?"

"I doubt it, but I'd like to see you. Can you pick up lunch from the café and meet me here during your lunchtime? It won't take long. And, put the lunches on my bill. They know I'll pay."

"Sure, Melvin. What would you like?" Louis scribbles the order in the little spiral pad he keeps with him for taking notes as he does his rounds in the building. He also wonders why his boss wants to see him during lunch. That usually is an honored time for all the staff. When you're off, you're off. When you're on, we want your full attention.

*****

Louis has come up the ladder here, having begun as a techie right out of college. He'd been brought on when the company first started installing electronic security systems and wanted someone who knew the language. Over time, though, the support staff and maintenance team seemed to be surprised that a man of his complexion holds such a position, they also seem to appreciate the fact that he respects them regardless of their job inside or outside, up high in the building or in the sub-basement. He greets them with a smile, not a grin. He listens but does not encourage long chats. He seems to recall their family members and sometimes asks about them. In other words, he has earned their trust, and most have been employed here for years.

Louis arrives on time for the meeting with his CEO, scans the office, and is pleased to see that it has been cleaned well by the staff. He whiffs a hint of lemon they use for polishing wood surfaces. Melvin, dressed in his trademark soft beige and grey Brooks Brother blazer, directs Louis to a small table in the corner where Melvin has set out a couple of bottles of iced tea he keeps in the compact wood-front fridge.

If a visitor didn't know it was a fridge, they'd think it was a cabinet. It blends well with other walnut paneling in the office. Once seated, Louis bows his head to say a silent blessing. When he looks up, he sees that Melvin's head still is bowed. Then he remembers, "Yeah, Melvin's a Christian, too."

Melvin is not just giving thanks for his food; he also is praying for direction on how to bring up the topic in a way that honors his co-worker as a Christian ought and falls within the realms of employer/employee relationships that will not be regarded as sexual harassment. It's tricky with these new laws!

"Need sugar?" he asks sliding a little bowl with saccharin and sugar packets.

"No, Man," Louis chuckles. "I don't drink my sugar. I eat it. That's why I added a couple of these sugar cookies to our lunch today."

"Right on! Well, let's eat and get right to the matter at hand. Someone came to me last week. The word is out that you're a homo and having a relationship with a guy who works here in the building."

"What do you mean, 'the word is out.' Out where?"

"I'm not sure how "out it is." But I did hear guys mention it in the lav the other day. Of course, I also have seen you. I'm not judging you for your sexual orientation. It's just that I'm surprised, even disappointed to learn that a married man is having an adulterous relationship. Male or female. Both seem wrong to me. But I've asked you here as your CEO, not your judge. Now that folks are talking, I was wondering how the rest of the managers will feel working with a man so well respected as you when they think you're in an adulterous relationship with someone who works right in this building. How do you guys do that?"

"Okay, Melvin. Let's get things straight. I'm bisexual. I am married and the father of three marvelous children. My wife, unfortunately, is just learning about my sexual orientation because I've been careful. I've not been hiding because I'm ashamed. I have been cautious because not many people understand bisexualism. I am as God made me. He's made me a father, so I want to protect my children from the scorn that I felt in your look when I walked in here today."

"It's not scorn, Louis. It's a puzzlement. Want to tell me about it. I don't understand bisexualism either."

"Simple, Melvin. It just means that I am drawn to both men and women with equal passion. I had just begun a relationship with Claude, my first and only homosexual partner, when I realized we both wanted children. You weren't here when I first came, but I'd regularly been having lunch with Lillian, who works on the fifth floor. She and I were among the first African Americans hired to work here in any position other than on the janitorial staff. We'd just graduated from college and often had lunch together. I learned that she also wanted to have children, but as a Christian, was not interested in doing so until she got married. So, we decided to get married. That was over fifteen years ago.

"Claude has been like a member of the family, for pretty much the same reason. He, too, was new to town living in one of the new apartment complexes built for those who'd arrived recently when all those good jobs opened here in town. He and I realized we'd been at the same college and started hanging out together. Soon, we were drawn together sexually but knew that few would understand such a relationship, so we've not made it public.

"Anyway, he was the best man at my wedding and now is an honorary Uncle to my children. Lillian has appreciated the role he has played as our go-to-babysitter, too. He now lives upstairs in the two-family home we bought last year. Claude even attends the same church as we do."

"You mean you all still claim to be Christian even though you are in a homosexual relationship?"

"Sure, why not? We both have given our hearts to the Lord and strive to live according to Christ's teachings at home and at work. You have a problem with that?"

"No. As a matter of fact, I've admired you since I came and was glad you were the man in charge of so many teams vital to the smooth running of this building. You have demonstrated Bible principles in the way you interact with the folks around here. But you're a homo!"

"No, I'm bisexual. That's different. What has that to do with you and my employment here?"

"Nothing, I guess. We're talking Bible here. Jesus taught us in Matthew 7:1 to *Do unto others as you would have them do unto you.*" The Golden Rule has always worked for me, so I'm going to apply it here. I'd want you to stay out of my personal business. So, I'm going to do that here. However, please know, if news of your lifestyle choices negatively impacts the work here, we'll have to "talk" again. Both you and I are responsible for the work we're hired to do. But, as a brother in the Lord, I'd have to add, "Think of your family." Your wife may have entered your marriage just to have children but now that you have them, think of them."

"I am. We haven't told them yet 'cause we're waiting till they finish their AP exams this week. That's why I'm surprised that you've heard something already. Claude hasn't said anything about anyone here saying anything to him."

"Oh, it's not new, Louis. I've suspected something since I saw you and Claude in the parking garage over the holidays. I knew you knew each other but was caught off-guard seeing you in that intimate position."

"So, why are you just speaking to me about it now? This isn't something that falls under sexual harassment, is it?"

"No Louis. I'm not harassing you because I'm not your judge. I'm not sure, but I felt led to say something today. When I was doing my devotions this morning, the Scripture in Luke 12:2-3, about what's done in secret will come to light seemed to suggest that I do something about what I was thinking."

"Well," Louis replies, crumbling the paper that wrapped his sandwich, and then wiping his mouth and hands with a napkin before stacking it on top of the waxed paper. "Thanks for the head's up. I imagine others will have noticed something between Claude and me but haven't had the guts to bring it up. I appreciate you for speaking to me.

"Just want you to know that Claude and I are planning to move in together. We just told Lillian about it just last Saturday. But we all are thinking of the family – Lillian and the kids. Being bisexual is a challenging way to live. How can I be me and not hurt my family if I'm honest about it?"

"That I can't answer for you, Louis. But know that whatever the Bible says should be your guide. My take is that "family comes first."

"But Claude is part of my family. I'd just like to feel confident that those who know will not scorn our relationship. It is love; you know."

"No, I don't know that kind of love. But I also know, I must not judge you for the choices you make. Please, Louis, pray about the way forward."

"I will. Let's start now. May I count on you to keep our family in your prayers as we deal with what we know is coming? Few are likely to be as gentle as you. Please know, that I appreciate your speaking up and letting me know that stuff is likely to hit the fan soon."

"Sure, my brother. And keep in mind that my job here is to see that the work gets done. If your work does not suffer when the word gets around, your job is secure as long as I'm here."

"Ding. Ding. Ding."

Melvin reaches over to turn it off.

"Oh! That's my timer. Lunch time's over. I'm meeting with the security guys to take care of an issue in the parking garage. Thanks for lunch."

"Sure, man. See you around. Take care. Thank you, Melvin."

The men head to the door and drop their lunch leavings in the half- filled trash can. Louis knows the janitorial worker on this floor will be by soon, to check and empty this receptacle. Once out of the office, Louis and Melvin turn and shake hands, then walk in opposite directions down the hall, both shaking their heads in wonder of what's to come. Both know the truth of what bell hooks is known to have said, "What we do is more important than what we say or what we say we believe." What are these men going to do?

Old Neighbor Becomes New Neighbor

What a delightful surprise, this time two years ago when she hears on the back porch of the house next door the voice of a childhood friend. Lillian Adams. Oh my, she thinks. She hadn't seen her since their families lived in the same trailer park near the Iroquois tribal lands along Lake Ontario! She knew the house next door had been on the market for some time. A flipper bought three of the houses on that circle when the families who owned them moved out west when land was going so cheap in Idaho.

One of the men traveled a lot and he convinced his other empty-nest neighbors to go along. "What the heck. We may as well get our retirement homes bought now while we can afford it." So, the three soon-to-retire couples who'd raised their children here, sold to a flipper and probably bought from one out in Idaho! The realtor who had bought the houses was finding it taking more time than he thought to upgrade them to sell at a price folks were willing to pay to live on this lovely cul-de-sac.

"Hey, Lillian!" Lillian twirls around, wondering who knows her here and would be calling her name on this new to her section of town.

Andrea Mekonnen had forgotten about the juniper pines that obscured Lillian's vision because she didn't know where to look to see the neighbor working in the flower gardens on the side of her wraparound porch. The house the Robertson's were buying is statelier, just a single portrait shaped two-story rectangle with an upstairs and downstairs flat. Andrea had only been living here a year, so she hadn't known the owners of the house the Robertsons bought.

Andrea decided to scramble up and go over to speak to her and the handsome man with her. He is just a couple inches taller than she, but heck, she's 5'8" herself. Andrea pulls aside the prickly juniper branch and steps through the arboreal property line. Yes, it's Lillian! She introduces her childhood friend to her husband, Louis and tells her about her three children. Andrea, too, has three, but they're spending the weekend with their paternal grandparents. The kids will meet when the Robertsons move in the first of June.

They don't talk much that day, but once the family moves in, the two ladies meet for coffee chats, usually sitting outside on their porches until the weather gets too cold. They often comment on the clear powder blue sky behind the powdery white clouds, wishing their problems would float away that quickly. It turns out that their children are about the same ages and attend the same high school, and even had some classes together. It eased the move to have "friends" already when the Robertsons moved in.

*****

Tuesday, after Mother's Day, I'm sitting on my patio, next door to the Robertsons. I'm noticing the just sprouting green shoots in my backyard vegetable garden. The recently planted flowering annuals sway above the stone pots seated at the corner of the patio. The soft crisp breeze whistles through the junipers.

I'm winding down from a stressed day of work, sipping a glass of fresh ginger tea with a little brown sugar Truvia sweetener. I hear the doorbell and wonder who it could be at this time on a Tuesday evening. Turning towards my handsome French doors, I pull one open, step inside, straight ahead I see a silhouette outside the front door. I walk the long hallway enjoying the beautiful oil paintings that depict my heritage land, Ethiopia. I look through the peephole before opening the door. What a sweet surprise, my sister-friend coming to see me. But her beautiful smile of many years, now looks twisted. Eyes puffy and darkness around her eyes. Such a sad look.

Lillian steps into the house. I shut the door and she falls into my arms. I hug her tight, as she releases a flood of tears. Asking no questions, I walk her to the patio and get her settled in a lawn chair then go inside for tissues, and a glass of tea.

Although I love to talk, as a counselor and life coach I have learned to listen more, than speak. This helps me not respond too quickly. Thus, patiently I wait to hear her voice. Eventually she speaks in a raspy tone.

"I can't believe he's sexually engaged with a man, a queer. I've been married to this man for almost 20 years. We've slept in the same bed for all these years and just recently he tells me his best friend, a guy he met at work who went to the same college, is his lover! I've never felt this way before!"

"Lillian what way do you feel, and what is a queer? Is that another term for homosexual?"

"Yeah, I think it is. I feel like I could strangle him for living and leading me through a lie for these many years. I know we never said we loved each other, but it hurts to hear him say he loves Claude and wants to move upstairs and live with him. What the world! Who says' craziness like this? As for the queer, I guess it means a person that engages in same sex. Maybe it means they feel liberated. "I really can't focus my thoughts on this explosion in my life. I've seen things blown up in the movies and that's how it feels; my life has been hit. Louis dropped a bomb and I'm broken into pieces."

"Lillian, I am sad for you, as I've never seen you upset like this. Typically, you are a mild-mannered person, and see the best in people. It is unfortunate that this bomb, as you say, has been dropped on your house. As your friend, I'm here for you and glad that you came over. I know this situation is fresh and I don't want to press you to share too much, but I don't want you to leave here the way you came in the door. Just sit and relax and I'll wait."

To change the subject, I redirect her attention to her song last week at church. "It was a blessing to hear you singing at church last week, Lillian. I pray that the lyrics of "Just a Closer Walk with Thee" will speak to your heart as they did to mine."

190

Lillian looks at me with sad eyes and questioning words, then nods. "Yes, the verse, 'I am weak, but Thou art strong, Jesus keep me from all wrong' has been my prayer this week. So far that's working. I've been able to talk with Louis, most days, and have received wise counsel from my sister and my department chair, Virginia. In fact, she's loaning us her family cottage in Letchworth State Park. That's where Louis and I have decided to have a family meeting to tell our kids about their dad's sexuality and his plan to move upstairs with Claude.

"Andrea, I didn't think I would have been able to sing last week, but Brother Jesse had me warm up first and then the choir sang, "O Happy Day!" as our warm-up song. It wasn't a happy day for me, but the song redirected my attention to the reason for our gathering. to worship and celebrate the life and gift of Jesus Christ. Of course, Pastor's sermon that we should be strong and courageous because God is with us has been feeding me ever since. But, alas, moments arise like today when all that strength seems to drain right out of my feet."

"You betcha, Sister. We always talk about how God never leaves nor forsakes us. He will be with you through every melodic note of this family decision as He got you through that song last week. As I said, what a blessing."

"Louis' news hit me, but Andrea. But you are right, I must process this situation. I need peace of mind. But my thoughts keep going to what will the children say and feel and, as much as I love our Beth-El congregation, I have no idea how they will treat us once this news gets out. This church is my family. Do you think they will put us out?"

"Lillian, that does not make sense. The leadership is always teaching and preaching on love and forgiveness. They will align with that. Lillian let's stop right here and let me pray.

"Father God, bless your daughter Lillian. Protect her mind and give her peace that surpasses her understanding. Remind her of Your love and calm her troubled heart. Help her to see that although she feels a bomb has been dropped on her, You are able to mend and help her pull the pieces back together. Help her not worry and stumble but give her concerns over to You. Give her strength and clarity of mind through this journey. In Jesus' Name, Amen."

"Thank you Andrea, for that prayer. I feel a bit of release. A little less tense."

"Lillian, I want to remind you of that passage from Philippians that our moms made us memorize when we were cutting up so much in middle school. You know, Philippians 4:7."

Lillian nods, and we repeat that verse together, "'And the peace of God, which surpasses all understanding will guard your hearts and your minds in Christ Jesus.' How the Word of the Lord works when we let it."

"Yes, Andrea, I believe that scripture and will keep it in my mind. I will meditate on it as I prepare for whatever is coming next. I'm feeling a bit energized and know with God I will sing my way through the next few days in a "melodic" tone as you say."

Consulting with Marriage Counselor

What a day. What a day. What a day! They have gone, but I have much to reflect on. It's not often that my clients come with a complex problem like this.

The Robertsons arrive after a day of work, and both look it. I imagine the stress of their family responses to Louis' announcement is taking its toll on their physical and emotional strength as well. I invite them to be seated side by side in lightly upholstered curvy slant back chairs with armrests. I set the chairs at an angle so couples can see each other if they wish but are not facing each other if they need another view as they talk, listen, and respond. This semi-circle arrangement, with my chair with them not behind the desk, gives a sense of collaboration that seems to help my clients relax. In the corner of the room, is a peppermint incense candle burning and releasing an aroma that calms the body and sharpens the mind.

Lillian Robertson made the conjoint appointment because they both want to understand the circumstances that have led to this time in his life and their marriage. In order to counsel effectively, I must find out what we have going on here concerning Louis' claim of, "bisexuality." What does he mean when he says, "I'm bisexual"? How strong are those feelings, and how does his acting on that drive compare with loving his wife? In this setting, it's going to be a triple challenge because the couple is Christian, and each wants to understand the psychology of bisexuals as well as Biblical guidance regarding sexual practices. Lord, help me!

*****

"Come in, come in. Welcome, Mr. and Mrs. Robertson. I am Dr. Manguel and am pleased to have this opportunity to share with you my understanding of your case. You see my credentials on the wall and know that I'm a licensed psychoanalyst who also has training in our local seminary. The Lord has helped me to combine psychology and theology in my practice as a marriage counselor. A psychoanalyst seeks to understand ways that prior experiences influence current behavior. And, of course, theology looks at the relationship of the client's circumstances in light of a Holy God who has revealed Himself in the Judo-Christian Scriptures."

Louis waits until his wife is seated, then sits in the chair next to her. When both are seated, I hand them each a bottle of water. She sets hers on the side table with the purse from which she's extracted a small spiral notebook and pen. For some reason, having something to do with their hands is another way that clients seem to relax as they begin to share some of the intimate issues that motivated their contacting me for professional reasons.

After chit-chatting for a minute or two about their day, their children, and the weather, we get right down to business. The following is a video recording of that session.

*****

"Louis, I understand that the reason for coming is that you have made a declaration that you are bisexual, and you want to express this God-given reality with others. Lillian made the appointment to try and understand what is going on and what can be done about it in light of your marriage. While these are two separate issues, the fact that they are occurring in one man and one family, we must address them one at a time, and then the three together."

Louis nods and Lillian's face wrinkles in confusion, as though I'd forgotten her reason for coming. I look directly at her,

"And you, Lillian, want to talk about how the marriage can remain viable with this new revelation. Today we're looking to provide an understanding of what marriage is, and how the notion of fidelity enters into this. After all, fidelity represents the exclusivity of marriage consisting of a couple."

Now, the wrinkles fade as she nods, recognizing that this will not be two men against one woman. "We three are here to gain insight and understanding."

"Louis, I am glad that you sought out treatment concerning this issue about your sexuality as being bisexual. We need to talk about how you understand that and what are the ramifications of this for your relationship with Lillian."

"Yes, I want to be here and receive some professional Christian counseling on this. I just want Lillian to see that God has made me this way and I know He will still bless our marriage because of that. I know that I can still love Lillian as my wife if she will only understand my quest for authenticity!"

Lillian, speaking to me while looking at Louis, "We really need to be here because I don't think that God has made Louis bisexual and caused him to act in ways that threaten our marriage. He wants to do things that are just inconceivable to me as his wife. God wants us to glory Him in our marriage not destroy it by what he wants to do! Does not the Bible say, "the marital bed shall be undefiled" That's in Hebrews 13:4, right? I would not want to be with him sexually after he had been with a man!." Lillian weeps and wipes as I hand her the box of tissues.

I wait until she regains some composure and then address them both but focus first on Louis's issue. "It is important that you present very clearly what you each want concerning being together as husband and wife. So, with that in mind, I would like to answer your questions imbedded in the statement, "God made me this way," as it relates to the Biblical purpose for marriage and also what this acknowledgment of yours, Louis, is all about. In this, I will cite appropriate scriptures to help see if we can discern God's view of this. Lillian, your bringing up the Hebrews 13:4 verse is a good place to start."

Lillian "Good, I would really like that."

Louis, speaking directly to me, "I know that this is important, and I want to be educated Biblically; but please understand my plight. I feel there is nothing I can do about what I feel, and it is a horrible thought that my sexuality could end our relationship!"

"Yes, I will make sure that we will spend ample time going over this in our later sessions. Today, I would like to talk about the two areas I shared with both of you just now. Just listen and reflect. We can interact about this at the end of our session tonight and certainly more next week. I now offer Hebrews 10:24-25 as our Biblical invitation for this session tonight. It says, 'Let us hold fast our confession of our hope without wavering for He who promised is faithful; and let us consider how to stimulate one another to love and good deeds.'

"First of all, Louis. I have some important questions for you to think about concerning the nature of your bisexuality. You can answer these when we have our discussions at the end of the session. Designations like homo, hetero, and bi, sexuality are usually defined by overt behaviors. That is, you seek out or are with the other because you feel a strong enough attraction to actually act that out in real life.

This is more than just playing a scenario in your own mind. If you had the chance, you would definitely act out on it. Now you may say, "What if the person is too shy or too afraid to actually approach a person and ask to become sexual with him?" This is important and has to be taken into consideration, but if this is not the case, as you have stated, then the lack of any completion in behavior needs to be explained.

"This leads us to the more "internal" or attitudinal aspects of this. What kind of fantasies do you have about being sexual with men; are they of the same kind as with women? How are they different? Is the arousal the same with both men and women? Do you climax in the same way with both? Do you dream about both kinds of partners, if so, is either one an ascendant? This means to the different genders are equal as partners in the dreams.

"Finally, is your sense of emotional satisfaction the same when your actions are completed; do you think and feel that your desires have been fulfilled? This will help us to understand more closely what, "motivates" you may have from moving into the stage of acting out these desires."

I pause a moment to give both husband and wife time to consider what is being asked. Though I'm addressing Louis, I make clear that the issue of sexuality is one experienced by any gender.

"By making these issues clearer we will be able to posit some causality concerning your experiences of your own parenting, traumatic sexual experience, and early childhood encounters and relationships that shaped your sense of self-esteem or produced feelings of self-denegation. I think it needs to be clear to you, Louis, that studies concerning the biological, physiological causes for homosexuality are still inconclusive. As a psychoanalyst, and as a marriage counselor, I look at the relational dynamics first of all in the etiology of any sexual identity formation."

*****

I hit the pause on the tape. I have to think about these issues myself. What behaviors and experiences help people decide their sexual orientation. If it is automatic, why are there so many differences? If it is natural, why are there so many theological teachings that decry differences? Lord, help me. I must be prepared when this couple comes back next week. I understand the psychology of sex. I know the Bible. Help me, Jesus, to pull the two together in ways that honor You and teaching about marriage. That's what I am, a marriage counselor guided by Biblical principles. I start the tape again.

*****

"Now Louis, I know that you are feeling some sort of sexual desires for men as well as for women and that you do not report that your desires for Lillian have diminished whatsoever! Therefore, these feelings, desires and imaginations of bisexuality have provoked in you the conclusion that this is now a major part of your identity and therefore your life; for as the proverb in chapter 23, verse 7 says, 'As a man thinks in his heart, so he shall be.'

"This brings me to the second subject that I want to share with both of you this evening. That is the biblical view of bisexuality as it pertains to Christian marriage. In what ways is it not compatible with what the Word of God states what marriage is in itself and what does it say about our relationship with Jesus the Christ?

"Genesis 2:24-25 says this: '*For this reason, a man shall leave mother and father and cleave to his wife and the two become one flesh. And they were both naked and were unashamed.*'

198

"This is the original intent of marriage; its original description. It speaks of mutuality, complementarity, and one flesh relativeness as its expression to the rest of creation. The experience of closeness, intimacy, and oneness that this kind of commitment in marriage makes possible is to be the norm of the relationship. The statement found in verse 25 about being naked and not being ashamed speaks to why this kind of intimacy, a freedom to be naked together in every way, here creates the depth of oneness in the total body, emotional, the equitable union that is signified by the shamelessness of mutual orgasm on the physical plane. It is the body's contribution of a union of spirits as persons created in the image of God!"

Lillian begins to nod her head as though she's glad we're talking about marriage fidelity.

"We will now turn to Paul's letter to the Ephesians chapter 5 verses 31-32. It first cites the declaration found in Genesis 2:24. It is speaking to the leaving, cleaving and one flesh relationship as described in the garden of Eden. Verse 32 goes on: '*This mystery is great. But I am speaking in reference to Christ and the church*' Paul is saying the aspects of the marital relationship such as, mutuality, complementarity, intimacy, and oneness are applicable to the relationship that Jesus has with the church.

"The church is the bride of Christ. In Ephesians, the apostle describes the many-faceted union that Christ has with His bride. In verses 28 and 29 Paul says, "'*So husbands ought also to love their own wives as their own bodies. He who loves his own wife loves himself; for no one ever hated his own flesh, but nourishes and cherishes it, just as Christ does the church*.' And just so you both know, Lillian and Louis, Wives are to love their husbands also as you'll see in Titus 2:4.

"Scripture puts an immense value on marriage as being between a man and a woman. In saying this, Scripture also acclaims that the expression of a husband/wife relationship is to be the only one that can be called a marriage. Again, not having this, creating some other kind of constellation or caricature of the husband/wife twosome is to be in violation of Hebrews 13:4; the marital bed would be defiled. It would not be pleasing to God because it would be made up of behaviors such as that which could be considered as fornication, and or adultery. Therefore, the marriage would stand under God's judgment. The writer to the Hebrews does not pull his punches!"

Louis grimaces. The battle raging in his face. It's as though question marks are streaming from his eyes into the air between us. "How can this be? If God created me male and female, why is expressing this causing so many problems for my marriage?" "This may feel hurtful to you Louis, and we will talk about this openly soon. All that I have just said can mean a lot of things. But one thing that it does is dismiss the position of bisexuality as a biblical/theological understanding appropriate for marriage."

Louis, as if speaking to the air, "Wow, there is a lot here to digest; a lot for me to take in. I am glad that Lillian decided to take notes. I do have one question for you, Doc. Your comments on this Biblical understanding on marriage leaves little wiggle room for me to be able to have any bisexual relationships. Is there not any grace here for a man such as me?"

"There is, Louis, though they are in some ways that we have not discussed here tonight. God understands your sincerity and your love for Lillian. We have much to discuss in this vein. Your homework is to go home and talk together about anything concerning what you have heard today. See you both next week."

Tape stops. I write my name, "Dr. Manguel" and the date in the subject line for the MP4 tape, then write a few notes in my journal to prep me for the meeting with this couple next week. On the one hand, I am excited to see how this will unfold, but more am delighted that my confidence in the Lord will help me counsel this couple with confidence.

Time is Taking Its Toll

This evening in the second week since Louis made his revelation, Claude is out back grilling again, He hardly notices that Lillian has silently pulled into the driveway.

*****

Usually, it would startle me that I do not immediately sense her arrival, but I'm on high alert today. What I don't like about this entrance to the property that Louis and I had paved last May is the silent and sudden approach of people in the driveway. Between the quiet hum of her green Honda Civic hatchback and the carefully cleaned and smooth asphalt in the driveway – or the Mekonnen's lawn mower next door buzzing its way through a spring day – I wouldn't hear it. A silent approach, perfect for an unwelcome arrival.

Maybe it's because I'm used to hearing the car approaching. The sound of the gravel under the weight of the car. The skip in my chest of when it would be coming. He could be coming. I remember when Daddy would come home because I always seemed to know. So did Mother. I learned to stay off the main road because I never knew when the next explosion would come. Daddy's explosions usually came at Mother, but sometimes I was in the line of fire. I was too quiet, not confident enough. I heard things he'd say to her.

"You don't push him hard enough; he won't be man enough for the real world with your coddling." What's "man enough"?

Lillian's pulling up the driveway and I'm certain she's sensing this is not a normal family friend arrangement. How could it be?

I learned the art of the cookout from Mother, and it feels safe here. Solid. Masculine. Unbothered by the approaching car. Lillian's door shutting like the sounds of my Dad talking about my gender that I'd just heard inside my mind.

It's a delicate balancing act, and I marvel at how folks always said that. But who is doing the balancing? What is lying in the balance? Jangling your keys while talking on the phone. The jangling keys are creating symphony – in your pocket and in my mind. A diversion. Today the balancing act is happening in my left pocket, while my right hand turns the blood-red cuts and I peer over the cover of the smoker. Cutting myself is a way I've dealt with stress for far too long. This living arrangement is not a long-term solution. That's why, a couple of weeks ago, I insisted to Louis, "Something has to give." I can move on.

*****

"She has to know. We have to tell Lillian." Louis doesn't respond. He is now cleaning off the glass table we have out here in our spacious backyard that backs up to a treed space between ours and the property on the next cul-de-sac. Louis doesn't take the bait or appear to hear my offer to leave. Leave my home, where I've lived with Lillian and Louis, albeit upstairs for the past couple of years. As Uncle Claude to the children.

"It's my family and this will break them," Louis says as he wipes back and forth, exchanging the damp paper towel between his hands to leave no surface or corner untouched. We'd bought this patio deck set together before we'd moved into our new home.. Lillian had trusted me to pick it out.

"Louis, they are my family, too. I know it will break them, but at least we'll be honest."

202

"I can't do this to Lillian or my children."

"God is watching us, Louis," I say, now slowly flipping the burgers. After my Mother finally left my Daddy, we focused on meal rituals.

Cleaning rituals. Church rituals. Family rituals.

Last fall, I had told Louis that this couldn't continue. That we could just be friends. In a way, back in college, I had done this with Andrew, too. I can break away now and make my peace with God later.

I avoided Louis for three weeks after that declaration that things had to change. Muttered hellos, but still took the teens for our monthly luncheon last month. Consented to help the girls work on wood crafted jewelry for the GEMS event in July. Attended Lou Jr.'s last game but danced around any actual discussion. Hugged Lillian. Yet kept distant.

I managed to avoid Louis most days, appearing to be the neighbor and family friend upstairs, simply hiding that there is anything wrong. Our story is unfolding and I'm telling it here with the grill on. The story is playing out and I've lived it before. I've got to talk to Pastor Jackson before I fall apart.

I'm telling the story now, even as I notice the tongs trembling in what I thought was a firm fist.

*****

The adults thought it would be a good idea to hold off telling the teens about their dad's sexual orientation because it would give Louis, Lillian and Claude time to adjust to the planned changes in household arrangements. True, Louis called Rev. Zusman after he'd heard his sermonette on the radio, Claude has met with the pastor, and Lillian has been talking with her sister, Glendella.

203

But, alas, holding in the secret from the children is taking its toll on them all.

While they are trying to maintain the guise that everything is normal, it isn't. Louis said things would not change if he moved upstairs to live with Claude, his longtime lover. Lillian can't really imagine things looking much different to the neighbors or their church family. The three would be living in the same house, going and coming as usual. The three have been members of the same congregation for nearly two decades. What's the difference now?

Teen Neighbors Talk in Text

Thursday, the twins' have their AP exam, and apparently, Alysa is distracted. She's left her friend, Sean's cell phone on the counter in the kitchen. He had forgotten it last night when he'd come to do a crash review for their exam today. Lillian, who's working from home today, turns over the phone when she sees it vibrating along the slippery ceramic tile. What? Oh no! Lillian can't resist and fingers up the screen and reads down the message between a teen who lives across the street and a Playstation 4 buddy. Now she knows why Alysa probably left the phone there in disgust.

The two students, Sean and John, while playing video games in a PS4 party, chat about what they've observed. Sean, who just got turned on the Playstation 4, lives across the street in the house, a mirror image of the Robertson two-story flat, except for the landscaping.

****** `

*Sean starts PS4 party. *John joins the party*

John: Sean bro you know LJ?

Sean: Naw ion know him.

John: The n... on the baseball team bro?

Sean: Oh yeah the dude who just got a scholarship?

John: yeah bro but listen his pops is gay bro

Sean: whaaaat you fr?

John: istg bro n apparently he been cheating on his wife for a lon
g a.. time w they upstairs neighbor

Sean: Claude? He work w my momma

John: Yes bro he gay too

Sean: How you know bro?

John: My moms go to they church i heard her talking abt it
 to her friend or w.e

Sean: d... bro thats messed up ik she sick John: My moms?

Sean: No n... LJ moms

John: oh yeah thats crazy but hop on 2k bro

Sean: Alr bet

Oh, God, Lillian cries, I must be the only one who's been blind all this time. Why now? Why is all this coming out now? Looking back at the teens' conversation on the phone, Lillian is surprised at how much she understands the text talk. She did have to look up some of the expressions in the online Urban Slang page. While she knows her kids know Standard English and use it at school, she's pretty sure they talk like this to their buds, too. Maybe not with the profanity she sees in this message, but teen talk is teen talk.

And the word is out. Out in the street and now out on the web. She'd been raised with the Scripture, *"What's done in the dark will come out in the light!"* but never knew how it would feel to be the outed till now. The thing is, she's not the one who is gay! But, because the two became one, now three, she's part of the mess.

Thankfully, her sister Glendella, is coming by for lunch, but for now, Lillian's got to get back to work. First, however, she strips the bed in the master bedroom. Louis has been sleeping at home all week, but Lillian can't abide the thought of continuing this habit until things are resolved. This weekend, they've got to talk to the kids. She's tired of holding everything in at home when she's learning so much is already out there.

*****

"Whew!" Alvyra exhales coming out of the test room where the sophomores have just completed their World History Advance Placement Exam. She and Alysa agreed to head straight home so they could go over their answers together. They didn't want anyone else to know if they'd misinterpreted any of the writing prompts. It wasn't cold this morning and it's nice and sunny this afternoon, so they've decided to walk. They know Mom is home working; they know she'll probably have a snack ready, so they don't have to stop by the local ice cream parlor where most of the kids will be gathering to unwind. Sometimes, you just need to be with family. Today, having a sister who understands is what Alvyra needs right now.

"Hey, Sis," Alysa calls across the exiting teens who are as eager to get out of the room as she. "Yeah, I'm ready. Gotta get my bookbag out of the locker. See you in a sec." When she gets outside, she is aghast. When Alysa reached in her backpack to pull out her cellphone, she remembers she'd left it at home. Thank the Lord, she'd been able to set what she'd seen aside for a couple of hours, but now it's flowing back. What's that with Dad and Uncle Claude?

"Alvyra. You been on Playstation4 recently?"

"No, what's up?"

"There's word out there about somebody with our Dad's name and some guy who is gay."

207

"Ah, you know Louis is a common name. Couldn't be our Dad. Come on. Let's do a brisk walk. We gotta stay in shape for basketball. You know we're to meet in the park next Tuesday for the GEMS meeting. Ms. Delphi's friend's gonna have us run through some moves. Sorta like a basketball camp with no scouts." the twin explains, trying to get her sister's mind on something more positive. Alvyra, too, has been a little concerned about the rumblings she's been hearing, too. That's why she'd stopped by her English teacher's classroom after school, that day.

Reveal at Letchworth

How pleasantly surprised the Robertsons are to coast into the driveway of the stately home Virginia, Mom's department chair is letting them use for the weekend. The teens, of course, are oblivious to the core reason for this bonus, so they just jump out and run around the property. After all, they've been on the road for three hours and are just about sick of being together even in their spacious SUV.

One thing the Robertsons have done for family car trips since the kids were young is to allow each family member to pick a CD, in the earlier days, then, in more recent years, bring along their own 6-8 songs playlist. Whichever parent is in the passenger seat takes care of the music. As they listen to the songs, family members periodically make comments about the lyrics, rhythms, or melodies they hadn't noticed before. They usually giggle when Dad pulls out a Motown CD or playlist because the Temptations were his grandmother's favorite secular quartet. When Louis was young, he often danced to the tunes when Grampa was out.

Louis' favorite CD, *The Temptations Greatest Hits* is the one he brought today. Mom brought one of her favorite CDs by the Brooklyn Tabernacle Choir. and the teens' playlists run the gamut from Mali Music to the Walls Group to Koryn Hawthorne - Unstoppable ft. Lecrae.

The family generally starts with the choice of one of the children, then a parent, child, parent, and end with one by child number three. The order of child choices varies from trip to trip, but the alternating pattern generally remains the same. The last song on the teen's playlist, Isaac Caree singing "Her," has just finished as Dad brakes on the smooth tiny gravel driveway in front of the spacious grey stone house on the broad green treed lot.

They know that each family member must take in their own luggage, so after a rousing run around the property, the teens scamper back to the rear of the SUV with the backend raised so they can get out their own belongings. Mom has the keys and is just unlocking the front door, She, too, is somewhat overwhelmed by the setting they'll have this weekend.

The house itself is a traditional two-story home that Lillian learned from Virginia, had been the family homestead. Over the years, the adjoining lots had been sold off and to date, only a couple had been purchased by downstaters who used them for weekend retreats. The two lots on either side of Virginia's family home have pre-fabs. This home where the Robertsons are staying had been custom built when Virginia's great grandparents "struck it rich" after World War II!

When Lillian, ever one to check out things ahead of time, asked Virginia for the address, Lillian looked up the place on the VRBO website. There she found this description, "Located inside Letchworth State Park, this two-story, four-bedroom house sits on the main park road directly across from Inspiration Point, one of Letchworth's most magnificent overlooks.

"The Stone House is beautifully furnished and features a living room with fireplace and stereo system, dining room, sunroom, patio, fully appointed kitchen, and two and a half bathrooms. This house is perfect for family retreats and weekend getaways."

What a blessing to have a generous department chair like Virginia; Lillian breathes in a word of thanks. Lord, you sure are taking care of this matter for us. Not just because we're getting a weekend free here at the Grand Canyon of the East, but because we're having the opportunity to get away as a family, to tell and hopefully, prepare the kids for the changes our family is certain to face. We'll surely need this space and time to react in private before the teens face the public, at home, at school, at work, at play, and at church. You know, of all these places, I am most curious about the response of the church family.

She wonders how she, herself, would respond if she learned the same facts about someone in their congregation. She just didn't know. Perhaps, this weekend, she'll learn more about her own thinking.

Louis, too, is overwhelmed with the place! He did not really believe the cottage would be this nice and the grounds this open, but at this point in his life, anything he can do to ease the time for his wife, he's willing to do. It has been tough, these past three weeks not spending as much time with Claude as they usually do. The children haven't mentioned it because they've been otherwise occupied with the end of the school year activities, Louis's excitement about the scout talking to him personally at baseball camp, and the girl's plans for the GEMS event for the fourth of July.

Delphi, whose husband Malcolm had often joined Louis and Claude on men's days out, is now widowed and is so deeply invested in her GEMS events that she gets started early on everything! Her rule of thumb is to plan in time to be able to replan if necessary. Louis also thinks Lillian has told Delphi about him and Claude because he sensed a different look from her when he picked the girls up last week.

It was raining that day, so rather than having them walk home, even with the umbrellas they'd taken, Lillian gave him the look when it was about 7:45. The GEMS meetings ended at 8 pm.

"Well?" her eyes asked then rolled over to the clock.

"Yes, dear! I'll pick them up. I was watching the clock and planning to leave right when the commercial started. You know they almost always have several long ones the last fifteen minutes of any of the popular news shows."

"Okay. Louie. Just a couple more days and we can get this off our chests. Maybe tonight we can go through a couple more of those questions on the marriage counselors' list. Why pay a professional, if, with prayer, we can work this out ourselves? I must confess, that I've been surprised and pleased that you've put off moving up with Claude until we tell the kids. How's he taking it? Really?"

"Well," says Louis as he pats his pocket to confirm his car keys are there, "We're making it. Let's talk about this later. I've got to leave now to get a place to park close to the door where the girls will be exiting the building."

"Sure, Louis. We can talk about this when you get home. Tell the girls, I'll have a snack ready for them. Delphi just serves drinks at the meetings but will send home a snack pack for anyone who chooses to take one. This is just in case one or more of the girls may not have had dinner. Delphi is a health nut, and fresh healthy food is expensive. So, she only budgets for drinks. From what she says, not many of the girls have indicated that they arrive for their 6:30 meetings without having had dinner."

"Bye, Babe. See you in a few." Louis clicks his heels and gives her a smirk and a salute. This gesture is just one of the many fun things they smile about when he lets her know he's doing what she has asked, but that he would have done it anyway.

*****

Now, here in Letchworth, sitting on the front porch in the slant back wooden chairs, Louis looks around the place. Giant trees that escaped the early logging industry in this part of the state shade the front, but don't block the view. He can't see the waterfalls but are sure the family will be able to hear them intermingled with the whisps of the winds through the leaves and the activity of birds nested nearby. He hears the "cheep-cheep, chirp chirping, cheep-cheep, chirp chirping." circling in the trees overhead. Being mid-May in upstate, few of the local birds have yet become parents of newly hatched eggs.

As expected, when the teens learned they'd be coming, they started doing online searches to discover what they would probably see and hear this time of year. Among the birds, Lou Jr. mentioned in the car coming up, were the common merganser, turkey vulture, ruffed grouse, wild turkey, pileated woodpecker, red-breasted nuthatch, and dark-eyed junco. Other than the turkey and the woodpecker, these are new species to Louis. He hopes to view some of them and expand his knowledge of the aviary residents in this part of the state.

"Dad," Lou Jr. calls. "You know there's a barbeque grill outback. It's gas, so we can heat it up and prep for dinner. How 'bout you and me cook tonight. I know Mom packed some hotdogs and brought a Tupperware bowl of macaroni salad. Let's not make her cook tonight. She looks a little pooped. She okay?"

"Good idea, son," Dad responds, not answering the question, and redirecting Lou Jr's attention. "You go get things turned on out there. I'll check with Mom. She's probably through giving the house an inspection. In fact, she said she is going to take pictures with her cellphone camera to help us make sure we leave everything in place before we return home. She's some kind of stickler for details. But it is true this is her department chair's family home and Mom wants to make sure all is well when we leave."

"Yeah, I know my mom. See you out back in a few," calls Lou Jr. as he quick steps around the house to the backyard, "Hey, Girls. Dad and I are gonna turn on the barbeque grill and fix some dogs. You two gonna go in and help Mom get the other stuff out of the cooler and into the fridge? She can use your help. This is her vacation weekend, too."

"Yes, Big Brother!" Alvyra replies with an attitude. "We're on our way."

"And we don't have to be told," Alysa adds. "You're not the boss of us, you know!" she says with equal attitude. The twins chuckle and each hop up the steps on one leg, holding on to the ancient wooden stair rail that probably came in handy as Virginia's family members aged. Yes, they let the door slam when they went in. And, yes, Lillian called them on it. All in a typical Robertson family weekend!

*****

That evening, after clearing up the dishes from the hot dog dinner, Louis gathers the family in the front room. Though it is late May, it's still rather cool up in the mountains, so he decides to light the logs already lying in the fireplace. There are plenty more in a pile by the backdoor probably from when Virginia's family was here last weekend. Surrounded by shiny maple wall paneling reflecting the flickering flames of the not yet settled fire, the teens pull their chairs closer and await the start of the Family Meeting,

Each has different thoughts about what the topic will be, but all are eager to get back outside to watch the stars in the now clear night sky. The teens decide to be cooperative and do what they can to speed along the meeting.

"Well, kids, "Dad begins, "Let's open with a prayer of thanksgiving. We arrived here safely, have had a tasty meal and from what you say, you all believe you earned at least threes' on the APs you've taken these past couple of weeks. Hey, with the positive news from the baseball scout from State College that may mean a scholarship for Lou Jr. and this gift from Lillian's boss loaning us this lovely cottage for a weekend retreat, we have loads to be thankful for.

"Let's go round the circle and do sentence prayers. Mom, you start, then you, Alvyra, then Lou, Alysa, and then I'll close. Mom, how 'bout you start with a song. That always gets us on track for praying together." Lillian doesn't really feel like it, but wants to appear cooperative, so she starts a family favorite,

> Jesus loves me, this I know,
> for the Bible tells me so.
> Little ones to Him belong;
> they are weak, but He is strong.

The sisters join in harmonizing, and, on the chorus, they start bobbing their fists like nodding heads. Ms. Delphi had taught the girls in the GEMS club that the bobbing fist is an American Sign Language symbol for yes. And touching the middle finger of your dominant hand to the center of your non-dominant palm is the symbol for Jesus Christ, our Savior, reminding us that because He loves us, He allowed himself to be crucified. He hung on the cross with nails that pierced through His Hand.

Yes, Jesus loves me! The Bible tells me so.

They all sway and join the bobbing, singing, and signing, smiling at the memories of the family learning these signs the first year the girls were in the club. Now, they all are five years older and are more familiar with the Bible, but for some reason, all are feeling "little" and glad to be in the circle with their family. Too bad, the teens think, Uncle Claude's not here. He, too, loves to sign this song!

The song ends. They look at Louis, then follow his lead and bow their heads. Quiet. A crackle and a shutter as burning wood shifts in the fireplace. Quiet. Then, Lillian remembers she's to begin. She prays her sentence of thanks. They each do the same. Louis concludes and invites them to repeat the Lord's Prayer. Dad is slow to open his eyes and when he does, all eyes are on him. "So, Dad, what's up?" Lou Jr. leads. The girls nod and look at the clock above the fireplace mantle. They'd really like to get out before the clouds come in and hide the sky.

"Well, Mom and I wanted to be in a neutral place when we tell you…" The kids all sit up!

"Tell us what?" the girls lean forward. They've all had friends whose parents announced they are divorcing and that's the first thought that comes to all three!

"Tell you that I am bisexual and am coming out of the closet, so to speak, and plan to move upstairs to live more openly with Uncle Claude."

Silence.

Louis' eyes pan the circle to see how they're taking the news. Then Lou asks, "Is that all?"

"Is that all?" Lillian exclaims. "Isn't that enough?"

"Sure, Mom, but it's no surprise. I've figured for a couple of years that the relationship between Dad and Uncle Claude is special. But, because he's always been welcome in our house and you didn't seem to mind, I decided not to bother talking about it. Everybody's family has something different or odd. Heck, how many black families do you know have a white, red headed Uncle living upstairs from them?"

"I didn't mind, 'cause I didn't know. Dad and Claude have been living parallel lives since your dad and I got married." The twins' heads swing back and forth from looking at Mom to looking at Dad. Lou Jr. is right. Their family has always been different, but this different. Wow!

"Is that it? Can I go out now? I wanna see how many of the constellations we can identify tonight. Girls, you coming?" Lou pushes his chair back from the circle and reaches for his sneakers. Dad had made them take off their shoes to keep the hardwood floors nice and clean. Lou bends down to pick up his shoes, looks up and sees Mom's pleading eyes, and hears Dad's commanding voice.

"Sit yourself back down, young man." Dad reinforces the order with his pointing finger. "This meeting is not over."

216

"Why not? You've made your announcement. Is there something you want us to be doing to prep for the hike to the Middle Falls tomorrow? Can't we do that in the morning?"

"Sit down! Things are going to be different. Mom and I want the family to be prepared."

"Daddy," whines Alysa, a little surprised at her shock. "What's going to be different? We already share a house and folks are accustomed to seeing you and Uncle Claude together all the time anyway." Alvyra's eyes dart back and forth from Mom to Dad trying the gauge the temperature of each. Dad seems hot. Mom seems cool, but not calm.

"That's true, Honey," Dad explains, "but when folks know why, they may treat you differently."

"Why would they treat us different? We're still the same family," Alvyra inserts. Lillian is watching and listening and wondering if she has made a bigger deal of this news than is necessary. If the only change is going to be where Louis spends more time, what will that really matter? He's not asking for a divorce.

Now, the family disperses without saying anything more. The teens head outside. Louis, goes out the back door as if to get more wood. Lillian is left inside, alone, wondering if this will be her life from now on. Alone.

Lou Jr. pretends to be going out to watch the constellations. He waves his sisters away from the log that is long enough for the three of them to sit comfortably. They sense his wish to be alone on this spacious lot. As speculatively as he, the sisters saunter around to the other side of the stone cottage. How glad he is that there is a place to be alone with his thoughts.

He reflects back on the week, what he'd seen, what he'd heard, and now what he is seeing and hearing from his parents. What's this going to mean for him, a rising senior and possible baseball scholarship recipient? Will his parent's lifestyle compromise his candidacy, application when they ask about his parents when they see two different apartment numbers and one address on his application? How will the three of them appear to the team of evaluators?

THIRD WEEK

Sunday morning, the Robertson family members each pretend that all is the same as though Dad had revealed nothing startling. Love hides a multitude of faults and all their parts. Each is feeling a little guilty for not feeling differently.

Louis followed the lead of Lillian who had gotten up early to prepare a cold breakfast. Before leaving home each of the teens had packed the boxes of cereal they wanted, and Lillian had added boxes of fruit juice for them all. They'd stopped by the small store in town to pick up two quarts of fresh milk. The kids drank whole milk, but their parents limited themselves to the 2% version. It is early in the season for fresh fruit, so Lillian brought a couple cans of fruit cocktail which she is spooning into small dessert bowls she'd found in the kitchen cabinets.

It seems that Virginia's family had not stripped the cottage of the fine china their grandparents had used while this was their primary residence. Apparently, the families who rent through the VRBO plan have been careful, because most of the sets of dishes seemed to be complete. Lillian noticed just one missing dessert plate when she was washing and restacking the dishes after dinner last evening.

The kids enter the kitchen, looking around as if taking the temperature of the room with their eyes. Mom and Dad seem to be working together. Dad is setting out the silverware and Mom is folding colorful paper napkins and placing them next to the cereal bowls already set on the old-fashioned wooden round oak table, the kind with smooth curve legs and club feet. It's large enough for the six high-back wooden chairs to encircle the table and seat the diners with plenty of elbow room.

The family is seated by the time Lillian brings the pot of coffee to the table which she sets on the round lazy-susan in the center. Dad reaches out for the hands of the twins on either side. Lou Junior grasps his Mom's hand and that of the older twin, Alvyra. Mom holds Alysa's other hand. They bow their head and following Dad's lead, say their regular blessing, "Thank you God, for this food, Amen." Each picks up their box of cereal, tears the strip on the top and the flakes and dried fruits tumble into their shallow bowls.

Thankfully, Louis brought in his tablet tuned to a playlist with Christian songs of various tempos. Playing now is Whitney Houston singing "The Lord Is My Shepherd" the family first heard in the movie, *The Preacher's Wife.* Before everyone has added milk to their cereal bowls, all are bobbing their heads to the music. Alysa starts singing, then gulps when Dad gives her the eye. "No singing at the table, young lady. You know better."

"Sorry, Dad. But I couldn't help it. I'm thinking of our walk after breakfast, up to the Middle Falls. I can almost hear Whitney singing the song with us as we walk through the valley. We'll be able to hear the waterfalls. Oh, Mom. Please let us send Ms. Virginia a thank you gift for letting us use their cottage this weekend. We haven't gotten good news, but we're having a great time anyway. We can send her one of those woodsy necklaces Uncle Claude helped us make." Everyone gulps, looks down, and pretends they haven't heard anything odd.

"Yeah, Dad. The stars were spectacular last night," Lou Jr. interjects with a mouth full of cereal. He gets the stink eye from Mom.

"Young man! No talking with your mouth full." All three of the kids giggle and pick up their napkins knowing if they're not careful they'll all spew chewed-up cereal across the table.

"Lil, Honey," Louis asks once he clears his cereal-filled mouth with a gulp of coffee. "What time will you be ready to start our hike up to the Falls? Lou Jr. and I are going out back to refill the woodpile. We burned more wood than I anticipated last evening. We want to leave everything the way we found it. Since we're gonna be heading back home right after our walk, I wanna make sure everything is in place before we leave. In fact, kids, thanks for bringing down your linen this morning. They should be dry by the time we finish getting the luggage packed in the van. We'll make up the beds and I'll do the inspection before we leave."

"Aye, Aye, Captain," Lou Jr. teases as he scrapes the last of the cereal from his bowl. He scoots back, gathers his leavings, and carries them over to the black plastic-lined trash can. He knows it'll be his job to check the wastebaskets around the cottage and see they all are emptied before they tie the top of this bag and put it in the dumpster out back.

"Girls, you decide which of you will wash and which will dry the dishes. I'm going to freshen up the bathrooms. I know you cleaned the bowls after you washed up this morning, right?" Their mom usually included an instruction in her questions, just in case.

"Yes, Ma'am. We know the ropes." Alysa reports. Lou Jr. knows them, too, so Lillian is certain it won't take her long to shine the bowls with the paper towels she has on the counter. She already collected the washcloths and bath towels and they're ready to go in the dryer as soon as the bedclothes come out.

As Louis turns from the door to the backyard, he looks back at his family as they scatter to do their jobs before they reconvene to take the hike through the valley, along the Genesee River, and up to the Middle Falls. Thankfully, it's nearly ten o'clock and the sun is shining brightly. No thoughts of the "valley of the shadow of death" today. Just, "Thou are with me" and "Surely goodness and mercy will follow…"

222

Am I willing to lose all this just to spend more time with Claude? Why do we have to change anything? We were doing just fine these past couple of decades. Now in just a little over two weeks, everything is all topsy-turvy. Maybe this walk will give me a sense of the direction God wants me to go. I thought coming clean would clean things up.

*****

Little does any of the family know what is going on back in town between Glendella and Claude.

*****

With the stone cottage all cleaned and their bags packed in the trunk of the van, the Robertsons each carry a light backpack with bottles of water, their cellphones, and notebooks. The kids know Mom is going to stop somewhere and ask them to write about their experience out here in the park. She was always telling them of their heritage as descendants of the Iroquois who lived in this section of the state. They, like most Native Americans, live in harmony with nature and she encourages her children to do the same. That means, stopping and letting plants and trees, water and winds, fish, fowl, and beasts of the fields speak to them. Today, here in this Grand Canyon of the East State Park, they probably will encounter and interact with all seven forms of creation!

"Ding a ling, Ding a ling, Ding a ling."

Whose phone is that? "Buzz, Buzz, Buzz"

They all recognize that as Dad's Motorola cell phone. He pulls it out and flips it open.

"It's Claude. What can he want? He knows we'll be back late this evening. Hmm. He already told me that he'll have cooked something on the grill we can heat up if we get back much past dinner time." Louis stops to read the text. "What? What does he mean, he's got good news?"

"Ding a ling, Ding a ling, Ding a ling."

"Mom," Lou Jr. says, "That's your phone, isn't it?"

"I know. I know. I know." Lillian recognized the sound and scrambled to reach the phone that's below the other stuff in her shoulder bag. But, before it rings again, she's got it and is looking at the phone screen as Louis tells what Claude has texted. She pushes the side button on her phone and see's the message is from Glendella. "Hey, Sis. I got good news for you. Can't wait till you guys get home. You'll be stoked." Lillian reads her message aloud but does not verbalize her thoughts. What's this "good news" that Claude and Glendella are talking about? Hmmm. Maybe they're gonna get married to provide a cover for us, like Virginia's aunt did with her lover and his wife? Won't that be something!

Lou Junior Reflects on the Reveal

Upon arriving at the cottage in Letchworth, Mom and Dad had asked us, the family to meet after dinner to talk about new plans. I immediately assumed we were planning a trip or maybe they were going off on their own, still in the 15-year anniversary mode. And after all, we kids are older and can stay by ourselves with Uncle Claude living just above us. During dinner mom certainly wasn't her usual inquisitive self. She's always so interested in our activities. Asking for the details of our adventures.

We all gathered in the old-fashioned wood paneled room with the fireplace. Yes, I was excited because I knew something new was brewing. Still, like I do at home, I picked the chair near the window in case I got bored. I could gaze out and even daydream. At home, our neighbors were usually working in the yard. Keeping up with the Joneses was part of the landscape, and our yards were among the best. Here in the stone cottage, I could hear nothing from outdoors, but could see peeps of the night sky through the tall narrow windows on the left wall.

Mom sat with a sober look on her face. I wondered could this be something other than what I had imagined. Was she sick or was there some financial crisis? Should I be worried or was it just my imagination.

Then the bombshell hit. Dad announced that he is gay and that his partner is Uncle Claude. We would remain in the same home; however, he and Uncle Claude would be living together in the upper flat. Dad would be there for us as always. Nothing would change except that the two of them would be cohabitating just above our heads.

I couldn't quite understand what he was talking about. Yes, I'd seen them together sometimes, but I couldn't understand what was happening and what this would mean. I was stunned. Once I wrapped my head around what he was saying, the thought raced into my head that one day he is my father, and the next day, I don't know what to think. I can imagine what would have happened if I'd spoken up.

*****

"Why couldn't this stay a secret?" I blurt out……" I've kept my secret to myself."

Mom darts her eyes at me, "What secret is that?" Oh wow! I didn't mean to let the cat out of the bag.

Dad asks in his you better tell us voice. "Junior, you have something you haven't told us about. "

"This isn't about me right now, it's about you, Dad and you, too, Mom."

"Junior, it's actually about us as a family and how we transition to this new lifestyle," says Dad.

"Louie," Mom interrupts, "what is this secret you've been keeping?"

I sigh and explain that a while back, I had seen Dad and Uncle Claude in an intimate embrace. I never mentioned it to anyone. But ever since then I have been unsure about my own relationships with other guys.

"I have been worried about building close friendships. What I saw makes me afraid that I might be… you know "that way. I don't have anybody to talk to."

*****

My family, parents and sisters would have looked at me like I'm crazy. Alvyra would sit pulling on her ear. Alysa's mouth would just hang open. They seem to think I should be stronger. It's not strength here; it's wonder, even worry! I haven't been able to open up to anyone about my feelings. There's a lot of pressure on us as athletes.

And at that moment, I remember one of our Sunday school lessons. *For there is nothing covered, that shall not be revealed, neither hid that shall be known.* that we found in the King James Version of Luke 12:2.

IT IS WHAT IT IS…..

No, it isn't, my mind is flooded with all kinds of thoughts. What will my friends say to me? Are they going to look at me differently? Am I a product of "like father like son"? I have his name, I have his genes, do I have his hormones, too?

IT IS WHAT IT WILL BE…..

Twins Call Camp Counselor

Susan Wagstaff, church camp counselor recalls evenings at summer Camp Otte Canaan, when it was time to share something about themselves that Alysa and Alvyra didn't give much information about their family. Over the week of camp, the first year the twins attended, Susan did gather that they have an older brother, and they live with their mother and father and an uncle with whom they spend lots of time.

Susan is a veteran Christian counselor who sensed something bothered the girls. But she'd not pushed them. Instead, she watched and prayed. What a surprise to get an email from the girls who'd not been to camp for two years. When she opened the letter, it was an invitation to meet with them online in an hour. The note went on to ask, "Can we talk to you about some troubling news we received from our parents last night? It is really kind of embarrassing to share, but we need to get some understanding from an unbiased person. We'll send a link to our Google Chat account. Then we can see each other. Okay?"

Susan smiles in a puzzling way but is glad the girls think to call her. As a camp counselor, she had seldom communicated with the campers between summers. She's so thankful that this past year the Board of Directors encouraged the counselors to use social media to stay in touch in-between times. That's one of the reasons she'd sent e-cards this past Christmas. Next summer, she will collect birthdays and add those days to the time she sends personal notes to her campers. *****

Once they are logged on, adjusted the tablet on Alysa's lap and volume on the audio so all three can see, hear, and be heard, they catch up briefly. The girls jump back and forth with comments about their GEMS group, a recent basketball game in the park, and their first-time taking AP exams.

Susan knows AP testing is not the real reason they call after all this time, so she gets to work, to focus on that reason. But first, what's that behind the girls? "Sure. I'm so thankful you consider me in that role. Where are you now, by the way. You girls outside? I see tree limbs waving. That's not one of those fake ZOOM backgrounds is it?"

"No ma'am. Those are real trees. We are outside. Our parents had us at Letchworth State Park for the weekend. And me and Vyra took our tablets so we could take pictures and write about our visit. We had no idea we'd be using it for a Google Chat with our camp counselor once we got back home."

"Yeah," Alvyra jumps in, "We're out back in our sorta new house. We got lots of trees between our house and the neighbors on the next block."

Alysa enthuses. "It's really cool after living in that apartment in the village for so long!"

"You got that right," pipes in Alvyra. "Um, Counselor Susan is homosexuality a sin"?

"Why do you ask, Alvyra?" "Well, umm…"

"Go on, you can talk to me in confidence."
 "Well, my father and mother have been married over seventeen years and we always thought they were a happy couple and I guess my mother was happy. But, this weekend, my father has told us that he has been living a double life."

Alysa continues, "We go to a Christian Church that teaches us that you must be born again and when you are a Christian you don't practice sin."

"That is correct Alvyra, if you are a Christian you don't practice sin. However, if you do sin, you can ask God to forgive you and then not continue to do those sinful things any longer.

"In I John 3:4-6 in the NIV it says, *Everyone who sins breaks the law in fact, sin is lawlessness. But you know that he appeared so that he might take away our sins. And in Him (Christ Jesus) is no sin. No one who lives in him keeps on sinning."*

"Now Alvyra, why are you asking about homosexuality"?

Alysa jumps in here and explains, "Well, Counselor Susan, last night during a family meeting, my dad told us that he has been having a homosexual relationship with our Uncle that lives in the upstairs flat in our home. Dad says the relationship has been going on since before we were born. "

As usual, her twin knows what's needed for clarification, so she continues, "He and Mom got married because the three of them wanted a family and he knew he couldn't have children with a man. Now he's tellin' us he wants to move upstairs and live as a couple with Uncle Claude."

"And is your Mom just learning about this parallel relationship? "

"Uh hunh," the girls nod. On her computer screen, Susan sees the worried lines in the girls' foreheads as though they are having second thoughts about revealing this information.

"How do you girls feel about his decision?"

"Well, "Alysa admits, "I am very embarrassed about it, mainly for my mother's sake. I am sure it is humiliating for her to find out after all these years that her husband is queer and has been having an affair right under her nose."

"Yeah," her sister continues, "I would be so ashamed to have any of my friends come to our house and see my father and another man together like husband and wife."

Alysa turns to ask her sister, "You don't' really believe he would do anything like that in front of our friends, do you? He and Uncle Claude have been living this parallel life for so long, we never notice anything unusual about them when they are together. Do you think our friends would notice something different?"

"Um, I don't know. We didn't notice anything. Maybe our friends won't either. Vyra, Um. Counselor Susan, Is our daddy wrong for having sex with anyone other than my mother, his wife,"

"Yeah, having sex with a man! Ugh." Alvyra says with a shudder. "That is just disgusting to even think about. I've seen same gender couples on TV, and it always turns my stomach. I know Mom has to decide whether she wants to keep living with Dad under these circumstances or to move out.. Yuck! I don't want to live in the house where my father is living upstairs with another man as his love partner."

To refocus the girls' attention on the questions about sexuality and sin, Susan Wagstaff suggests, "First of all girls, before we go any further. Let's see what the word of God has to say about homosexuality. So, we don't lose our connection here on the Google Chat, one of you take out your cell phone and look up Leviticus 18:22. That's in the Old Testament."

"We know, Sister Wagstaff. Our GEMS leader, Ms. Delphi, made us memorize the books of the Bible by singing a song!"

As Alysa looks up the verse, the girls smile and sing, "Genesis, Exodus, Leviticus, Numbers, Deuteronomeeeee."

"Hey, I got it. What chapter again?"

"That's Leviticus, Chapter 18, verse 22. Read it aloud, please."

Alysa looks up into the tablet screen her sister is holding and confirms that their Counselor is watching. "I got the NIV. Is that okay?" She continues when she sees Susan nod her head. "Okay, it says, *'Do not have sexual relations with a man as one does with a woman, that is detestable.'*"

Sister Wagstaff, with her teacher hat on, sends the girls to a passage in the New Testament. "Now, let's look at I Corinthians 6:9-10. You read this one, Alvyra. Got it?"

"Yes, Ma'am. It says,

'Or do you not know that wrongdoers will not inherit the kingdom of God? Do not be deceived: Neither the sexually immoral nor idolaters nor adulterers nor men who have sex with men[nor thieves nor the greedy nor drunkards nor slanderers nor swindlers will inherit the kingdom of God.'

Watching the leaves flutter in the wind behind the girls, this experienced camp counselor, remains silent. She is giving time for the Word to do its work. In the silence, the girls can cogitate, ruminate, and thoughtfully consider how these passages of Scripture apply to their family situation. She then summarizes,

"Now we know what the Bible says about homosexuality. It is a sin and people who practice that lifestyle will not go to heaven unless they repent and turn away from that ungodly behavior."

In the angle of light through the tree limbs, Counselor Susan sees tears welling up in the girls' eyes. They've leaned together and both are visible on her computer screen.

"However, I am sure that your father loves the two of you and your brother very much. Please do not start disliking or disrespecting your father because of this. Continue to show him the Love of God and pray for him to change his ways and turn away from the sin he is committing with your Uncle Claude."

"What about our Mama?" Alysa asks and Alvyra nods. Suddenly, the Google Chat screens starts flickering.

Speaking a little more rapidly, now, Counselor Susan goes on, "Your mother has a big decision to make. She'll be wrestling with her thoughts. She'll have to decide whether she is going to continue living in the house with your father and uncle living upstairs as a couple or move out and find somewhere else to live."

"Move?" Alvyra yelps. "But we just got this house. Where we gonna be moving? All our friends live around here." Suddenly the girls see this issue is bigger than they thought. The counselor realizes they need more than words. They need to sense she understands their current worries.

"Calm, down. Calm down, girls. Let's not jump the gun. Now girls, When you go back inside, please don't put any pressure on your mother to make a decision. Show her lots of love and support and be very patient with her and give her plenty of time and room. She, too, needs to feel she's doing what God wants her to do."

Alvyra and Alysa nod thoughtfully, hoping the Google session won't shut down now because they have a couple more questions. But, Counselor Susan says, "Let's close this discussion with prayer before you girls go back inside and face your parents with this expanded information."

All three bow their heads. A bird chirps overhead as though confirming their decision to pray to their common Creator.

"Dear Heavenly Father I ask you to give Alysa and Alvyra peace in the midst of the storm they are going through. Lead and guide them and their mother as she makes some very difficult decisions concerning her family. Please help them to be an example of your love as they interact with their father and uncle, Claude. Bless that home and help the family to get direction and allow you to lead them as they work things out in the marriage. These blessings we ask in Jesus' name. Amen"

"Thanks, Sister Wagst...." the screen shuts down. But the girls aren't upset about the technology. It's spirituality and sexuality that's on their minds. They do feel somewhat better knowing what the Bible says in the Old and New Testaments. They'll understand why folks may look at them funny. But these sisters also know that God will be with them. They know they have a role to play and the song from First Sunday comes to Alvyra and she begins to sing softly as she pushes the side button to shut off her computer tablet. She stands up, then reaches down to pull up her sister.

It's me, it's me, it's me, Oh Lord,
standing in the need of prayer
!   Not my mother, not my father,
but it's me, Oh Lord,
standing in the need of prayer!

"Yeah, Vyra. Mom's gonna need us. And so will Dad and Uncle Claude!" Alysa checks her phone, then, scrambles up from the log on which they've been sitting and brushes the damp leaves from her jeans. The two amble through the lightly wooded area, back to their house, confident that whatever they face, they'll not be alone. Pastor's sermon that Sunday told them that God promised never to leave or forsake them. They hope that will be true of their parents, too.

Sisters Journal about the Reveal

At a GEMS overnight at the start of the Fall semester last year, the girls had played around with numerology to see if their birthdates had any significance to their lives. Alvyra and Alysa though twins, were born on different days, Alvyra on March 7, and Alysa on March 8. Using their birthday month and date as a three-digit number came up to 307 and 308 proved interesting. The group of girls used their phones to look at the Angel Wings number website to see how accurate the description of the angel with the number matches each girl's birth date. If the girls couldn't find the exact number for their birthday, they looked at three numbers in their birth date to see what came up.

Folks always teased, "How can you be twins with different birth dates?" In a way, though, the girls like having differences, being their own person. They enjoy many of the same things, same foods, same music, even some of the same classes at school, but each seeks to be her own person. Now that they have learned about their Dad's desire to move upstairs to live with Claude, his longtime lover, the girls wonder if they'll respond in the way their birthday numbers suggest.

Later that evening back home after the startling weekend spent at Letchworth State Park and then the Google Chat with Counselor, Susan Wagstaff, Alysa pulls out the journal she had written about the significance of the numbers of her birthdate. As she reads, she notes that she'd picked up three statements from that website in hopes that those would help guide her choices as she listened to the Scripture the girls were studying that weekend.

Their GEMS leader, Ms. Delphi, had asked them to write down three quotations: one positive, one negative, and one aspirational. The leader clarified that numerology is just a way of looking at life, not the answer. The answer, she assured them is in Scripture. What would Jesus do is what she always asked them to consider. Anyway, this is what Alvyra had written in her journal:

"It consists of two prime numbers – 3 and 7. They mean new ideas, life achievements, and a positive ending."

Such people do not know how to keep their mouths shut and often talk too much. Impulsiveness manifests itself in the form of rash decisions and hasty conclusions, and low self-esteem leads to unnecessary bragging.

Such persons will not tolerate injustice and will try to correct the situation in any way possible. They strive to acquire the skills they need and enjoy filling knowledge gaps. Over time, these people share their experiences."

Alysa closes the journal but leaves her thumb between the pages she has just read. She senses something behind her and turns. Yep, it's her. Alvyra clasping her burgundy leather book behind her back, peeks into her twin's room. Ah, there's Alysa sitting with her light tan journal in her lap. Alvyra's not really sure she wants to share what she's been thinking but is not at all surprised that her twin has pulled out her diary, too. Early on, their Mom had encouraged them to write out their thoughts instead of blurting without thinking.

The girls have been journaling since elementary school. Sometimes Mom would send them to their room after dinner to write three sentences about their day. Occasionally, the family gathers to share what they have written. They'd been doing less and less as the kids reached their teens. But, habit is a habit and the girls have continued writing regularly. Alvyra wonders sometimes if Lou Jr. still does the daily writing. But, she hasn't asked. He'll think she is criticizing him, or something.

*****

"What's that behind your back?" Alysa queries when she feels her sister standing in the doorway. They've only been living here a little over a year, and neither is yet used to having her own bedroom and a bathroom they don't have to share with their older brother. No more Louie mess to contend with. The sisters had shared a tiny little room with double-decker twin beds for the last ten years of their lives.

Dad had worked hard to fix up this house when he got a good deal from a real estate flipper. The girls had overheard Dad, Mom, and Claude talking about how much money they would save if they did some of the remodeling and interior decorating themselves. Dad is a techie who is skilled with his hands, and he has contacts with suppliers in the area because he knows them from his job as a building manager at the eight-story office building downtown.

236

The girls are proud of their dad who supervises the security, indoor and outdoor maintenance, as well as the janitorial teams there. Mom knows numbers and helps Dad figure out how much they might save if they bought early and did the work instead of waiting and buying after someone else had done the remodeling.

The sisters picked up from grown-up conversations, that he'd negotiated a pretty good deal. That's why their family was able to move into this up-scale house after being cramped for so many years in an apartment chosen for its accessibility to public transportation. In the old days, their dad said, getting to live in this house would have been moving "across the tracks." In the old days, when redlining was the rule, few people of color would have been able to buy a home over here, even if they could afford it. In fact, he admitted, the original deed to the house where the family now lives had a "do not sell to Negroes or Jews" written in the earlier version of the document. That "do not sell" covenant agreement some communities had is no longer enforceable, but that's how things were not all that long ago.

*****

"You looking at your journal, too?" Alvyra notes as she steps inside her twin's bedroom. The colors are different from what she chose, but fine for her twin. She likes lilac. Surprisingly, her twin likes the traditional girly pink.

"Yeah! You, journaling, too?

"Yeah. Um.. I was thinkin' 'bout what Ms. Delphi had us writing when we did that numbers thing last Fall. We were gonna be startin' high school and she said it was time for us to start thinkin' about who we are now and who we want to become. Being a Christian, she said, is just the first step.

"You right. She always sayin 'Once we establish our relationship with our Creator, we still have choices to make and consequences to live with.' That sounded scary."

"I know what you mean, Sis. Well, when we did that numbers thing, using our birthdays as starters, I was reminded yet once again that we twins, but our birthdays aren't the same day. I wonder if that will be significant as we grow up."

These studious teens like using polysyllabic words and try to add one or two a day. Their middle school homeroom teachers would have a new word on the whiteboard each day and challenge the young teens to use the word of the day correctly at least three times that day – either in writing or in speaking. Sometimes the young teens sounded a little pompous, but they were learning.

"Who knows? Well? What did you write about being a 308? That Angel Wings website Ms. Delphi had us use was strange. Almost every number had positive and negative characteristics. I'm glad she had us just search for one positive, one negative, and one aspirational. I had to look up that word, 'aspirational.' Glad we were working on tablets so no one would tell I didn't know that word!" she grins. Alvyra hates to look ignorant. She is usually a pretty good student, and she wants to retain that reputation now that she is in high school.

Alysa, challenges, "I'll let you see what I wrote if you let me see what you wrote." Alvyra looks over at her sister, then glances out the window at the fluttering flowers tipping the crab apple tree. Ah, beautiful.

"Sure, okay. Here you are." The sisters exchange journals and sit back-to-back on the floor next to Alysa's bed. This is something they have done lots of times. Back in the apartment, they shared a bedroom and had no chairs on which to sit; it was the bed with the upper bunk where they'd bump their heads, or the floor. Mom had gotten them some color-coordinated spongy bath rugs. The cushy cushion rugs buffeted their bottoms.

The siblings, used to sitting on the floor, wiggle a bit to adjust their shoulders, and raise the soft-covered journals and begin the read. The rustle of the trees outside the screened windows calms the girls as they cogitate the changes coming to their family.

Dad always tells them to use natural air conditioning to keep the circulating air fresh and the electricity bills low. It has to be really hot before Dad would let them turn on the air conditioning. He'd had one installed with the new furnace, but they couldn't keep the automatic temperature setting all that low. "Gotta save money where we can" is Dad's motto. But he isn't a scrimper. Just careful. Anyway, the cool breeze feels fine and smells pretty fresh, too.

Because the lot on which their house sits had established trees, as new homeowners, the family didn't have to wait to experience the growth of new plantings. There is a full-grown flowering crabapple tree in the side yard with the sweet-spicy aroma of the blossoms. Alvyra inhales deeply, then starts reading. She knows from science class that the pinky-white blossoms only last a few days, seldom more than a week. But other things are on her mind today.

But (not sure if the double but is for emphasis) the fluttering leaves keep drawing her attention away from the issues at hand. She wants to enjoy the fragrance and view today. The window in her room sits on the opposite side of the house, so she doesn't get this view or these fragrant fumes. Instead, a handsome row of juniper pines provides a little privacy from their neighbor, Ms. Andrea's house next door. They have visual privacy, but usually can hear people talking when they sit on their wrap-around porch. Alvyra opens her twin's journal and reads the quotations she has written about Angel number 308, the numbers of Alysa's March 8th birthdate.

"The number 308 suggests that you do not think negatively about what you are doing, and do not doubt whether or not you are doing the right thing. … However, don't expect everything to fall into your hands promptly. Ask for help and ask what to do, only then can help reach you."

"Be sure that all the decisions you are making have been carefully thought through and analyzed, seeking the most perfect harmony between your desires and your possibilities."

"Spiritually, 308 represents practicality: it awakens the idea of pursuing your goals and facing the adversities of the way little by little, with patience and perseverance, but always with hard work and divine help at decisive moments."

The siblings just sit, read, and say little about the quotations each had chosen that memorable Fall evening at the GEMS overnight. It now is the month of May and they have completed the AP exam for the World History class. Both had thought that course was an eye-opening experience.

But, now with what they are learning about their dad's sexuality and talk about moving upstairs to live with Uncle Claude, whom they now know is dad's lover, they know their own history will be significantly different than they ever imagined. Thankfully, they have Aunt Glendella.

Aunt Glendella has shared with them one of the ways she and her husband learned to deal with the tensions of military life. Many evenings when they were together, their aunt and her husband, Uncle Quentin, would stand and pray these lines from Psalms 46:10 (KJV) "*Be still and know that I am God*". Instead of just quoting the lines and going to bed, they would repeat the lines, dropping the end word each time, and focus on the new last word.

The sisters found that doing this same ritual seemed to work for them to. So before splitting up for the night, Alvyra and Alysa stand and repeat.

Be still and know that I am **God**

Be still and know that I **am**

Be still and know that **I**

Be still and know **that**

Be still and **know**

Be still **and**

Be **still**

Be

Without saying anything else, Alvyra taps her cell phone screen activating the YouTube channel with May Iglesias Gaza singing a song, with the words of this Psalm. The twins sway to the music as Alysa turns back her bed covers. By the time, the song winds down, Alvyra has returned to her room humming the song to herself.

Claude and Glendella Plan

Sunday afternoon, Claude and Glendella meet in the park across the street from Beth-El Community Church, where they all worship. The Robertsons miss the service today because they're weekending in Letchworth State Park, spending two nights in a vacation home Lillian's department chair has loaned them. While there. Lillian and Louis planned to tell the children about their Dad and Claude. Glendella is a little skeptical about the future of the family because each of the Robertson's teens will probably take the news so differently.

The four adults, that now include Glendella, have been praying for guidance and seriously considering what is the right thing to do when what has been done so far is because of love. As the protective older sister, Glendella is exercising God-given control of her tongue. She wants to lash out at anyone who gives any member of her family a funny look.

Lillian has met with the Pastor. Louis and Claude have spoken with the chair of the usher board. No one knows who overheard whom, but Glendella overheard chitter during the snack time after service today. Yes, she's noticed that the church members who now are aware of the relationship between Louis and Claude are shying away from her, too. All the years of faithful service in the church seem to be overshadowed by the honesty of this pair of men. "Well," Claude asks. "I need your help to finalize a plan that will not hurt the family so much. Can I count on you?"

Claude hands Glendella a bottle of cold water he pulls out of his briefcase. She accepts it and takes a deep pull on the refreshing liquid, then leans back on the park bench. She'd rather be on the swings but knows Claude wouldn't have invited her to this public place if he didn't have something private to talk about. It may be serious. So, she goes along.

"The family! What do you think you've been doing all these years, Claude? Why now?"

"Pastor Jackson's been preaching about being open and honest with those we love. I love this family and they've welcomed me into theirs since Day One. Louis and I have been cloistered about our relationship all this time because we know few people understand bisexuality and would probably not welcome us in places that are important to us. Our church and our workplaces. Lou and I thought, our reputation as faithful church members, employees, and workmates would overshadow this misunderstanding about the sexuality God gave us."

"Claude, please don't go there. I don't understand it either. I do know about Lillian and when the kids learn, they probably will be hurting as much as you and Louis are now. So, what can you and I do to alleviate some of the pain? I'm a widow. Lil's my baby sister. We're adults with no living parents. You guys are all we have. See, there I go. I see you as family, too."

"I'm glad, Glendella. And it's for that reason I'm coming to you to help me work out the details."

"What details?"

"I'm leaving."

"Leaving? When? Going where?

"Well, I've spoken with an Episcopal priest who has connections with the mission work with the Dinka Christians in Sudan. I started the process the Monday after Lillian sang. I've been offered a job there and I'm going to take it."

"You're leaving?" Glendella jerks up, looks Claude in the face, and sees he's at peace.

"I put in my two-week notice at work.. For my job here, I keep my passport up to date, and with the aid of the council, I should be able to get a Visa with no trouble through the Sudan Embassy. My record's clear and so it should be smooth sailing. You know when we all went to the altar, God spoke to me then. I felt confirmed since I've seen the stuff hit the fan."

She's not sure about his plan because she knows how much the kids will miss their only Uncle, the man who has been so close for so many years.

"Why are you doing this? This seems pretty wild!"

"Not really. You know that song, "I Have Decided to Follow Jesus"?

"Yeah, of course, I do!" and to get her mind off the hot topic at hand, Glendella softly sings the first verse:

> I have decided to follow Jesus;
> I have decided to follow Jesus;
> I have decided to follow Jesus;
> No turning back, no turning back.

Claude harmonizes with her on the second verse.

Though none go with me,
I still will follow;
Though none go with me,
 I still will follow;
Though none go with me,
 I still will follow;
No turning back, no turning back.

They both take another deep drink of the water, sit and gaze across the street at the sturdy house of worship where their church family meets. The modest steeple has a cross on the front between the steep A-shaped eaves of the red-tiled roof. The tip of the A seems to be pointing toward heaven and the red tile could be perceived as the blood of Christ flowing down, but not hitting the ground.

"You serious about this, Claude? You really gonna leave and go live in South Sudan. That can be dangerous."

"It could be, but life can be dangerous anywhere. I feel led to leave.

When I asked the Lord where, He told me South Sudan. Glendella, you know Jamal is Louis' middle name."

She nods, "Yeah, I know he's name Louis for his grandfather and Jamal for his Sudanese father who came to this country as an orphan student sponsored by the Episcopal church. Oh! I get it now. It's because of Louis you're planning to go to Sudan!"

"Yeah, It's because of Louis' family heritage and because the Episcopal church will have me."

"Does Louis know about this?"

"Not yet. I'm talking to you first because I need your help."

"How can I help? I know I've traveled much of the world with my husband! Heck, we spent tours of duty on four of the seven continents. Even had a short assignment up in Iceland. But I've never been to the Upper East Coast of Africa. Just to Kenya and Uganda."

"I don't need help with travel. The Episcopal council is taking care of that. It's the family here."

"Sure. What can I do?"

"Well, you know, as Uncle Claude, I've been helping with various aspects of parenting since the kids were born. I also have some assets I'd like to share with the family before I leave."

"What do you mean, "assets"?

"Well, to start. I will ask Louis if I can sign my car over to Lou, Jr. The car is paid for, Lou has his driver's license, but he's still not an adult. If he keeps his grades up, insurance for him should not be too much for the family to carry until Lou finishes school and gets a job earning enough to take over expenses himself."

"That's generous of you, Claude. You know Lou will be stoked. Who among his friends is driving a burgundy Toyota Prius! You know the school colors are burgundy and blue. He'll be on top of the world!"

"And the twins. I wanna do something for them, too."

"You gonna leave them your bicycle and shop tools so they can keep up with that weird artsy craft stuff you've been teaching them?" "Hmmm. That's a good idea!" Claude chuckles and looks around and up. A red-breasted robin is chirping in the tree above their heads. When Claude and Glendella stop and look, they notice tightly woven straw nestled between the inner branches. A proud father, protecting his family!

"That's a good idea, Glendella, about the bike and tools! But, right now, I am talking about something further down the line. Just as your parents worked hard to see that you and your sister got more education than they got, Louis and Lillian want the same for their three. I wanna help."

"How're you gonna do that?" "With your help."

"My help? All the income I have right now is what I get as the widow of an airman who died in active duty. It's enough for me right now. But…"

"You can help by encouraging the girls to keep up their grades so they can qualify for scholarships or low-cost grants. I have some CDs, you know, certificates of deposit I got through my credit union. Those CDs are due to mature in five years. When they do, the girls will be twenty years old and probably in their third or fourth year of college. The CDs should be enough to help pay for two years of tuition at the state college."

"You'd do that for them?" exclaims Glendella, incredulously.

"Why not? They're my family. This is what family does for one another. What good is money to me if I can't share it with those I love?"

"But Claude. You're not their blood-kin."

"Yes, I am. We're all Christians and, therefore part of the family of God!"

"Yeah, but! Wow! I can't believe you'd do this."

"Why not? Like I said, God has blessed me to earn good money since I graduated from college. I've lived frugally, but have always had enough, so I've been saving. Once I began to partner with Louis and the family welcomed me so graciously, I've just been doing what family does. You know, I, too, am an orphan, now, so it's just us."

"Wow! So, how can I help? It sounds like you've got it all worked out already."

"Not all of it. I need you to do one more thing. Really three things."
"Three? What three things?"

"First, I want to know that you will stay close and help the family through the coming months as they deal with the fall out of Lou and me coming out. And I'd like you to take over the lease of the upstairs flat. I have a lifetime lease for that."

"You know I'm gonna be there for my sister and her family. And now, you want me to move into your flat! How much is that gonna cost me? Sure, it'll be convenient 'cause the apartment building where I am now is among those being gentrified down in the village. We already got notice to be out of there by the end of June."

"Well, you know as a life tenant, you'll have full control of the flat as long as you live, and you also have a legal responsibility to keep the property up. You can rent it out, and also make improvements on it. I don't 'think you'll have to do much for a few years. It's in pretty good shape right now. Of course, if you accept this offer, you can redecorate to fit your taste."

"That's quite a lot, Claude. But I may be able to swing it. Wait a minute! How'd you know about my apartment issue?"

"Oh, that? I heard about it at work. One of the chaps in the office next door mentioned it. You know, our staff shares a break room with the folks in the other offices on our floor. They keep the coffee pot going and the water cooler in there. I heard him talking about his having to move. In fact, that was when I got the idea of signing over my lease to you.

"You'd have your own place so you could get away when you need to. It's really quite private for being in a shared space. The sound abatement is really effective. You can play your keyboards as loud as you like and if the windows are closed, no one will hear you! Almost no sounds can be heard from the Robertson's place on the first floor."

"Well, that's good to know. I mean about the sound of my keyboards. When I'm working on a new piece, I sometimes forget how many times I play and replay the same few bars! If I forget to put in my earphones, which automatically turn off the external sound, I can be pretty annoying! So, my Quinten reminded me more than once. That was quite a man! I miss him so much!"

"I'm sure you do, Glendella. And I'll miss the Robertsons, too. But I must do this. In a way, it's my fault they're going through all this. I was the one who was feeling guilty about not telling Lillian, especially with that sermon series Pastor's been on recently. I've known about Louis' bisexual orientation from the beginning. I knew I was sharing him with Lillian. In a way, it's been a bonus for me that I've accepted as a blessing. I got a family, too."

"Claude. I don't know how you can do this. Leave the family and leave your money, too."

"What's that song we sang? I have decided to follow Jesus, who sacrificed his life for those He loves. What's He teach us about giving our all?. Taking up our cross and following Him. Remember Pastor's sermon that first Sunday about being courageous. That God would be with me. I trust in His Word, Glendella."

"Yeah, I know all that, Claude. Pshaw! Those are just Bible verses," Glendella throws back at him, flipping her hand toward him as though she puts little stock in the Word.

"Not to me, Glendella. When I became a Christian, I committed myself to living the Word as I understand it. I never heard any preaching about homosexuality, but I'd seen and heard lots "out in the world". So I just assumed that like Paul's "thorn in the flesh," keeping that aspect of myself was something I'd have to bear as a child of God."

"I never thought of it that way, Claude. That keeping a secret about the way you believe God made you could be a thorn in the flesh."

"Yeah, well. It's not my sexual orientation but my love that I believe is motivating me now. If I stay, the family will not heal. I've met with the pastor. We've prayed about this. I've taken a vow of celibacy and will try to live as a widower who has known love."

"How you gonna do that, Claude? You're not yet fifty years old! I'm a widow just a little older than you and I understand the temptation when you no longer have a spouse."

"That's the third thing you can do for me, Glendella. Keep me in your prayers. It's going to be hard enough being away from my family, but equally challenging to live without the physical relationship I've shared with my partner of eighteen years!"

Delphi's Admission

I had to do it. I called her and invited her to come to tea. Lillian was ready. I open the door and face my dear friend, wondering just how to broach this delicate subject of her husband's sexuality. She and I have a light lunch, talking about the upcoming GEMS event for the fourth of July as though nothing else was important. Then, sipping coffee, I turn to her.

"Lillian, I know about Louis"

"What?" She spews, grabs the napkin next to her plate to catch the tea, then wipes her eyes, trying to hide the tears now slipping down her cheeks.

I slide my chair close enough to embrace her gently, offer a tissue, then escort her into the living room. We sit. A lampstand casts light on the floor between our two chairs. When Lillian, finally, composes herself, I begin to speak.

"The girls told me everything. They are pretty shaken up about it. Alysa is divided between her loyalty to you and her love for her dad. Alvyra, is more volatile, though. She denounced God and family and anything that ever meant anything to her!"

"Oh, my babies!" Lillian is shocked, but before she says more, I continue. "I'm sure that's just a knee-jerk response to not having control over her life. Believe me, 'been there, done that.' My biggest concern is for you. How are you doing?" Lillian looks down at the floor. Tears drip from her eyes again. "I know Louis didn't marry me for love. We both wanted kids and there didn't seem to be any prospects in the near future and my clock was ticking……..

But I never, ever, thought that he was…. GAY! How could I have missed that?" She screams louder than she intended, then looks around to see if anyone else can hear her.

"We see what we want to see, Lillian. He is attentive and kind and he adores the kids. A lot of women with "straight" husbands would kill for that. Don't beat yourself for not seeing what you were not seeking."

This seems to ease Lillian's mind knowing that I am not judging her ignorance. "What am I expected to do?" she says, more to herself than to me.

"What do you want to do?"

"I don't know! Louis is a good man, and I don't want to stir up trouble, but this really has thrown me for a loop!"

"A 'good man'?" I clench my teeth, trying not to scream, "Are you serious?! Would a "good man" mislead you for 17 years? Or keep a lover on the side for 17 years? Would a 'good man' discuss your marriage and living arrangements with his lover, but not with you, his wife to be?!!" I realized that I was getting louder with each question, so, I settled back down and looked at her, caringly.

"Sexual preferences aside. Can you call him a "good man" when he went into this marriage with the forethought of keeping his lover close to him; so, close as to bring him into your home?" I interrogate much more gently. "Remember, Genesis 2:24 says, *'Therefore shall a man leave his father and his mother and cleave unto his wife: and they shall be one flesh.'* I would think that it means leaving his lover, also!" I say, barely keeping the disgust out of my voice.

"Well, I guess so," Lillian concedes, her forehead wrinkling in thought. "Genesis 1:28 says, "*So, God created man in his own image, in the image of God created he him, male and female created he them.*" Lillian recites more to herself.

"Do I even have a marriage in the sight of God?" she wonders aloud. "We vowed before God to love, honor, and keep……, but that was a lie, at least on his part!" Lillian laments and questions. "Have I been living with a liar!"

"I can't say if your marriage is real or not, but you do have a decision to make. one that will affect not just you. My, unsolicited advice is this; if you deem Louis to be a "good man" then, stay with him. If not, believe God will forgive you for not living a lie."

*****

The friends talk and pray together through the afternoon. By early evening when Lillian leaves, she has a made-up mind and quieted spirit. And Delphi Louise gives her dear husband, Malcolm, props for being right all along.

Basketball Coach Wonders

James Milton, one of the basketball coaches who assists with GEMS club physical ed activities, runs along the sidelines serving as coach and referee. Now that the weather is nice, his friend, Delphi asked him to supervise a GEMS outdoor event at the park across the street from Beth-El Community Church. Neither of them attends services in that building, but they do have permission to use the restrooms with the showers in the church basement. Since there will only be girls this evening, they can use the facilities set aside for both genders. And gender identity is one of the issues that is creating stress for a couple of the GEMS girls. Not theirs. Their Dad's.

*****

All I can think when I watch the teams out on the park court is, "Those poor kids." Alvyra and Alysa just found out their parents may be divorcing. The reason? He's bi. And he's been in love with his best friend, who has been like an uncle to the girls and their brother their entire lives. I can't imagine what the family must be going through right now.

As a coach who has worked with Delphi's club for a couple of years, I've become one of the trusted adults in their lives. While we're supposed to only care about winning, *I* do my best to care for the young people's emotional and mental health, as well. They seem to be doing okay out there today. But it's hard to know from looks alone.

*****

"Go, go, go!" I yell as Alvyra crosses the court and makes a basket. The other girls clap. "No slacking, though. Give me 10 free throws, Alvyra." She makes a face, but the court clears as the girls make room for her to shoot. As one of my team's shooting guards, it's important for her to practice all kinds of shots.

"Can we try some alley-oops now?" Alvyra asks after she makes the tenth free throw.

"Sure thing. Alysa? You ready for this?" Alysa jumps up from the bench where she was taking a break.

"I'm in, Coach!" she replies. I step back to watch the twins do their thing. Alysa, even in her Goth attire and dark eye makeup is one of the best point guards I have coached, especially when her sister is playing shooting guard. "Gabriella and Destiny, you do the same at the other basket." They jog over to the other side. "All right! The rest of you, defense." Most of the girls groan in response, but I cut them off with a whistle. "I don't want to hear it!" and they quiet down as they begin.

I focus on the sisters with half an eye on the defenders. Alysa and Alvyra seem pretty in sync today. They usually are, but with what's going on at home, I want to be extra sure. Once I'm satisfied with the number of successful shots, I whistle again. "That's enough for now. Hit the showers!" The girls gather their backpacks with towels and soap and straggle across the street to the church. My wife stands there with the Beth-El janitor who has come to unlock the doors.

"Alysa, Alvyra, stay back a second, please." I wait as they change directions to head back my way.

Alysa starts, "Coach, is this about--" "Our dad?" her twin finishes.

"It is. I just want to make sure you're both alright. I heard about the possible divorce."

"We're all right. Mom is taking it harder." Alysa replies.

"Yeah, we just see it as gaining a third parent!" Alvyra adds and Alysa nods. "There are worse things than getting a third parent."

The way they're avoiding my eyes, it looks like they are trying to convince themselves of that. As I debate what to say next, I hear sobbing hiccoughs. I see tears welling up in their eyes. Alysa's cheeks soon have streaks as her dusky eyeliner joins the waterworks. Her sister uses the corner of her oversized tee-shirt to wipe the tears of her twin. They head across the street, clinging to each other as if their lives depended on it. Maybe they do. Are they faking it or making it? Time will tell. Now, it's time for me to collect all the basketballs and go out with my wife to dinner.

FOURTH WEEK

The Robertson Family have much to consider in the days, weeks, and years to come, as does this congregation. Before praying the benediction, this Sunday, Pastor Jackson signals the tech team leader to play the video.

Reveal at Beth-El

Good morning, my Beth-El Community brothers and sisters. If you're seeing this, I'm likely already on a plane to New York City to begin orientation for my new life. Yes, this red-headed man you see is Brother Claude Rupert and I'm on my way to minister with my Episcopalian Brothers and Sisters in the Dinka area of South Sudan.

I am leaving the video so all will know that what they suspected is true. I am gay. I have been in a loving relationship for nearly twenty years. My partner married and now has three children. A couple of months ago, I got greedy and began pressuring him to tell his wife and family so that the two of us, who had become one family, now with three children could live more openly.

Gulps roll across the Beth-El sanctuary like ocean waves on the shores at the height of hurricane season. Eyes dart around trying to figure out who Brother Claude is talking about.

Then, the first Sunday of this month, while standing here in our Beth-El sanctuary, the Lord spoke to me and said you must leave. I met with Pastor Jackson and my usher chair. They agreed and accepted my resignation from the usher board. They also will affirm that I've taken a vow of celibacy. I made a commitment to live my life as a celibate widow serving the Dinka Christians in South Sudan and will not return to the United States during my lifetime.

Finally, please know that I believe in an omniscient, omnipresent, and omnipotent God. I have not been living a life hidden from Him, just not transparent to you, my brothers and sisters. I believe in an omnipresent God who will be with me as I serve Him in another country, and also with you as you come alongside the Robertson family who will be adjusting to this new reality of life without Uncle Claude.

Another wave of gulps rolls across the sanctuary. Eyes angle toward the fifth row on the left where Louis and Lillian Robertson, their son Lou Jr., and daughters Alvyra and Alysa sit stiffly as though wearing steel armor. How could that family come to church this Sunday when they know what is coming?

Most importantly, I believe in an omnipotent God, who will empower us all with courage to live out our convictions and commitment to live a life pleasing to Him.

So, Sister Glendella, please begin playing the song that Brother Jesse Vincent will lead as my prayer for my Beth-El Community Church family. Yes, please sing all four verses as you let marinate in your hearts and minds that I, a gay man, am confident that I am living the life as God made me. I cannot remain here if it will hurt the family I love. Like the Apostle Paul, I am trusting in the Lord to sustain my living with this "thorn in my flesh" until we meet on that Heavenly shore.

Pastor Jackson signals the congregation to stand and sing as a closing hymn that Fourth Sunday in May, God be with you till we meet again; loving counsels guide, uphold you, may the Shepherd's care enfold you; God be with you till we meet again.

Refrain:
    Till we meet, till we meet, till we meet at Jesus' feet.
    Till we meet, till we meet,
    God be with you till we meet again.

    God be with you till we meet again; unseen wings,
    protecting, hide you, daily manna still provide you;
    God be with you till we meet again. [Refrain]

    God be with you till we meet again;
    when life's perils thick confound you,
    put unfailing arms around you;
    God be with you till we meet again. [Refrain]

    God be with you till we meet again;
    keep love's banner floating o'er you,
    smite death's threat'ning wave before you;
    God be with you till we meet again. [Refrain]

In his benediction, Pastor Jackson asks for God's blessings on them all and calls on the church family to remain silent during snack time. He knows that few would be able to do it, but he encourages them to hold their tongues and opinionate responses until they get home. Let the message from their Brother Claude marinate as they continue to fellowship by eating and drinking, but not talking.

As they are leaving the sanctuary that fourth Sunday in May, Pastor Jackson who's decided to join the congregation during snack time instead of retreating to his office to unwind and reflect on the service, has something to hand the church family members. He, saying nothing, as he advised the congregants to do during snack time, slips into the hands of each member of the Beth-El church family a plastic-covered note card imprinted with New International Version of I Corinthians 13.

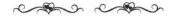

If I speak in the tongues of men or of angels, but do not have love, I am only a resounding gong or a clanging cymbal. 2 If I have the gift of prophecy and can fathom all mysteries and all knowledge, and if I have a faith that can move mountains, but do not have love, I am nothing. 3 If I give all I possess to the poor and give over my body to hardship that I may boast,[b] but do not have love, I gain nothing.

4 Love is patient, love is kind. It does not envy, it does not boast, it is not proud. 5 It does not dishonor others, it is not self-seeking, it is not easily angered, it keeps no record of wrongs. 6 Love does not delight in evil but rejoices with the truth. 7 It always protects, always trusts, always hopes, always perseveres.

8 Love never fails. But where there are prophecies, they will cease; where there are tongues, they will be stilled; where there is knowledge, it will pass away. 9 For we know in part and we prophesy in part, 10 but when completeness comes, what is in part disappears. 11 When I was a child, I talked like a child, I thought like a child, I reasoned like a child. When I became a man, I put the ways of childhood behind me. 12 For now we see only a reflection as in a mirror; then we shall see face to face. Now I know in part; then I shall know fully, even as I am fully known.

13 And now these three remain: faith, hope and love.
But the greatest of these is love.

I Corinthians 13 (NIV)

*****

Well, with that video taken care of Claude had one more financial issue to address that he did not share with Glendella last Sunday. Conscientious Claude has also purchased a burial policy with instructions. He wants to make sure there are funds there to return his physical remains to be buried in the family plot he and Louis, Sr. purchased years ago. Though they can no longer live as partners here on earth, when the time comes, they do want their physical remains to be buried in the family plot.

Decision Time

Louis and Lillian have chosen to work together, with the help of the Lord, to restore their marriage. They understand from all that has hit the fan that the goings will be tough. But Louis is a paladin. His wife is a Wonder Woman in her own right. The song "Onward Christian Soldier" had been his marching orders since he was a child tagging along with his grandfather, when they served with church outreach ministries, but he's found a new song that he's shared with Lillian. The lyrics serve as an affirmation for them both.

> I mean to go right on until the crown is won;
> I mean to fight the fight of faith till life on earth
> is done. I'll nevermore turn back,
> defeat I shall not know,
> For God will give me victory
> if onward I shall go.

> *Refrain:*
> I'm going on, I'm going on,
> Unto the final triumph,
> I'm going on;
> I'm going on, I'm going on,
> Unto the final triumph, I'm going on.

265

Should opposition come,
should foes obstruct my way,
Should persecution's fires be lit,
as in the ancient day—
With Jesus by my side,
 His peace within my soul,
No matter if the battle's hot,
I mean to win the goal.

EPILOGUE

No Dinking with the Dinka

Sipping refreshing tamarind juice, a newly acquired taste for him, and unwinding in the slightly cooler evening after the 90 degrees day here in South Sudan, working in the fields gathering straw for thatching cottage roofing, Claude recalls a conversation just last week.

Some of the Lost Boys of South Sudan have returned home to minister with the Dinka Christians in their home country. One such man, Amani, challenged him the other day.

*****

"Are you dinkin' with the Dinka, Claude?"

"What do you mean "dinkin"? I know the Urban term means fooling around and not being serious. You don't think I'm serious in my commitment to live and learn with the Dinka?"

"I don't know for sure. While in the US as one of the orphans who immigrated there during the political and religious conflicts here, I saw the movie, *Hawaii* with the teens in the family who fostered me. In that movie, based on the novel by James A. Michener, some of the Christians who were supposed to be missionaries betrayed the Hawaiians and took their land. Once the sugar plantations started bringing in big bucks, a group of American sugar planters under Sanford Ballard Dole overthrew Queen Liliuokalani. You're not here to do that to us are you?"

"No, Man. You clearly understand urban slang, so I'll call you that. You also are a Christian, so I'll call you, Bro. I'm here to heal. I was in a gay relationship that was destroying the family of the man I love. He is bisexual with a wife and three children who warmly welcomed me as brother and Uncle Claude. Now, however, I've taken a vow of celibacy and am here to serve the Dinka peoples who are in the heritage line of Louis Jamal, my partner, whose dad was one of the Lost Boys of Sudan. You know the orphans who immigrated in the 20th Century. He found love there and fathered my lover."

"Whoa, Man! You're a queer!"

"I guess that's what you'd call me. But I'm no longer practicing that lifestyle. I'm here to learn to plant and grow with my Dinka brothers and sisters. You know, Amani, I'm so glad you reached out to me to let me know you are skeptical of my coming. I'm thankful, too, that you seem to be open to teaching me how to do the work as I heal. I truly appreciate your holding your tongue and not getting the folks here to shut me out. Instead, the church members have opened their hearts and daily let me use my muscles to help where I can."

"You bet, Old Man. We need all the muscle we can get. Heck, I saw you out there with the guys on that irrigation dig. It'll be great to have a fishery here. I'm glad you're not here to do us dirty!" Amani leaves and Claude continues to ponder their exchange.

*****

Exiled, like me. When the Sudanese civil war began there were only five Dinka congregations along the Nile, but today, we have hundreds of Christian congregations representing multiple denominations. My voluntary expatriation has been a mixed blessing. I'm learning to follow the services in the church where I now fellowship. The rhythms are different, but the message of Christ is the same.

Here, I think often of Louis and Lillian and the kids. I wonder what they are doing. I'm not sure it came to me naturally or if it's because they were Louis' children. Children of God. Children I hadn't had. I had longed to be the father for Lou Jr. that maybe Louis wasn't – and certainly the father I didn't have. I do get a few postcards. Letters from Lou Jr. and the girls.

*****

"Will you write us, Uncle Claude?" Alysa implored when we met on Zoom that first week in June. By that time, I was in New York staying with a couple Glendella knew from her time in the military.

"You're gonna stay in touch aren't you?" Alvyra pled. "We can't lose you forever!"

"Of course, I will. You two better be getting ready for your SATs. I remember how important it was to do well on what they used to call the Scholastic Aptitude Test and later the Scholastic Assessment Test."

"Who cares about those now?" Neither twin wanted to be distracted when I urged them they could use the summer to prep for those subject matter assessments created by the College Board. Many colleges used those scores to determine admission to their institutions of higher learning.

Since then, Alysa has been the only one of the children who stay in regular touch. Soon after meeting with my Beth-El Pastor and creating the video he promised to show during Fourth Sunday service at my home church., I'd left. I had gone to stay with Audra, a military friend of Glendella's. Used to moving around themselves, Audra and her Fujian husband understood the need for some stability before a new move.

They allowed me to stay there for the six months it took to finalize plans and begin orientation to the new culture before my move to South Sudan. Learning specific things like gestures, private spacing, history, and values. It opened my eyes that knowing Blacks in the United States was not the same as getting to know their Black brothers and sisters in a new culture. It is culture and language, not melanin that made the difference.

What a blessing that Glendella had consented to help implement my plan for the family, even consenting to take over the lease of my flat in the upper floor above the Robertsons. The family is staying together. All but me. Now it is an Aunt up there, instead of an Uncle Claude.

Living here in the Bor village, I spend lots of time outdoors. While planting trees I think back to when we bought the house, back home. Yes, I still call it home. Louis and I got straight to work on the yard making sure to protect the natural barrier of juniper trees between our house and the neighbors. We had freezing temperatures and extreme heat, so we had to be careful about what we planted there. Here in South Sudan, the planting is strenuous. After all, I'm no longer a young man. But I've been strong enough to help with the irrigation dig to set up the fishery.

Here, along the Nile, it's verdant. Things grow. Plants change. Here, the plants are usually green, but some varieties semi double in white, pink, magenta and red, reminding me of those crab trees back....

It has taken more than six months, but the pain in my heart feels less sharp. More dull, like the first year after Mother died. As I pull up the weeds from the earth, the sharp pain is lessening. Clearing the land is allowing me to heal. Following the advice of the therapist I had consulted while in New York, I begin each day practicing yoga. Then I help in the kitchens to prepare breakfast. I still like to cook and though the herbs used here are different, the skills are similar. Know when the meat is done.

I'm starting to feel whole again. Forgiving myself and Louis – and even Lillian. I'm finding forgiveness to be a tougher road than I imagined. Stewing on the pains of the past. Loyal servant that I am, taking heat and bearing witness to ugliness – but for the brief moment of pushing back, of telling myself I'm more than this abuse.

In the end, was it all worth it? I gave up the man I love so his family can be whole again. I gave up my dreams to be a side-line figure. A character in the narrative.

I savor fond memories. The two – Louis and Lillian, the one family, the three children. Glendella and I are family, too. That's how it can be. Family is all. True, I miss the children the most. Adults tend to be complicated beings after all. Then, I pull out the card Pastor Jackson had slipped into my hand during our last meeting at Beth-El. Yes, indeed. I need the Word to help me through it all. I, too, am "Going On!"

> I mean to go right on until the crown is won;
> I mean to fight the fight of faith till life on earth is done.
> I'll nevermore turn back, defeat I shall not know,
> For God will give me victory if onward I shall go.

> I'm going on, I'm going on,
> Unto the final triumph, I'm going on.

Acknowledgments

The multiple perspectives and points of view reflected in this work of Christian fiction could not have occurred without the authentic voices of more than a dozen contributors. After reading my SEED STORY, which has become the opening chapter of this book, I asked, "Whose voice needs to be heard?" and "Will you write a first-person narrative in the voice of that character?"

Then, to those who consented to write, I sent some guidelines written in much the same way I, a retired educator, would have given an assignment in one of my classes.

As you write the first-person narrative that you flesh out with the STEAL character elements (Speech, Thoughts, Effect on others, Actions and Looks: physique and attire) and description of a specific place that includes sensory images that appeal to sight, sound, taste, touch, and smell, consider ways
the scene you are writing will show your relationship with the characters named in the story before, during, or after they learn of Louis' revelation and plans.
the dialogue with Lillian or Louis that may have occurred prior to the SEED story.

The thoughts, however, should reflect the way you believe the character you've chosen will/would respond to one or more of the characters mentioned in the story once your character learns of Louis' revelation and plans.

I invite you to pray about your writing. Ask the Lord how the threads in your story will help round out the picture showing ways people respond to the news Louis reveals.

Many of the readers consented to do the writing. Others recommended key issues the story should address. My task, writing in the omniscient point of view, was to weave those individual voices and perspectives into a story that shows the theme for this book:

When people are confronted with behavior or news about something or someone that is frowned upon by society or decried by their religious teaching, they are challenged, based on their relationship with those involved, to consider or reflect on the impact their responses have will or have had on the people involved.

TWO, ONE … NOW THREE: How Can That Be? has contributors from all across the United States who range in age from 18 years old to their early 70's, who represent a variety of racial and ethnic groups, different denominations of Christianity, and who are professionals in medical, education, church leadership, counseling, and more.

My heartfelt thanks goes out to the following contributors who are listed in alphabetical order by their last names.

Bonnie Burke, George Davis, Shannon Hayes, Xavier Johnson, Rochelle Jones, Dorien McKay, Allison B. Miller, Verneal Y. Mitchell, Kate Moore, Donna Russ, Kayon Tompkins, Gary Ventimiglia, Constance Vickers, and Annette West.

It is our prayer that reading our work in the form of Christian fiction will provide a mirror, window, or sliding glass door through which you will experience more because you now have seen, heard, and reflected on Lillian's question, "What would Jesus do?"

Discussion Questions

General Reflection on the Writing and the Message

1. What is the significance of the title? Did you find it meaningful? Why or why not?

2. Would you have given the book a different title? If yes, what would your title be?

3. How important was the period or the setting to the story? Did you think it was accurately portrayed?

4. How would the book have played out differently in a different historical time or place?

5. What scene resonated with you most on a personal level? How did it make you feel?

6. What motivates the actions and reactions of different characters in this book?

7. Which characters remind you of someone you know, have observed, or have read about in other fictional works.

8. How do the way the characters see themselves differ from the way others see them?

9. Which characters did you relate to the most? Why?

10. Did your opinion of the characters change as you continued reading the story? Why?

11. With what characters were you rooting the most?

12. Were there times you disagreed with a character's actions? What would you have done differently?

13. Which moment in the story promoted the strongest emotional reaction for you? Why?

14. What ideas does the author illustrate? What message is the author sending?

15. How would you summarize this book using the Five W's and H? Who? What? When? Where? Why? and How?

16. Were there significant plot twists and turns? If so, what were they? On what page(s)?

17. How did you feel about the ending? How might you change it?

18. What quotes or passages stood out to you? On what page? Explain.

19. Who could you see playing the lead characters if this was a movie?

In what ways have your personal views changed because of this book. Reflections on Historical and Theological Ideas

1. What historical incidents did the author present that intrigue or inspire you to explore more?

2. Which seemed strongest to you: the novel's nuanced characters, the spiritual world, or the compelling plot?

3. What helpful fresh revelations or new thoughts did you receive as you read? In what ways does your knowledge of the topic expand?

4. Did the author point to a Scripture passage that was new or unfamiliar to you?

5. In what ways did reading the lyrics of hymns enhance your understanding of characters, plot, and message?

6. What part or parts of this book did you find encouraging? List some adjectives that describe your overall impression.

7. What was your main takeaway? Or could you share a couple of takeaways?

8. What was the overall tone of the book?

9. What in-text references compel you to investigate more, or maybe you investigated already? What supplemental material was suggested?

10. How has reading this work of Christian fiction influenced your opinion on the topic(s)? Negatively or positively?

11. Does the author create a core call to action in the book? Where did you feel that call to action? What do you personally plan to do about it?

12. To what friends would you recommend this book?

After completion of responses, consider sharing your responses with me. Send to my email at ajroseboro@comcast.net

About the Author

Anna J. Small Roseboro is a wife, mother, retired educator, and author of books in multiple genres: fiction, poetry, and textbooks for teachers. She currently uses these experiences and skills as a mentor and writing coach. But, because she is first and foremost a child of God, she intentionally shares her Christian journey in devotionals, anthologies, and online interviews. This book *TWO, ONE, NOW THREE: How Can It Be?* reflects her passion for storytelling and belief in the power of collaboration. She invited more than a dozen contributors who consented to share fictional narratives in the persona of characters she has woven into this work of Christian fiction.

Anna is the author of this intricate novel because others have shared secret eyes of life based on their experiences, observations, and reflections on sexuality, family life and Christianity.

See more on her website https://ajsmallroseboro.wordpress.com/.

Anna also is the author of other publications that may be of interest to readers of this novel.

ON ZION'S HILL: Funny and Frank, Fanciful and Faithful (2015)
SWEETHEARTS OF ZION'S HILL: A Collection of Stories (2016) Editor
EXPERIENCE POEMS AND PICTURES: Poems that Paint/Pictures that Speak (2018)
RAINBOW REMINDERS: What the Colors Tell Us (w/Nancy White) (2022)
CINDY AND SANDY: The Elephant Girls (2020)

Made in the USA
Columbia, SC
02 October 2022

68275285R10152